MELODY

HILL

A prequel to the aw...

The Gomorrah Principle

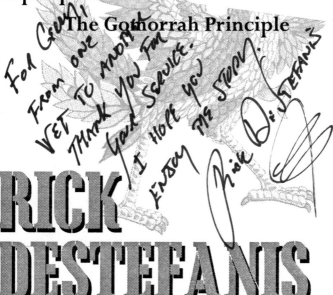

For Greg,
From one
VET TO ANOTHER
THANK YOU FOR
YOUR SERVICE.
I HOPE YOU
ENJOY THE STORY.
Rick DeStefanis

RICK
DESTEFANIS

ISBN: 1508742162

ISBN 13: 9781508742166

For My Readers

Writing true-to-life military fiction necessitates the use of military jargon and acronyms. For that reason I have included a glossary of terms at the back of this book. This story faithfully adheres to the historical events of the Vietnam War era, as well as its organizations and operations; however, other than public figures, the characters depicted herein and their actions are totally fictional. I wish to thank my cover designer Todd Hebertson, editor Elisabeth Hallett and publishing consultant Sara Ann Zola. And most of all I wish to thank my dear friends and critics Ellen Morris Prewitt, Chris Davis, Brian Patterson, Tish Pierce and Rachel Lau for their steadfast support.

CHAPTER ONE

The Hills of Tennessee
1966

Duff Coleridge stood over a freshly killed deer, one he hadn't meant to kill. It was a stupid mistake, one a seasoned hunter shouldn't have made. He had watched a buck threading its way along a distant wooded ridge that late afternoon. Visible one moment and hidden in the shadows the next, the buck reappeared far back in the trees as Duff steadied his rifle. This was his last opportunity to stock the family freezer with much-needed venison before leaving. Again the buck disappeared, but then it was there in his crosshairs. At nearly four hundred yards, Duff found only the deer's front shoulder visible. That was all he needed. Holding fifteen inches high, he squeezed off the shot.

There weren't a lot of deer in the area, and conservation laws forbade the killing of does, but after the long walk to the top of the ridge, Duff found he had done just that. Somehow, the buck had traded places with a doe, one he hadn't even realized was around. Duff ran his hand gently over the deer's grayish-brown hide. She wouldn't go to waste, but neither would she have any more fawns. His foster brother, Brady, who was hunting nearby, would arrive in a while to help carry the deer down the mountain. Duff would have to admit to a careless mistake. It was a hell of a way to end his thirty-day leave.

After making quick work of field-dressing the deer, he pulled it out to a high bluff on the edge of the woods where he awaited his brother. Far below, the waters of the Hiwassee spilled over the rocks in shimmering ripples and swirling eddies, curling their way to the distant horizon. Out beyond where the river disappeared into the hills, the winter sun offered a silent requiem to another day, and it brought back another ache that never quite left his heart.

Duff loved the Tennessee mountains and the town of Melody Hill. Growing up here had been as close to heaven as he could imagine being, but it was a bittersweet love, because despite all their beauty, it was these hills that had taken his father. And if he had learned anything the day they buried William Coleridge in the church cemetery, it was that life could come and go as quickly as summer rain. Perhaps this was what drove him to leave—to go, before his life, too, passed like the clouds on the horizon.

It wasn't going to be without risk, but the military was his ticket to life, and he had taken what was offered. Duff had enlisted in the army, and he had no misconceptions about Vietnam. During Basic, and later at Fort Polk, the drill instructors said this new war was a bad one. Not that any war was good, but this one was like none before. There were no front lines. There was no easily recognizable enemy, but they left calling cards everywhere in the form of booby traps. Over the years, many of the men from around Melody Hill had done it—gone off to war. Most came back—some didn't.

He looked down at the dead deer lying at his feet. There would be little room for mistakes like this in Vietnam. He had to get his head right. Duff's orders had come after jump school at Benning. He was going to the First Brigade of the 101st Airborne, Phan Rang, Republic of South Vietnam. In five days his military leave would end. He was a paratrooper going to war.

Duff gazed out at the distant mountains. It seemed a natural progression of events had brought him here, almost as if his entire time growing up he had been guided by some invisible hand. Even as he played with Brady and Lacey in the hills and streams around home, every experience had somehow brought him to this point, experiences like the day down in Etowah when they saw the trick marksman. Only now did he realize it had been a seductive siren's call.

Duff remembered that magnificent autumn morning with its Indian summer sun shining brightly on colorful handmade quilts. His mother had sewn the quilts to sell at Trade Day, but she had three kids to keep busy that day. She gave each of them, Duff, Brady, and Lacey, a quarter, and turned them loose. Feeling like a twelve-year-old rich man that morning, Duff struck out across the grounds with his siblings. The Tennessee hills rose all around as the three kids kicked off their shoes and tromped barefoot through the thick, cool winter rye, talking, laughing, and soaking up the autumn sun.

Duff was almost a year older than the others, a little taller and burdened with the responsibilities of a big brother, even to Brady, who was as much a friend as he was a foster brother. With his two siblings in tow, Duff led the way as they wandered through the vendors' booths searching for the one trinket they had to have—as long as it didn't cost more than twenty-five cents. It was midmorning when the crisp mountain air cracked with the sound of a rifle. It came from the far end of the grounds.

Etowah Trade Day was as much a community fair as it was a market. Guitar, mandolin, and fiddle players sat in a clutch of chairs circled beneath the sweet gums, while people plied wares that ran from home-baked pies to pickled okra and live goats. The kids ran along a row of cars and pickups parked in the grass as they heard more shots and the oohs and aahhs of a crowd gathered in the field beyond. It was a man doing a marksmanship demonstration.

Duff turned. "Come on, guys, hurry up."

Brady was with him step for step, but Lacey was in no particular hurry as she ran her little fingers over jars of honey on a vendor's table.

"Come on, Lacey," Duff pleaded.

She turned and ran his way, and Duff led them toward the sound of the gunshots. The kids squeezed through the crowd of adults to the front row. A man wearing a white shirt with a dark brown vest and khaki trousers held a rifle high in the air. He was smiling, and his vest was filled with colorful championship patches.

"This, my friends, is the Remington Arms, Nylon 66, .22 caliber longrifle, and this particular model is the Apache Black version with a chrome barrel and receiver. It holds fourteen rounds."

"Whoa, check it out," Duff said.

The reflection was almost blinding, as the shiny black and chrome rifle glistened in the morning sunlight.

"Yeah," Brady said, his eyes wide with amazement.

Lacey shaded her eyes with her hand and squinted, but said nothing.

"On the fence rail behind me you see seven cans filled with water," the man said. With a quick but incredibly smooth motion, he pivoted and fired seven rounds inside of two seconds, sending each can bursting into a shower of water, jerking and tumbling through the air.

"Wow!" Brady said. "He's good."

The men in the audience hooted, cheered, and clapped, and the marksman held up a small object. The anticipation built as he waited for total silence. The last of the mumbling in the back tapered off as the crowd grew quiet with expectation.

"This, my friends, is your common, everyday black walnut, the wild variety, hardly fit for consumption, unless you own a sledge hammer to crack it."

A ripple of laughter filtered through the crowd.

"I have several of these tasty little morsels, but I have no hammer. So, let's see if we can do it another way."

After setting them on a small table, the man began rapidly tossing walnuts one at a time into the air with his left hand, firing at them with the .22. As he did, each burst into a black cloud of fragments and dust, until he had shot seven in all. More applause and a loud whistle came from the crowd, and Duff, too, found himself clapping in amazement. The man began reloading his rifle, and Duff looked around at Lacey and Brady. The crowd behind them had grown to at least thirty people.

"For my final demonstration of the morning," the man said, "I'm going to fire a bullet through the hole in this washer."

He held a large metal washer on his index finger for the crowd to see. Another round of chuckles circulated through the crowd.

"Oh no, I'm not joking," the man said.

With that he tossed the washer high into the air. His motions weren't jerky, but fluid and focused as the rifle came to his shoulder. When the washer reached the apex of its climb, the man fired a single shot. The crack of the Nylon 66 quickly faded in the distance as the crowd remained silent and watched the washer fall to the ground.

"Wow," Duff exclaimed.

The man beside him patted his head.

"It's a joke, sonny boy. He didn't really shoot through the hole."

Overhearing him, the marksman said, "Oh, but I did, sir, and it's even more difficult to shoot two washers with two shots at the same time."

With that, he quickly turned and tossed two more washers, and fired two more shots. Both washers fell, seemingly untouched, back to earth.

"Bull feathers," the man said.

"No, sir," the marksman replied. "It's not."

He tossed yet another washer into the air. The crack of the rifle was followed instantaneously by the zing of the washer as it rocketed away.

"You see, I can hit the side of the washer if I want."

"So, how are you gonna prove you really shot through the hole in them others?" the man asked.

The marksman smiled.

"If I can prove it, will you take a friendly wager that I can shoot through the holes of three washers on the same toss, say a quarter a shot?"

"I reckon so," the man said.

"Would anyone else like to make a bet?" the marksman asked.

Men began stepping forward and tossing their quarters, dimes, and nickels on the table.

"Heck fire," another man said. "I don't doubt you, but reckon I'd pay seventy-five cents just to see you do it."

When they were done, the man quickly counted the money.

"There's eighteen dollars here," the marksman announced. "Anyone who placed a bet, regardless of the outcome, is entitled to a free box of Remington .22 longrifle ammunition, courtesy of Remington Arms Company. Just pick it up here at the table."

He pulled a wrinkled twenty from his pocket and laid it atop the money on the table.

Duff had never seen so much money at one time.

"Now," the man said as he laid three more washers on the table. "I'm going to place a postage stamp over each of the holes in these washers."

He licked the stamps and stuck them to the washers. When he was done, he held them up for everyone to see, then picked up the Nylon 66. Again, washers sailed upward. Again, the marksman fired shots. Again, the washers fell back to the ground, seemingly untouched. The marksman laid the rifle on the table and turned to Duff and Brady.

"Would you boys mind going over there and finding the three washers with postage stamps?"

The boys scrambled forward and searched the grass. Brady found the first one. Holding it up to his eye, he peeked through the small hole in the stamp. Duff picked up the second. It too had a .22 caliber hole. When they had found all three, there came applause and the crowd began dispersing, but Duff, Brady, and Lacey lingered as the boys admired the shiny new Nylon 66.

"How did you learn to shoot like that, mister?" Duff asked.

The man smiled.

"Practice, practice, and more practice," he said. "Do you own a rifle?"

Brady and Duff nodded together. "Yes, sir. We both do, but they're just old JC Higgins single shots. My mama got them for us here at Trade Day last year."

"Well, those old JC Higgins rifles will shoot just as accurately as this rifle," the man said.

"Really?" Duff said.

"Really," the man answered. "You just have to shoot them. Like I said, practice, practice, and practice."

"We do, when we have bullets," Brady said.

"Do your rifles shoot .22 longrifle cartridges?" the man asked.

"Yes, sir."

He reached into a box on the table.

"My sponsor, the Remington Arms Company, supplies me with free ammunition. I'm sure they won't mind my sharing a few boxes. Here."

With that, he placed two boxes each in front of Duff and Brady.

"Wow! Thanks, mister."

"Just be safe. Don't aim at anything you don't intend to shoot, and remember that ninety-nine percent of making a good shot comes from that little knot-head of yours."

That had been almost seven years ago, and Duff had since become an exceptional marksman, but the dead deer at his feet presented a new realization. Such talent brought with it a huge responsibility. From the opposite side of the mountain came the distant sound of chimes from the Melody Hill church, signaling another day's end. With dusk quickly fading into nightfall, he decided to go find Brady. Having his help carrying the deer down the mountain would make the task easier. He turned, and there came a soft whistle from back in the trees. Duff whistled back. A moment later, Brady appeared from the shadows.

"You're not going to believe what I did," Duff said.

Brady looked down at the deer.

"I was looking at a buck," Duff said, "and I don't know how, but—"

"Stop your worrying," Brady said. "We'll get her skinned-out and in the freezer. You've got more important things to think about."

"You mean like leaving?"

"Exactly," Brady said.

Duff nodded. "Reckon you're right."

There remained only five days before he departed, and though it was late fall, they planned to spend the next afternoon down at the river. A rocky shallows of gravel bars where the kids hung out, the shoals were part of the Hiawassee where they built campfires, floated the rapids with inner tubes, and often had their first taste of liquor. Tomorrow it would be just the three of them, Duff, Brady and Lacey. It would be their last time together down at the river—a time for Duff to say his good-byes.

* * *

Duff sat at the kitchen table that morning drinking coffee with his mother. Brady and Lacey had left for school, and only the ticking of the wall clock broke the silence as Emma Coleridge stared out the window. She was not one for idle talk, especially since his enlistment, but now she looked down, fidgeting with the dish towel in her lap, and Duff knew she wanted to say something.

"What is it, Mama?"

"I reckon we've talked enough."

"Mama, I know there's something else you want to say. Might as well tell me."

She looked up with moistened eyes. "Okay, but promise me you'll stay and hear me out."

"Is this about me and Brady, again?"

"You are so much like your daddy, Duff, and that's mostly a good thing, but you are being stubborn."

Duff didn't respond as he sipped his coffee.

"You owe Brady an apology before you leave. It would mean a lot to him, but it'll mean more to you."

"He knows I'm letting it go."

"But you really haven't, and he knows it."

"Mama, I love Brady like a brother, but—"

"Then bury the hatchet, son."

Duff looked down into his cup.

It had happened after a mid-season football game last fall. They'd built a bonfire down at the shoals that night to celebrate their sixth victory in a row, and the teenagers were passing a bottle of whiskey around. Several of the ballplayers stacked more driftwood on the already huge fire as Duff's aches and bruises faded in the warmth of the alcohol buzz. He looked around for Brady. Little brother didn't need to drink. After all, he was just a junior. But he was nowhere to be seen.

The bottle came around again, and Duff took another long swallow of the whiskey. Afterward he wandered outside the light of the fire. The rippling waters of the river sparkled orange with the reflection from the flames, and the stars were brilliant in the cold night sky. Upriver there was the silhouette of two people sitting together on a log. Duff walked along the rushing rapids toward the couple, and only at the last moment did he realize they were locked in a passionate kiss and embrace.

Quickly turning away, he started back toward the fire, but a sense of familiarity struck him and he looked again. Even in the darkness he recognized him. It was Brady. And the girl—he looked closer. It was Lacey. He strutted toward them.

Grasping Brady by the shoulders, Duff snatched him from the embrace. Lacey went sprawling in the gravel as Duff spun his foster brother about and drew his fist back. Never backing away from a challenge, Brady was always willing to engage in a good scrap, but it had always been play. This time he merely stared at Duff in confused shock. Duff opened his fist and back-handed him across the face.

"Stop," Lacey screamed. "What are you doing?"

Brady stumbled backward, and Lacey jumped to her feet.

Duff stiff-armed her, and she fell back again, landing in the gravel.

"No!" Brady shouted as he lunged at his foster brother.

The two boys rolled across the gravel bar, both coming to their feet as they faced off.

"You keep your hands off of her," Brady said.

"Yeah, and you keep yours off her, too."

"Stop!" Lacey yelled. "Both of you…"

She broke into sobs.

Brady threw up his hands. "What the hell, Duff?"

"You tell me," Duff said. "She's your sister, for god's sake."

"We aren't blood kin."

Brady shook his head as his eyes teared up. "I mean…I love her, and—"

"I'm the one started it," Lacey said. "He never would have—"

"You shut up," Duff said.

Lacey scrambled to her feet and again started toward him.

"No!" Brady said. He held her back and turned to Duff. "You've been drinking."

"Doesn't matter," Duff said.

Brady rubbed his jaw. He looked more hurt than angered.

"I wish I'd never come to live with you," he said.

Brady's words stung worse than a punch on the nose, but Duff was puzzled by his own reaction more than his foster brother's. His anger had gotten the better of him, and he didn't even know why. There was nothing he could say. He turned and walked away.

Duff looked across the table at his mother. Lacey had told her about the incident, and his mother was the only one who had spoken about it since. Brady and Lacey avoided showing affection when Duff was around, and Brady acted as if he had forgiven him. His mother was right. He owed them both an apology, but he still felt somehow cheated. It was as if something had been taken from him, or that he had become a lesser part of their threesome. Just the same, he thought it was forgotten, because they had gathered again down at the shoals last fall, a few days before the final game of the season. It had been just the three of them.

Duff had purchased a new Remington 700, thirty-aught-six, earlier in the week, leaving Brady heir to the old rifle they had shared the last few years. Despite the electrician's tape that wrapped the cracked stock and bluing worn to bare metal, the old rifle could drive tacks, and Duff wanted to see how his new one compared. Lacey sat watching from the river bank as Brady walked down the bar and lined several small stones on a log. After walking back, he began loading his rifle, but before he finished, Duff raised the new rifle and began shooting. He shot every rock from the log in rapid succession. As the booms echoed down the river, Lacey held a hand over her mouth, stifling her giggles.

"Don't laugh at that show-off," Brady said. "I can do the same thing."

"Okay," Duff said. "We'll just see. Line up nine rocks on the log. We each have five shots. We'll start on opposite ends, then we'll *see* who reaches the center rock first."

They lined the stones on the log and as Brady bolted the first of his five rounds, Duff turned to Lacey.

"You be the judge and say 'go' when you're ready."

"Go!" she shouted.

The boys shouldered their rifles and fired their first shots simultaneously. The rocks on either end exploded. Quickly they each bolted a second round. Two more hits. Then six, then eight, and as they each fired their last round, the middle rock exploded.

"Ha! See?" Duff said.

"What do you mean?" Brady said. "*I* hit that rock."

"No you didn't. I—"

"Hush!" Lacey shouted.

Both boys turned toward her.

"I'm the judge, remember?"

Sitting on the bank above, she grinned like the Cheshire cat.

"Yeah," Duff said. "So, tell him."

"You both hit it at the same time," she said.

Duff furrowed his brow, then broke into a smile.

"Not bad, little brother, not bad. I just hope you're that accurate throwing the football Friday night."

Brady nodded. "Yeah, I wish we had more of a passing game. We just need to get old Lanky open more."

"Don't worry," Duff said, "We'll just grind it out, like we have all season, you know?"

"We still need to pass some, to keep them honest. If Scooter could catch like Lanky I wouldn't be so worried," Brady said.

"Yeah, I can't believe he dropped that pass against McMinn," Duff said.

"And I hit him square on the numbers, too," Brady added.

"Maybe you surprised him," Duff said.

Lacey again burst into laughter.

"That's not funny," Brady said. "Stop laughing at him."

Duff threw his arm around Brady's neck. "Sorry, little brother. You know I'm just kidding. We're gonna win it all Friday night. You'll see."

And Friday night came that autumn day a year ago, but it was late in the fourth quarter and Cleveland, despite missing two extra points, had a nineteen to fourteen lead. All night, Coach had called Duff's number for three yards and a pile of dust, but the bigger, faster boys from Cleveland had worn him down. He was exhausted. Gil Owen came in with a play from the bench. They were on their own thirty-six-yard line, and Duff glanced at the clock on the far end of the field. There was a minute and eighteen seconds left in the game.

"Coach wants Thirty-six, Power Right," Gil said to Brady.

Duff looked out from the huddle across the line of scrimmage. Coach was sending him off tackle again for the twentieth-something time that night. Cleveland was stacked up tight behind the line, like they had been the entire second half. Polk County hadn't scored since the first quarter. Across the field, the Cleveland fans were beginning an early celebration. Duff turned to Brady. His younger brother's face was red and lined with sweat.

"We're running out of time. We've got to do something different."

"What the hell are we gonna do? They've kicked our ass the whole second half," Owen said.

Brady turned to him. "Never give up," he shouted.

"Calm down, little brother," Duff said. He turned to Lanky. "Lanky, I want you to do just like you've been doing all night. When we break out of the huddle, take your time and trot out there and split right, but you gotta look bored out of your mind."

"Then what?" Lanky said.

"When the ball is snapped I want you to take about two or three slow steps to the inside, real easy like you know the ball is going to me, then turn it up field as fast as you can go."

Duff turned to Brady. "I want you to run it like Thirty-six Power Right, and I want you to make a really good fake, then pull up and chunk it down to Lanky. I guarantee he's gonna be wide open. Just take your time and float it, so he can get under it."

"Coach is gonna kill us for not running the play," Brady said.

"Look here, little brother," Duff said, "I can't do this by myself. They've stopped us cold, and I don't have anything left. Like you just said, 'Never give up.' You can finish it. I know you can. Just keep your confidence and make the pass. I'll take the heat if it doesn't work."

Their eyes met, and Duff knew his little brother had what it took. He nodded, and Brady smiled.

"Let's do it," he said. "On two."

"Break!" they shouted.

Duff took his three point stance behind Brady, and for once that night, Cleveland's huge line with its linebackers and defensive backs edging closer didn't look so bad. If little brother and Lanky pulled this one off, they'd be the talk of the county. If not, they'd all probably run wind sprints till they puked, even if it *was* the end of the season. Duff glanced over at the bleachers. Everyone was standing, but no one was cheering. There was only a waning hope expressed by ragged silence. With the clock winding down, their hopes were hanging by the barest of threads.

Brady called the cadence, and the center snapped the ball. Stepping to his right he met Duff in the backfield as he pushed the ball against his abdomen, but he didn't pull it back. Instead he took one, then two steps with him as Duff charged off tackle. At the last possible moment, Brady pulled the ball back and Duff plowed into a linebacker. As he drove ahead, he glanced back to see Brady setting his feet.

Duff heard Coach's voice on the sideline, "No, No!"

Fighting free of the linebacker's grasp, Duff rolled to his knees to see Lanky loping all alone down the sideline. He was already past the fifty-yard line when Brady lofted the ball. Duff followed it through the blinding stadium lights, as the ball floated with only the slightest wobble, arcing high into the night sky. He looked back at Lanky. No one was within thirty yards of him as the ball began its downward arc. Lanky's arms were outstretched and his eyes bugged as he looked over his shoulder. Brady's pass was perfect, and it settled ever so gently into Lanky's outstretched hands.

As the referees ran down the field, holding their arms straight up to signal the miracle touchdown, Duff again heard Coach's voice, "Yes, Yes!"

The game was won, but what happened next had stuck with Duff ever since. He knew Brady had felt betrayed by the backhand across his face. He knew it was still there, this invisible barrier between them, but as he ran down the field Duff felt as if a locomotive had hit him broadside. Only later did he learn that one of the Cleveland players had clotheslined him in a fit of rage. And with his head spinning, he sat up in time to see the blur of his little brother coming like a mountain lion as he leveled the Cleveland linebacker. Then, not satisfied that he'd probably put his lights out, Brady turned and pounced on him. It took both coaches and the referees to pry Brady off of him.

Duff was lost in his thoughts and didn't realize his mother had gotten up and gone to the stove, until she began refilling his cup. He looked up at her. "You're right. I need to figure out how I'm gonna say it."

His mother smiled and pulled his head against her breast. "You're a good man, Duff Coleridge."

* * *

For a November afternoon it was relatively mild, but with the sun setting, there came a renewed chill off the river. Brady and Lacey were behind him stacking driftwood and building the fire while Duff skipped flat rocks across the water. With only four days remaining before he left for Vietnam, he needed to clear the air, and this was probably his last opportunity.

The fire climbed quickly as Lacey sat on the trunk of a fallen sycamore picking out *Wildwood Flower* on her guitar. Brady joined him skipping rocks on the water. Duff realized his baby sister was in a somber mood, still angry because he'd gone into the military. At least Brady understood, but he, too, had been asking questions and wasn't exactly enthusiastic about his leaving.

Duff returned to the fire to warm his hands. The sunset sparkled on the rippling water, and Brady walked around and sat on the log beside Lacey. Duff had watched the two growing ever closer, and it now seemed they were beyond teenagers with a mad crush on one another. Brady held his arm across her back, while she continued picking the guitar. The amber light of the flames reflected on their faces.

"You two sure have it bad for one another," Duff said.

He was trying to find a way to say it was okay, that he was now at peace with their relationship. Lacey looked down at the fire and smiled. The flames sparkled in her big brown eyes.

Brady looked into the fire and shrugged. "Yeah, I reckon so," he said.

Lacey smiled. "He always sounds so excited about me, you know?"

Duff laughed.

"Well, he's not much of a poet, but I think he's pretty serious. You both need to stay clear-eyed, and don't do anything stupid that might keep you from finishing school."

"You're one to talk about staying clear-eyed," Lacey said, "going off to Vietnam."

Duff looked away. He couldn't say his apologies with Lacey harping about him leaving.

"Aw hell, baby sister, I can take care of myself. Besides, if I go, maybe this meathead won't have to."

He tousled Brady's hair.

"Who are you calling a meathead?" Brady said, grabbing Duff around the waist.

They tumbled from the log and rolled across the gravel bar into the water.

"You two stop clowning around," Lacey shouted. "This is serious."

Duff and Brady stood panting in the knee-deep water.

"And you're gonna get pneumonia if you don't get out of that river."

Duff shook his head. "Aw hell, baby sister, you gotta lighten up, it's going to be an adventure."

"It's a war, Duff. Don't you get it?"

Duff and Brady walked from the water and stood beside the fire. Lacey sat on the log, staring into the flames. A tear ran down her cheek.

"Maybe I don't want to work all my life and end up dying in a mine like Daddy?" Duff said.

"Oh, so you're just gonna get it over with in a hurry by going to Vietnam?"

"Stop worrying, Lacey," Duff said. "I promise, I'll be careful. Come on, let's go for a walk together."

"Your clothes are wet. You'll catch a cold."

"No I won't. Let's go."

He took her by the hand, and looked back at Brady. "Keep the fire going."

Brady nodded, and Duff led his sister down the long gravel bar. The rocks crunched beneath their shoes, and a barred owl called from far downriver. When they reached the far end of the bar, Duff glanced back upriver where Brady was silhouetted by the fire.

"Have you given any more thought to what you're going to do in May after you graduate?"

"Mr. Langston said he can get me a job in Nashville, and let me sing in his club on the weekends."

"You better stay away from that old snake," Duff said. "I don't trust him."

"Oh, it'll be an adventure, don't ya know? Sort of like you going to Vietnam."

Duff felt his face burning as it flushed. He'd never seen this side of his sister.

"Being a smart alec doesn't fit you," he said.

"Being mean to Brady didn't fit you either."

She'd come out of nowhere with that one. There was nothing he could say. She was right.

"You didn't have to hit him."

Duff turned and looked into her eyes.

"I'm sorry, Lacey," he said. "I didn't mean to hurt either of you."

She looked down, her face in a pout.

"You need to tell *him* that."

"Why don't you go to college or hair dresser school or something?"

"With what? I don't have any money."

"I told you, I'm gonna split my enlistment bonus between you and Brady."

"I'm buying a car," she said. "I can't do anything without a car."

Duff prided himself on his ability to see people as they really were. Lacey was sweet but naive, and he'd only met Langston a few times, but that was enough. The bastard had the heart of a snake oil salesman. He took Lacey's hand and led her back to the fire.

"Well, if you go to Nashville next spring, I want you to watch yourself around that old bastard. You hear?"

Lacey nodded. "I'll be fine. You just take care of yourself."

Duff shivered as he stepped closer to the fire and dried his clothes. He wanted to have a one-on-one talk with Brady, but the timing just wasn't right. His apology would have to wait.

* * *

Late that evening, Lacey had gone to bed, but Duff and Brady sat out on the porch. Brady was on the wooden swing, while Duff sat in a rocker, his feet propped on the rail. Neither had said a word for better than an hour, but they weren't compelled to fill the void, for in fact there was no void.

A million stars hung in a purple sky, tiny crystalline white lights, each giving its small part to a cosmos that left Duff feeling he was looking into eternity. Life was this way. Each person gave a tiny part, and he was going to give his, but he knew Brady was feeling lost with him leaving for Vietnam.

"You don't have to act big and brave," Duff said. "But you don't need to worry about me either."

The chain on the porch swing stopped creaking.

"What do you mean?" Brady asked.

Duff laughed.

"Please, don't play dumb with me. Lacey told me you're worried."

"So, you aren't?" Brady said.

"I'm not stupid. It's going to be an interesting tour of duty, but I plan on keeping my head down."

"You know we graduated almost the entire first string last year," Brady said. "I was the only starter left on the team."

"Oh, hell," Duff said. "Is losing those three games still bothering you?"

There was only silence, and he looked across at Brady in the darkness. His younger brother's eyes were ringed with glistening moisture in the shadows.

"Okay, enough of that shit. Leave the tears for Lacey. You've got to take care of her while I'm gone."

"I just—" Brady's voice choked into silence. Duff stood and walked to the swing. He put his arms around his little brother's neck and grasped the back of his head, pulling him close.

"I just want you to come back. That's all," Brady said.

Duff sat on the porch swing beside him.

"Do you remember what you said to Gil Owen during the championship game last year when he started whining?"

Brady shook his head. "Not really."

"You said, 'Never give up.' Now, you take care of Mama and Lacey while I'm gone, and don't ever give up. You hear?"

He put his arm across Brady's shoulders, and they sat long into the night. His little brother was tough as a hickory nut. He'd be okay.

CHAPTER TWO

Leaving Melody Hill
December, 1966

The morning sunlight sparkled like a thousand diamonds on the heavy frost that day as Brady watched Duff standing in the front yard. A striking figure in his army dress uniform, he wore spit-shined jump boots, polished brass insignia and his silver jump wings. Gazing up toward town, Duff seemed focused on the white steeple of the church rising above the leafless trees. The Melody Hill church was a landmark that could be seen from miles away in the valley below.

Brady sucked down a deep breath because he knew what Duff was feeling. He knew because he felt it, too. The town was surrounded by misty river gorges and the rolling Tennessee hills as far as the eye could see. Growing up here was a boy's dream. Its parts were inconsequential, a combination General Store-Post Office with a flag, a small restaurant, a gas station, and nondescript wood-framed houses—they were inconsequential until their whole was crowned by the church. A shining pearl in a sea of green during the summer, the Melody Hill church represented a people as steadfast in their beliefs as they were stubborn in their ways—those of their Scottish Highland ancestors.

Brady walked over and cranked the pickup, leaving it idling in the driveway. The thick white vapor of its exhaust pooled in the cold morning air. Mama Emma and Lacey were on the porch, shivering and waiting to say their final good-byes. Like them, Brady harbored no misconceptions about life's illusive passing, but all were resigned to Duff's departure and his journey to a place fraught with danger.

"What are you looking at?" Brady called out.

Duff turned, and walked back to the porch.

"Just taking a last look at town. Don't want to forget what it looks like."

Brady was driving him down to the bus stop on 411. From there Duff would catch a Greyhound bus to Atlanta, where he would board a charter flight to South Vietnam. Standing on the steps, Brady held Duff's duffle bag while Lacey and Mama Emma said their tearful good-byes. When they were done, he loaded the bag into the back of the truck and sat behind the wheel while Duff got in on the other side.

"You ready?" Brady asked.

Duff nodded and turned to wave a final farewell as Brady pulled out of the drive. Duff was still looking back as they coasted down the road to the edge of town. Up ahead a black and white squad car was parked on the side of the road. Its occupant opened the door and stepped out. It was Sheriff Harvey. He raised his hand, signaling them to stop. Brady pulled up beside the sheriff as Duff rolled down his window.

Harvey extended his hand. "I heard you were leaving for Vietnam this morning, son. I just wanted to tell you to take care of yourself, and don't worry none about your family. I'll be keeping an eye out for them."

"Thanks, Sheriff," Duff said. "I appreciate that."

"You've done a lot of growing up since your daddy died, Duff," Harvey said. Duff nodded, and Harvey looked past him at Brady. "Matter of fact, both you boys have done real good. You've become men before your time."

Harvey put his hand on Duff's shoulder. "You're gonna be carrying a weapon in a war now, son. Things can get pretty confusing at times. I know. I was in Korea. Do the right thing."

"Yes, sir."

Harvey stepped back from the truck. "You take care now."

Brady glanced at his watch. They were growing short on time, and he pushed the old truck up to sixty as they rolled down the mountain road.

"You're anxious to get me gone, aren't you?" Duff said.

"I wish you wouldn't say that. I just don't want you to miss the bus."

Duff laughed. "And I want to make it there in one piece."

Brady let off the gas. "Sorry."

"Besides, you're inheriting this old wreck for the next three years. You better take care of it."

Brady glanced over at him. "Really?"

"Yeah, just keep the oil changed regular, and try not to put any more dents in it."

It wasn't long before they pulled into the gas station parking lot on 411 where they parked beside the blue and white Greyhound sign. Brady let the engine idle and the heater run to keep the truck warm while they waited. Duff glanced over at him, then up the highway. It was evident he was wanting to say something.

"Look, before I go..."

Duff paused, and Brady knew he was struggling with an inner demon. The bus came over the hill, and Brady turned off the ignition.

"I never should have hit you the way I did last fall. It was wrong, and I'm sorry."

"I forgave you a long time ago, brother, but what about me and Lacey?"

Duff looked down.

"I know you two will do the right thing, whatever it is. Just promise me y'all won't do anything stupid before you graduate. You know what I mean?"

Brady knew exactly what Duff meant. He nodded. "You have my word."

"And take care of Mama, too, while I'm gone."

"I will."

Brady pushed open his door as the bus rolled to a stop in front of the truck. It wasn't exactly the blessing he'd hoped for, but at least they'd healed an old wound. The airbrakes on the bus hissed and the door opened as the driver stepped down to the ground. Brady handed him the duffle bag and turned to Duff. The emotion welled up inside him, but he fought it back. He wanted to show Duff he was strong, but only then did he notice that it was Duff who had become teary-eyed.

The two men embraced. "Don't worry about Mama or Lacey," Brady said. "I'll take care of them. You just take care of yourself."

"Better climb aboard, son," the driver said.

Brady stood leaning against the truck as the bus pulled back onto the highway. He tried to find Duff in a window to wave, but he couldn't see him. He waved anyway. He and Duff had shared a bedroom for the last twelve years. They played on the same football team. They hunted together, fished together, and they'd not been apart for a single night in all those years. Brady had never heard anything quite as sad as the whine of the bus engine as it disappeared in the distance.

CHAPTER THREE

The Republic of South Vietnam
December, 1966

Before jump school at Benning, Duff had never been on an airplane. If he had, the take-off of the ancient C-119 Flying Box Car packed with soon-to-be paratroops would have scared hell out of him. He thought the missing rivets, the bone-rattling vibrations, and the engines roaring at max RPMs were all normal. Only now, after experiencing the smooth take-offs and landings of the commercial airliner en route to Vietnam, did he realize the difference.

His ignorance had been a blessing back in jump school. There had already been enough tension with those first jumps, but now, as the big jet airliner landed at Tan Son Nhut, the tension had returned, and it ratcheted to a new high as Duff worried about what else he might overlook in the face of his ignorance. "You don't know what you don't know," the old drill instructor had said. "That's something only experience can teach you."

The commercial airliner had padded seats and air-conditioning, definite improvements over the old military aircraft at Benning, but these comforts quickly disappeared when the stewardess opened the door after landing. A steamy, almost smothering air filled the cabin along with an odor that was one part stench and the other chemical. It was diesel fumes, JP-4 jet fuel, and mildewed canvas hanging over an odor of rotted vegetation, smoke, and decay. Duff imagined it to be similar to the atmosphere of an alien planet.

The soldiers slowly shuffled toward the door, and an instant sweat broke on Duff's forehead. Not only did it stink, but the air was hotter than any he'd ever felt. It was as if someone outside were blasting the doorway with a huge propane heater, but it made no difference. He was on an adrenaline high. He was here in Vietnam, a place where history was being made.

Outside the aircraft he heard men shouting, the roar of jets departing on another runway, and vehicles crossing the tarmac. And as he stepped into the sunlight at the top of the stairs, there came a muted thunder in the distance. He instantly recognized the sound and paused, gazing out at the horizon. It was the crunch of artillery impacting in the nearby hills—the real thing. Other than the day they buried his father, it was the most sobering moment of his life.

* * *

After the excruciatingly long and uneventful flight from the United States, it seemed the army was suddenly in a hurry again as Duff and nineteen others stood in formation beside their duffle bags. They had been flown directly to a replacement company at Phan Rang where a young first lieutenant paced back and forth and addressed them in a manner totally out of character for the military. He raised his voice only enough to be heard.

"Shortly, gentlemen, you will be completing paperwork, including next of kin notifications. You will trade your cash for military scrip and receive your malaria pills from the company medics, as well as any inoculations you may still need. After that you will be issued field gear and receive an abbreviated in-country orientation. We have shortened it because the First Brigade has already departed out of Tuy Hoa for a major operation up in Kontum Province...."

By early afternoon they were handed off to a supply sergeant who wasn't quite as soft-spoken. He had them standing in front of wooden pallets stacked with piles of equipment.

"Sorry for the rush, fellas," the sergeant said. "But we didn't want y'all to miss all the fun."

The supply sergeant walked with a noticeable limp, as he directed the men to take certain items from each pallet, the first being a rucksack with a metal frame. By the time Duff reached the last pallet, he could hardly believe the weight of his field gear. Marching more than a few hundred meters with a rucksack that felt like it held a granite tombstone seemed impossible.

He was now the proud owner of a new steel helmet with a liner and camouflage cover, cloth bandoleers, a poncho, a quilted poncho liner, six pairs of socks, a flak jacket, green canvas jungle boots, rip-stop jungle fatigues, a field dressing with pouch, eighteen M-16 magazines, a cleaning kit, two canteens, a bayonet, and near the end of the line were several wooden crates with claymores, smoke canisters, boxes of 5.56mm ammunition, frags, white phosphorous grenades, and starburst flares. Last in the line were stacks of cardboard boxes containing C-rations.

"Fill each of your magazines with eighteen rounds, men. Draw two each of the frags and one smoke, and one starburst, but don't fuck around with the frags or the flares. No need blowin' your ass up right away. Charlie's gonna be trying to do that soon enough.

"Now, you're gonna be doin' a lotta humpin' for the next eleven months. You hear what I'm saying? You're gonna be dog-ass tired, but don't get stupid and throw any of this shit away 'cause if you do, two bad things are gonna happen, young troops. One: Charlie's gonna pick it up, and make a booby trap to blow your ass away. And two: If Charlie don't, I'm gonna bust your sorry ass myself for not turning my shit back in to me. And, oh yeah, there's a number three: Uncle Sam's gonna dock your pay for it, too."

* * *

The next morning, Duff lay prone on his poncho at a rifle range while another NCO and a range officer walked up and down the line behind the troops.

"I don't need no John Wayne shit," the NCO shouted. "Just take your time. Shoot a group so we can get your weapon zeroed."

Duff lined his sights on the target. The NCO, another leathery old sergeant with a wad of tobacco in his mouth, said the distance was a hundred meters. Duff noted a slight cross wind, adjusted his aim and squeezed the trigger. The little M-16 cracked and threw a small piece of brass off to one side. There was almost no recoil. Nothing about this weapon was like his Remington 700 back home or the M-14 he used in training. The M-16 reminded him of the .22 caliber Nylon 66 he'd seen the marksman shooting at Trade Day when he was a kid. He realigned his sights and popped off the remaining nine of the ten shots he was supposed to fire.

"Goddammit, cowboy!" the sergeant screamed. "What part of 'no John Wayne shit' did you not understand?"

He stood over Duff, red-faced, with his hands on his hips as he spit an amber stream of tobacco juice off to one side.

"Me and you ain't gonna get along at all, numb nuts. And if you don't learn to follow orders better, Charlie's gonna send your ass home in a body bag."

After a minute or two the other men finished their ten shots.

"Cease fire. Clear and lock open all weapons," the range officer shouted.

The sergeant returned, walking up behind Duff.

"All right, men," the range officer shouted. "Walk down range, and stand beside your targets."

The sergeant stood glaring as Duff got to his feet.

"Come on, dumbass, me and you are gonna be out here for a while."

Duff understood the sergeant was pissed because he'd fired his ten rounds too fast. Perhaps there was some peculiarity with this little rifle. After all, it did look more like a Daisy Red Rider than a real rifle. Duff stood beside his target while the sergeant studied it.

"How many shots did you fire?"

"Ten, Sergeant," Duff said.

There was one hole the size of a silver dollar in the paper. The sergeant dropped his steel pot on the ground and bent down, sticking his finger through the hole.

"Shiiiiuuuutt."

He looked up. He wasn't smiling, but he was no longer glaring. "Where'd you learn to shoot like that, troop?"

"Back home, Sergeant," Duff said.

"And where, pray tell, is home?"

"Melody Hill, Tennessee, Sergeant."

The sergeant picked up his helmet and called out to the range officer.

"Sir."

He motioned toward Duff's target. "You might want to see this."

The lieutenant walked up and stared at the target. After a moment or two he nodded his head.

"Mighty fine shooting, troop. What's your name?"

"Coleridge, sir."

"Might be a recon candidate, sir," the sergeant said.

The lieutenant nodded again. "Possibly. We'll see how he performs in the field, first."

As the lieutenant walked away, the sergeant turned to Duff. "Your shot-group is about an inch right. Do you know how to adjust your sight?"

"I think so, Sergeant. If the sight adjusts one minute of angle at a hundred meters, it probably needs a couple counter-clockwise clicks to—"

"Never mind! Just make the damned adjustments."

The sergeant walked away mumbling and shaking his head.

* * *

The next morning they boarded a C-130 to Kontum, and by early afternoon Duff and the new replacements sat at the edge of the base LZ. He checked his gear for the hundredth time. Choppers were coming to carry them out to the field, where the rest of the brigade had already deployed. In the distance came the thumping of helicopter rotors as they approached, and the men began standing, helping one another pull the heavy rucksacks onto their backs. Within minutes the rotors clacked loudly as the choppers flared, engulfing them in red dust as they settled onto the LZ.

They were Hueys, open-sided UH1-H helicopters that held four men on a side and a couple more in the middle. The pilots glanced their way as Duff and the other men stooped and ran toward the choppers. The rotors maintained a fast and steady beat until the door gunner gave the pilots a thumbs up. The RPMs increased and the turbines screamed, and when the pilot twisted the collective the chopper lurched skyward.

Duff looked around at the other replacements, but they were watching the ground slip away below. Turning, he looked over his shoulder at the OD green panel behind his head. It was stitched with silver bullet holes. His first impulse was to touch one with his finger, but he looked instead toward the cockpit. The copilot's windshield also had spider-webbed holes covered with strips of duct tape.

Duff tried to swallow, but couldn't. His wish for adventure was quickly turning to the reality that he was heading into a war. The door gunner had his arm draped over his M-60 as he looked down at him with a maniacal smile and mouthed something. The sound of his voice was mostly lost in the rushing wind and clattering rotors, but Duff heard, "Welcome to Vietnam, Cherries."

As the chopper lifted higher the steamy air near the ground gave way to a cool and almost refreshing breeze. Duff looked out across the Vietnamese countryside. Below, the green mountains were laced with fog. It was much like the Tennessee Overhill, but these were the Central Highlands of Vietnam, a place he had heard about on the television news and again at Tiger Land at Fort Polk. These mountains were covered with dense triple-canopy jungle and stretched as far as he could see, all the way to the horizon. Beneath the benign green canopy lurked the enemy, entire regiments of the North Vietnamese Army that called this terrain home. They were well trained and armed with modern weapons.

Duff looked down at his M-16. They said this mission was called "Operation Pickett." The only Pickett he had ever heard of was in history class when the teacher talked of Confederate General George Pickett's ill-fated charge at Gettysburg, the beginning of the end for the Confederacy. If his memory was correct, that attack resulted in over five thousand Confederate soldiers killed or wounded. Hopefully, this operation wasn't named for the same Pickett.

According to the officer who gave the mission briefing, they were heading up north to an LZ south of Dak To and thirty miles west of Kontum. The operations area was on the Cambodian border, the other side of which lay a huge sanctuary for several large NVA units. The Hundred and First had already taken casualties, and Duff and his comrades would be divided amongst the various companies as replacements. He was going into battle, and the vibrations of the chopper in his gut grew with the inner tension.

After a while he noticed the chopper dropping closer to the hilltops. The door gunner stood and snatched the bolt on the sixty, chambering a round. His helmet was decorated with graffiti, and the maniacal smile returned as he glanced around at Duff and the other new replacements. Seems, for whatever reason, new guys were resented and called cherries, newbies and FNGs. This door gunner was no different, and he seemed happy to deliver them into battle. The chopper made an abrupt dive toward the treetops. Duff gritted his teeth. The wind buffeted his face and the trees became a green blur. This was it.

* * *

Within minutes the choppers flared over the LZ, their rotors popping loudly as they scattered the green smoke streaming from a canister on the ground. Duff's throat was constricted with tension as he jumped from the skid and ran toward an NCO holding an M-16 and waving the replacements into the jungle. Before he reached the wood line, the choppers lifted off and disappeared into the hills. The men piled into a wooded ravine where they stood panting and looking about. Duff's new jungle fatigues had gone from chopper-ride dry to sweat-soaked in seconds, and he felt more beads of sweat rolling down his neck.

The jungle ravine was quiet. And though it was mid-afternoon, only the dimmest emerald twilight filtered down through the dense canopy. The oder of mold and rotted leaves permeated the damp, warm air, and there wasn't a hint of a breeze. Several NCOs were gathered around a lieutenant holding a sheet of paper. Duff held his M-16 at the ready. The only sound was that of the choppers fading in the distance, and the shadows gathered around him.

"When I call your name," the lieutenant said, "sound off." His voice was subdued, almost a whisper.

"Avery."

"Here."

"Aquadro."

"Yo."

"Booker."

"Here."

"You three go with Sergeant Jamison."

He went through the entire list, as the replacements were assigned to individual units. Duff and two others followed an NCO to a company CP several hundred meters away where they were assigned to platoons. Sergeant Collier, his new squad leader, led him down a hillside to where a single man sat smoking a cigarette on the edge of a hole. An entrenching tool was stuck up in the dirt beside him and he was bare from the waist up. The soldier's fatigue pants were faded and torn.

"Here's you a brand new cherry, Nobles," the sergeant said. "Try to take better care of this one, will you?"

Duff didn't miss the implications.

"Hey," he said to his new partner. He dropped his rucksack beside the hole.

The soldier looked up at him with eyes that were bloodshot and drooping with fatigue.

"They told me I was getting another cherry."

Duff reached for his rucksack. "Want me to go somewhere else?"

"No, no," the man said in a tired voice. "Just chill out."

"Well, don't call me 'cherry' again, how 'bout it? Name's Coleridge, Duff Coleridge."

The soldier smiled. "Hell, dude. I think I'm going to like you. I've been here better than twelve months and you're the first, uh, *new man* to get in my face. Jimmy Nobles is my name."

They shook hands.

"Twelve months?" Duff said.

Nobles shook his head. "Yeah. They talked me into extending my tour six more months. Don't ask why. I'm just a dumbass."

Duff didn't press the issue, but picked up Nobles's entrenching tool instead. "I reckon we need to make this hole bigger."

"Yeah, reckon so," Nobles said. "You never know when those motherfuckers are gonna show up."

Duff began digging, packing the dirt around the logs Nobles had placed in front. When he was done, he climbed out of the hole.

"I have a claymore," he said. "You want me to set it out down the hill?"

The surrounding jungle was quiet as a wake, and the men spoke in muted tones.

"I've got one down that way," Nobles said, pointing down the hill. The hillside was covered with thick grass and small trees. "Maybe another one over there in that little ravine would be good."

As Duff pulled the claymore from his rucksack, there came a peal of thunder. He looked up. Gray clouds had blotted out the sun.

"Looks like we're gonna get wet," Duff said.

"This is supposed to be the dry season, so maybe it won't last long. Gimme your claymore. I've got a couple trip flares down there. I'll put it out."

The first raindrops were big clotted ones that made an audible thump in the dirt beside the hole. The two men sat shoulder to shoulder in the foxhole wearing their ponchos as an early dusk fell and the rain became a steady downpour. Peeking over the log to his front, Duff saw nothing but fluttering leaves and a gray sheet of foggy rain.

"So, where are you from?" Nobles asked.

"Tennessee. Melody Hill, Tennessee. It's east of Chattanooga near the Carolina, Georgia state lines."

"No shit?" Nobles said. "I'm from Dalton, Georgia, just south of Chattanooga."

"Yeah," Duff said. "I know where that is."

"Better eat before it gets dark," Nobles said.

They broke out C-rations in the gathering darkness.

"These ham and beans smell like a fart," Nobles said.

Duff grinned. "Yeah, they're pretty awful."

Nobles suggested swapping two hours on, two off, and he would take the first watch. Duff realized that no one probably slept first watch, but he didn't argue. After all, Nobles looked exhausted, and seniority *did* have its privileges. By 2200 hours the water in the foxhole was up to his knees, and despite the plan,

Duff's adrenaline high left him unable to sleep. When it came time to wake Nobles for his 0200 watch Duff let him sleep. Nobles didn't budge, and Duff sat staring bug-eyed into a solid wall of rain and darkness.

Morning came but without the sun. The rain continued unabated in the first gray light of dawn. It came in steady, straight-line streams as if the entire South China Sea was pouring through a sieve above the jungle. A foggy mist obscured the hillside below, and the constant patter of the rain shrouded all other sounds.

Duff should have been drowsy. He hadn't closed his eyes all night, but the static of residual adrenaline still rattled around in his head, not as intense as it was in the dark of night, but still there. He looked over at Nobles. He was asleep, slumped over in the armpit-deep muddy water, his nose barely inches from the surface. Around them in the foxhole floated their empty C-ration cans, some sticks and leaves, and the edges of their ponchos. The rain drops spattered the muddy water into Jimmy's face and it dripped off his nose, but he didn't move.

Duff nudged him. "Hey."

Jimmy's eyes opened, and his head jerked upright. His momentary disorientation seemed to morph into instant alertness.

"What?" Nobles said.

"I think the dry season is over," Duff said.

"Dammit, Coleridge. You have a sick sense of humor."

"Aw shit, Jimmy, I just wanted to wake you up before you went completely face-down in the water. Besides, I think my poncho is leaking."

"Hummph." Jimmy wiped the water from his face with his bare hand as he looked around. He pushed away the trash and cans floating near his chest.

"I think you're a little too late to be worrying about your poncho leaking. How come you didn't wake me up for my watch?"

"You looked so peaceful, I just couldn't bring myself to disturb you."

Nobles smiled. "Okay, smart ass, you'll see. In a couple days you'll be able to sleep on an ant hill."

"I believe you," Duff said. "Just first night jitters, I reckon."

Nobles climbed up out of the hole and reached back with his hand. "Come on. Crawl your ass up here behind the hole and catch some sleep. I'll keep watch till we move out."

* * *

The rain ended, but the hills, rivers, and jungles were an agonizing treadmill of slippery climbs and muddy slides for the next few days. Staying off of the booby trapped trails, they pushed through jungle that held an eerie twilight in the middle of the day. They hacked through brush and vines with hooked thorns that ripped Duff's new fatigues. Walls of razor sharp elephant grass and towering bamboo thickets surrounded them, and danger, it seemed, could come from anywhere at any moment.

Although he'd learned to catch restless snatches of sleep, Duff's tiredness became all-consuming, and he fought its effects. It was easy to fall into the same catatonic state as some of the men around him, but he refused to let down his guard. They'd said back at Polk that when you least expected it, Charlie would be in your face, and if you weren't ready, your ass would come home in a body bag. This was his sixth day in the field, and the company was forming yet another perimeter that afternoon.

Duff glanced skyward. A gray overcast lent to the spooky silence that surrounded them. The company was spreading in an oblong perimeter along a ridge facing the Cambodian border. A stillness pervaded the jungle like none he'd heard since back home in the Overhill. The CO was quietly assigning sectors and fields of fire for each of the platoons. Duff's platoon leader motioned toward him and Nobles.

"You two—Coleridge, Nobles, over here," he said in a low voice.

The young lieutenant pointed through the trees to a secondary ridge down below.

"You men see the saddle on that ridge down there?"

They nodded, and the lieutenant held a PRC-25 up by its straps.

"Take this radio. You're going to be on LP tonight, call sign Charlie Whiskey One-Lima. Any questions?"

Duff could think of dozens, but he looked instead at Jimmy. Jimmy was the one who had been here for over twelve months, but he said nothing. Duff waited, thinking the lieutenant might give them more.

"Stay awake, men. That's Cambodia down there half a klick out, and recon has been finding enemy sign everywhere. Call in a sit-rep every two hours. Have a nice night."

Jimmy shouldered the radio and directed Duff to take the lead. They pushed their way down the ridge through the thick vegetation. The sun finally broke through the clouds, hanging low on the horizon.

"I don't know how we're supposed to see anything in this shit," Duff whispered.

"That's why they call it a listening post, dumbass. We're supposed to listen."

Duff took it slow, moving as quietly as possible. There was no breeze, no birds calling, not even the occasional distant call of a monkey. It was quiet as a church at midnight as the two men made their way toward the saddle below. It became difficult to tell where they were, but after a few minutes Duff thought they were getting close. He parted the vegetation with his left arm and led with the barrel of his M-16 as he took another step and stopped.

"What's wrong?" Jimmy asked.

Duff looked left, then right. He was standing on a wide trail, almost a road. He looked down. It was filled with footprints.

"It's a trail," he said.

"We're in the middle of nowhere," Jimmy said. "It's probably just a game trail."

"No," Duff whispered. "It's more like a dirt road, and it's full of tracks."

Jimmy pushed his way out of the undergrowth and stood beside him.

"Shiiiiuut," he muttered.

He looked left and right.

"This is a fucking highway. We better get back in the bushes and call it in."

He turned and parted the brush with his sixteen.

"Come on."

The two men stopped only a few feet from the roadway. Duff could see no more than twenty meters of the trail in either direction, but he maintained watch while Jimmy knelt behind him whispering into the handset of the PRC-25.

"Charlie Whiskey One, this is Charlie Whiskey One-Lima, Over."

Duff barely heard the tiny speaker on the handset as it broke squelch each time. He peeked through the undergrowth as he watched the trail.

"Charlie Whiskey One, this is Charlie Whiskey One-Lima, Over," Jimmy called again.

The speaker on the handset again broke squelch with a barely audible scratch. Duff caught movement out on the trail, or did he? With the fading light, he wasn't sure. He blinked as sweat ran into eyes.

A barely audible voice came from the handset.

"Go ahead One-Lima. What do you boys need?"

Duff caught movement again. This time he realized he was looking at a man. A soldier was less than twenty meters down the trail. The soldier slowly knelt as he held up his hand to stop whoever was behind him. It was an NVA soldier wearing a khaki uniform, and it seemed he was staring directly at them. Duff didn't move a muscle. He didn't blink. His thumb rested on the selector switch of the M-16.

Without looking back, he slowly extended his leg until he felt Jimmy. He pushed hard with his foot. Duff dared not move his head, but quickly realized he had Jimmy's attention. Neither of them moved. The NVA soldier also knelt statue-still, staring up the trail. Duff thought about tossing a grenade, but the enemy soldier's stare had him fixed in place, unable to move. Duff detected Jimmy making the slightest movement. He was inching his hand toward a frag hanging on his web gear.

The enemy soldier slowly came to his feet. Duff stopped breathing. With a waist-high scooping motion of his palm, the NVA soldier signaled his men ahead. He grasped his AK-47 with both hands and took a tentative step, then another. The soldier suspected something was amiss. Duff pushed the selector switch over to full-auto.

"Take him," Jimmy whispered.

Duff brought the sixteen to his shoulder in one smooth motion as he mashed the trigger. The soldier spun and fell backward, and Duff redirected his fire into the shadows down the trail, shooting until the magazine was empty. Jimmy threw a grenade and slapped Duff's shoulder.

"Let's go," he said.

Pushing blindly through the undergrowth they ran across to the opposite side of the small ridge before turning up the hill toward the perimeter. Duff inserted a new magazine as he ran. Everywhere around them AK-47 rounds cracked and zipped, shredding the leaves. The nasal chirp of the enemy's voices came from the jungle down the ridge. The enemy had apparently recovered from the ambush and were spreading across the ridge in search of them.

"Gotta go, gotta go," Jimmy said as he looked back. "We gotta go fast."

Duff caught up with him as Jimmy pushed his way through the undergrowth. They were less than a hundred meters from the perimeter.

"Stop," Duff said.

Jimmy glanced over his shoulder.

"Stop," Duff said again.

Jimmy turned, but continued backing through the brush.

"What?"

"Call and tell them we're coming in," Duff said.

Jimmy stopped.

"Shit. You're right."

Duff turned and held his sixteen to his shoulder while he watched their back-trail.

"Charlie Whiskey One, this is One-Lima, Over."

"This is Charlie Whiskey One. What the hell is going on down there, boys?"

Duff listened as he watched their rear.

"We found a damned highway down here, sir. Coleridge nailed a point man, an NVA regular I think. We're comin' back in."

There came the sliding whisper of an artillery shell overhead followed by a hollow pop. A flare lit beneath a parachute and drifted down the ridge. The jungle became a dancing collage of spooky shadows.

"Illumination," Jimmy said. "Come on. Let's get the fuck out of here."

"Coming in," Duff shouted as they drew closer to the perimeter.

"Come on," someone shouted from up the ridge.

CHAPTER FOUR

Pickett's Charge
December 1967

uff and Jimmy made their way across the perimeter to the company CP where they fell to the ground panting. It had been an uphill run for nearly a quarter mile through the thick undergrowth. Both men were laced with sweat and out of breath.

"Okay, men. Calm down and tell me what you saw."

As with all conversations in the jungle, it was sotto voce, but Duff recognized the voice. It was the company commander, Captain Shipley. With him were the company first sergeant and the XO, all mere shadows in what was now total darkness.

"I didn't see much of anything, sir," Jimmy said. "Coleridge was the one practically nose-to-nose with the dude."

"What did you see, Coleridge?" the CO asked. His voice remained low.

"One NVA regular, sir. He was carrying an AK-47 and looked to be a point man for a unit coming up a pretty wide trail going over that saddle down there. I couldn't see the others behind him, but I think he heard our radio. I had to take him out. Nobles threw a grenade, and we started back up the hill to the perimeter. I could hear a lot of voices behind us, and we took a pretty good bit of small arms fire."

"Are either of you hit?" Shipley asked.

"Not me," Jimmy said.

"Me either," Duff said. "But I think they're using that road to maneuver around our perimeter."

"Was he wearing a pack or other heavy gear?" the CO asked.

"No sir, just a couple bandoleers."

The CO turned to the first sergeant and nodded. "They're getting ready to probe us. Let's get some arty on their ass."

The CO turned back to Duff and Jimmy. "Okay, men. Mighty fine job. Go back down to your platoon CP. We'll wait and see what happens next."

As they made their way down the hill, there came the whisper of more artillery shells high overhead. Not sure whose they might be, they dove to the ground and waited. Bright flashes lit the night sky, followed a split second later by the shuddering *karoomphs* of 105mm rounds impacting on the saddle below. A trip flare lit the jungle in front of them as the men on the perimeter opened fire. After a few moments, someone yelled cease fire. It was quiet. Just a probe.

There came several more probes that night, but the men were ready each time.

* * *

The next two weeks were much the same, as the brigade hacked through the jungle, climbed hills, swatted insects, and walked until Duff didn't think he could walk anymore. There was only incidental contact, probes, watching from the perimeter at night and searching by day, but it seemed the enemy was biding their time. They were taking jabs when they could, taking on small units or a point man every once in a while, but they were waiting for the right opportunity and the right moment to hit hard. At least this is what Duff figured. It was what he'd do if he were the enemy. Jimmy agreed. Sooner or later the shit was going to hit the fan.

They searched, and they found villages and enemy camps with huts so elaborate they even had bamboo pipes for plumbing. They found bunkers with weapons caches. They found maps, tunnels, and supplies. They even found bowls of cooked rice and smoldering cook-fires, but they didn't find the enemy. What they found were booby traps.

"Coleridge, Garcia," Lieutenant Cupper shouted.

They were searching an abandoned village when only a minute earlier a huge explosion had ripped a hooch to smithereens. Smoke, straw, and the odor of cordite still floated in the air as Duff jumped to his feet and ran forward. Usually, there were calls for a medic, but this time it was only Lieutenant Cupper calling. Cupper was the platoon leader. He had a little mustache, but Duff figured he couldn't be more than twenty-two years old.

The lieutenant was on a knee talking into the radio. A medevac chopper was already inbound. Garcia, another of the new replacements who had arrived with Duff, trotted up behind him. The lieutenant motioned for them to get down.

"Atway went behind that hooch," Cupper said. "That's his helmet out front there."

He pointed to a helmet lying in the middle of the village in front of what remained of the hooch.

The lieutenant nodded. "It's time you cherries got a real taste of what this shit is all about. Coleridge, you get his helmet. Use a poncho, and the two of you police-up any remains you can find. We'll cover you from here."

So far, Duff had seen only one other man wounded up close. After stepping on a toe-popper, the sole of the soldier's jungle boot had been blown away and his pants were shredded with shrapnel. Much of his left foot was gone. As they pushed him into the chopper that afternoon Jimmy had reassured the man, "Don't worry, buddy. At least you still have your nuts."

Duff was pretty certain Atway wasn't going to be so lucky, and the irony of it all struck him. He shook his head as he came to his feet. Thinking a man *lucky* who had his feet and legs shredded by a land mine could happen only in Vietnam.

Cautiously, Duff eased forward, followed by Garcia. He reached the helmet and was about to pick it up when he saw a gray paste and bits of white bone inside. An acid bile rose in his throat. Behind him, Garcia had already gone down on all fours and was retching. Unable to avoid the human remains, Duff picked up the helmet with his thumb and finger and walked behind the smoking remains of the hooch. There was only a crater. The ringing in his ears grew until he heard nothing else.

Duff didn't know how long he had stood there when he felt someone grasp his arm. It was Jimmy Nobles. Garcia was still out in the middle of the village puking and retching.

"Come on," Jimmy said. "I'll help you."

Duff looked back at the crater.

"But there's nothing left of him."

Jimmy motioned with the barrel of his sixteen.

"There's some web gear and looks like part of him up there."

Atop the thatched roof of a nearby hut was all that remained of Atway, a portion of his upper torso tangled with his web gear. Duff felt the world jerked out from under him, and he landed on his butt. The ringing in his ears became a roar.

* * *

It was now dark, and though he realized time had passed, Duff had no recollection of leaving the village. Jimmy was beside him with a canteen, trying to get him to drink some water.

"Where are we?" Duff asked.

"In our NDP," Jimmy said.

Duff looked around. Jimmy had carved out a hole for their night defensive position.

"How'd we get here?"

"We walked. Hell, you don't remember? We humped another three klicks after we left the village."

Duff took the canteen and drank. After wiping his mouth with his sleeve, he looked around. His head was beginning to clear.

"I reckon I lost it back there."

"Anyone would have," Jimmy said. "Cupper's an idiot. He should have asked for volunteers or at least sent an old-head up with you guys. Ended up, Garcia lost it. We had to put him on the medevac."

* * *

Day after day the "hike in wonderland," as Jimmy called it, continued. The platoon captured one scout, caught hiding in a bamboo thicket, and a small VC squad was surprised on a creek bank and shot up, but no main-force units were found. It was damned spooky when someone saw enemy scouts in the distance watching them with binoculars. Days of monotonous heat, drizzling rain, and boredom were punctuated by moments of adrenaline-fueled terror.

Clashes with the enemy were seldom more than sporadic firefights, often lasting no more than seconds. Choppers would dive in above the trees, unleashing salvos of rockets, but there was seldom anything found afterward, except booby traps. These continued to be the worst of it. Every camp, every bunker, every hut and every trail it seemed was wired with grenades, punji stick holes, and an array of other lethal devices. So far they hadn't found any more 155 rounds like the one that all but vaporized Atway, but the booby traps still took a maddening toll both physically and mentally.

Duff and Jimmy were standing guard on a stream outside a newly discovered enemy camp that morning when they heard the muffled blast of yet another booby trap. Duff shuddered as word came that first platoon had two wounded and a KIA. A medevac chopper was inbound. This was the second in as many days, and Duff was beginning to wonder when *his* time would come.

"This is a crock of shit," he said. "How are we supposed to fight these people if we can't even find them?"

Jimmy shook his head. "Be careful what you wish for, partner. You should've been here back in June when the entire 24th NVA came at us."

Duff sank his canteens into the stream as he filled them.

"Didn't have to worry about booby traps that day. Hell, our people called in napalm on their own positions just to get the bastards off of 'em."

Jimmy tossed him one of his canteens.

"Fill mine, too."

Duff dropped halazone tablets in each canteen. "I reckon you're right, but this shit still gets to you after a while. LT said the brigade has taken more casualties from booby traps than anything else."

"Yeah," Jimmy said, "it's a mind fucker, but I'm telling you, it can be a lot worse."

Duff screwed the cap back on Jimmy's canteen, and tossed it up to him. "I believe you. I just wish we could do something else."

Jimmy shrugged. "Well, if you don't like this shit, they're always looking for volunteers to join the lurps."

"The lurps?"

"Yeah, L-R-R-P, long range recon patrols, they——"

"I know what LRRP's *are*, but why volunteer for them?"

"Lurps don't have to fuck with search and destroy. They go out and find these fuckers. It's mostly just recon, but the way I hear it, they do a lot of ambush, too, and when they get into shit it can be bad. You know?"

Duff nodded. "Yeah, but it has to be better than this."

"Whoa, partner," Jimmy said. "It was just a joke. This boy ain't volunteering to be no lurp."

"Why not?"

"Like I said, if they get into shit, it's usually bad 'cause they're outnumbered. Nope, not me. Those boys got big balls and little brains. I'll take my chances with the line company."

"So, how come you extended your tour six more months?"

The corners of Jimmy's mouth turned down, and he gazed up the stream.

"I really wish I had a good answer for you. It's hard to explain. I mean it's not like you can just turn it off when it's time to go home. The best way to explain it is that after you live this way for a year, it becomes a drug, one you know might kill you, but you want more. It's kind of like that Puerto Rican dude in Alpha Company who died from a heroin overdose last month. Poor fucker just couldn't leave it alone."

* * *

Word came just before Christmas that they were going on stand-down for the holiday. The brigade choppered back into the base at Kontum on Christmas Eve, and Duff had his first shower and hot meal in over two weeks. He was beginning to feel almost human again, and despite the constant booms of the outgoing artillery, the base at Kontum was a vacation villa compared to living out in the boonies.

The day after Christmas, despite having slept twelve hours, he and Jimmy lounged in the sun as they polished off their third hot meal in as many days.

"I never thought I'd say this about army food," Jimmy said, "but that shit wasn't half bad."

Duff smiled. "Yeah, beat the hell out of C-rations, and I can't believe I'm actually sitting here with clean fatigues and dry feet."

Mail-call had come, and letters from home seemed like Duff's only lifeline to reality as he sat reading them. It had snowed the week before Christmas, and Lacey wrote about how they had gone sledding on a bald out near the Brister place. That was one of their favorite hunting spots, too, and Brady wrote in his letter how they'd begun seeing coyotes there from time to time. With the heat and humidity, it was hard to imagine hunting, sledding, or doing anything that involved cold weather. Home seemed a distant memory.

Resting on a sandbagged bunker, Duff and Jimmy watched as twenty-four shirtless men played jungle-rules volleyball nearby. With twelve on a side, the ball was in play as long as it didn't touch the ground or go out of bounds, and the net was only a marginal guide as flailing arms and fists collided in something resembling a standing rugby scrum.

Folding the letters, Duff shoved them in his pocket, locked his hands behind his head and lay back.

"Nap time?" Jimmy asked.

"Reckon so," Duff said.

Sleep was a luxury they imbibed like drunkards, but the words no sooner left his mouth than the platoon sergeant shouted for them.

He was down near the volleyball court waving his arms. "Let's go," he said. "The CO is getting ready to give a briefing."

The volleyball game was stopped as more men streamed in from the surrounding hooches. Captain Shipley had arrived and was pacing back and forth as he motioned for the men to gather around. The red dust from the volleyball game had begun to settle.

"No need for a formation, First Sergeant," he said. "Let them smoke if they want."

"Okay, troops," the first sergeant shouted. "Gather up close and take a knee."

Duff was beginning to see his company commander as a man who was focused, but who didn't waste time with fanfare and bullshit when it wasn't necessary.

"Men, as most of you already know, we're going back into the field tomorrow. We're heading north this time to the Dak Akoi Valley, and this time we'll be doing a night assault. We're going in after sunset. As always, don't talk about this with anyone outside of this unit, no one. We don't need some hooch mama passing word through the wire about our business. We will move with speed and secrecy on this deployment. The LZ's will be cleared with Bangalores only hours before we land.

"There are at least two verified enemy units in the area, the 304th Viet Cong Main force Battalion and the 24th NVA Regiment. We will air assault in with the support of the 10th Combat Aviation Unit. I want all weapons cleaned, all ammo magazines emptied, cleaned and reloaded, and make sure your iodine and malaria tabs are dry. If anyone hasn't written home, do so now. I don't want to get letters from your mothers wanting to know why you haven't written. You will get more details from your platoon leaders after I meet with them. Enjoy the rest of your afternoon, but get some rest. We may be out for as much as twenty-one days.

"Oh, by the way, Brigade Headquarters is still looking for a few LRRP volunteers. No guarantee you will be accepted, but see your platoon leaders if you're interested."

A few snickers came from the men, and Jimmy nudged Duff. "There you go, John Wayne."

Duff grinned at Jimmy's sarcasm, and as they walked back to the hooch the platoon sergeant hailed them.

"How about you boys? Either of you want to go to the recon platoon?"

Duff stopped. To him, being a lurp made sense. Instead of the constant pressure of waiting for the enemy to strike or waiting for the next booby trap while rummaging through enemy camps, it put the initiative for making contact back in his hands. The sergeant continued walking, apparently assuming Duff and Jimmy weren't interested.

"I'll go," Duff said.

The sergeant stopped and looked back.

"Have you lost your fucking mind?" Jimmy asked.

"No, and if you had half a brain, you'd volunteer, too," Duff said.

Jimmy wrinkled his brow.

"What about it, Nobles," the sergeant asked, "you want to go, too?"

Jimmy didn't look at the sergeant. Instead he fixed Duff with his gaze as he answered. "Sure, sarge. Why the hell not? Sign me up, too."

Duff grinned.

"I must be out of my fucking mind," Jimmy said.

* * *

Later that evening the platoon sergeant returned. The CO had said "not now." He said Duff was too inexperienced, and they needed Jimmy's experience with all the new replacements, but he'd reconsider when they returned from the field in a few weeks. Duff shrugged. He knew too little to be disappointed, but Jimmy exhaled with an over-dramatic sigh of relief. Duff ignored him. Perhaps it was a good thing. Perhaps he wasn't seeing what Jimmy saw, and it was becoming more evident every day that what you didn't know could get you killed.

* * *

Duff sometimes found himself, if only for a moment, wanting to clear his mind of the ever-present tension. He wanted to relax and enjoy the beauty of the countryside, but as the choppers climbed out of Kontum late that December afternoon, he knew better. The emerald hills were laced with the amber gold of the setting sun and a foggy mist rose from the shadowed valleys, but it was a lethal beauty. Beneath its protective shroud, the jungle hid a determined enemy. There would be no respite, no relaxation, not this day or any other day in the next few weeks. They were headed into the Dak Akoi Valley.

Even with secrecy and surprise, the air assault was pretty much a non-event from a battle standpoint, which was okay with Duff.

The dry fatigues didn't last long, as they became soaked with a salty sweat. They were back into the grind of search and destroy, and somehow the army had found a way to have them walking uphill ninety percent of the time. Within days his neck was raw. His groin was raw, and his nerves were raw as they found signs of the enemy everywhere.

Jimmy was walking point for First Squad that afternoon, and Duff had volunteered to walk slack for him. While Jimmy chopped away with his machete and searched the ground for booby traps, Duff looked past him, searching the terrain ahead. The platoon was moving in squad columns abreast, about one hundred meters apart. First squad was moving along the side of a ridge, while Second and Third Squads took parallel tracks in the little valley below and Fourth Squad walked on the other side near the crest of the ridge. With the thickness of the vegetation and the strong wind, the units were having difficulty staying abreast of one another, and the squad leader was continually calling for them to speed up or slow down.

The afternoon sun filtered through the trees in a collage of dancing light and shadows as Jimmy pushed and hacked his way through the jungle. Duff was only a few steps behind him. The squad leader, RTO, and the rest of the men were strung out behind them. The strong breeze had been blowing all day, masking the sound of their movements. It also brought some relief from the heat and, considering the possibilities, it wasn't that bad of a day.

A thunderous *karooomph* sounded down the slope to their rear. Jimmy went down on one knee. Duff knelt beside him, his heart thumping in a full-bore adrenaline rush. A spattering of shrapnel fell through the treetops. They gazed into the small valley below where a blackish-gray smoke rose from the trees. M-16s chattered, and a few stray tracers shot above the treetops.

"What do you think?" Duff asked.

"I don't know," Jimmy said. "Sounds like Second Squad hit a booby trap, but I wonder what they're shooting at. I don't hear any AKs."

Duff noticed the hillside was more open up ahead.

"Let's ease up there, where we can see better."

Jimmy shrugged and came to his feet. From below came the shouts of the men from Second Squad. It sounded as if someone was calling for a medic, but with the wind, it was difficult to hear. Duff and Jimmy reached the open area on the side of the ridge and stopped. They watched the hillside below and listened. There came the sounds of men running. Second Squad was apparently maneuvering up the hill.

When the first soldiers broke from the cover below Duff thought they were friendlies. Three, four, six, all ran across the opening less than sixty meters away. Jimmy threw up his M-16 and fired a burst, then another as Duff stood momentarily dumbfounded. Two enemy soldiers tumbled and fell, but one came to his feet and began hobbling on one leg as he crossed the opening below.

"Shit!" Jimmy shouted.

He pulled his sixteen down and snatched the bolt back as he tried to clear a jam. He looked back at Duff.

"Shoot, goddammit!"

Duff recovered from his paralysis and threw up his rifle. Another five or six soldiers burst from the cover following the first group at a dead run. Instinctively leading the first man, Duff squeezed off a shot. He didn't hesitate as he went to the next man in line, and then the next before they disappeared into the jungle. When he stopped firing there were three more enemy soldiers writhing in the brush below.

"Jesus, Coleridge!" Jimmy said.

Duff went to a knee and fired three more shots at the ones still trying to get to their feet. They fell, unmoving.

"Son of a bitch," Jimmy said. "I think you got three of 'em."

"Shshhh," Duff said, putting his finger over his lips. "Let's move."

It was something he'd heard the old heads say, 'Never stay in one spot too long.' He sprinted across the slope toward a large ravine. Jimmy followed, and they squatted there in the grass, maintaining a watch on the clearing below. It was quiet for a minute or two, until Duff again spotted movement. A helmet slowly rose from the undergrowth across the clearing. It was Sergeant Collier, the squad leader. Behind him was Baker, the RTO. Both peered tentatively down the ridge, where the wind scattered the smoke through the treetops. Jimmy raised his hand and signaled across the opening, pointing to where the VC had crossed below.

Sergeant Collier told Duff and Jimmy to cover the right flank while the remainder of First Squad joined with Fourth Squad and swept down the hill. After a few minutes only the tops of their helmets were visible. Duff still felt his heart thumping in his chest, when there came the sound of a man moaning. He was somewhere in the direction the enemy had fled. A moment later came a barely audible voice. "Medic, medic."

The wounded man was apparently further down the deep ravine. Duff rose to his feet, pushing the brush apart for a better look.

"Get down," Jimmy said.

Duff glanced over his shoulder. "Why? That's one of our guys, probably from Second Squad."

"Get down," Jimmy said.

Duff knelt.

"I'm gonna crawl up there where I can see down the ravine," Jimmy said. "When you see me stop, I want you to call out loud and tell him you're coming. Toss a stick or a rock down that way, but don't move from right here. And stay down."

"Why?"

"Just do it!"

Removing his helmet, Jimmy crawled on his belly along the ridge until he reached the head of the ravine. Duff waited, and when he was certain Jimmy was ready, he called out, "I'm coming, man."

He tossed a large stick into the brush to his front. Jimmy came up on his knees and threw a grenade down the ravine. Only then did Duff realize what was happening. The zip and crack of enemy rounds filled the air. He opened fire with his M-16, as did Jimmy. Both men fired blindly into the brush and across the ravine as the explosion of the grenade filled the air with leaves and debris.

It was over in seconds, and Jimmy crawled back down to where Duff lay. Rolling on his back, he retrieved his helmet and looked over at Duff.

"You know, in some ways you're sharp as a tack, but in others, you're just plain ol' dumb as a fucking brick."

"How did you know it was the enemy?"

"You'll learn," Jimmy said, pointing down the ridge. "Our guys are over that way. Only the enemy went across the ravine. Besides, I've heard talk about them using that trick before."

"Yeah, but how did you know for *sure* it was the enemy?" Duff asked.

"Because," Jimmy said. "When our guys call for a medic, they say 'me-*dic*' not 'med-*deak*'."

* * *

Two weeks later Operation Pickett ended, and the company first sergeant sent for Duff and Jimmy. The CO wanted to meet with them. Captain Shipley came from the rear of the operations center and shook their hands. As they stood at ease in front of Shipley that afternoon he informed them that they were being awarded Bronze Stars for their actions after the last enemy ambush.

Duff hardly felt worthy. Second Squad had two men KIA by a command-detonated booby trap, a 105 round. Six others were wounded, three seriously. He knew them all well. He and Jimmy had simply been in the right place at the right time. Between them they had accounted for four enemy KIA and two wounded. Problem was the platoon had gained no ground. They simply traded with the enemy using the only commodity they had, the lives and crippled bodies of their buddies. By Duff's estimation, it was a poor trade.

"Nobles, you can pack your gear. You're going to the LRRP platoon," Shipley said.

"What about Coleridge?" Jimmy asked.

"They want men with experience."

"With all due respect, sir, I may have more time in country, but Coleridge is already ahead of me in a lot of ways. He knows more about this business instinctively than anybody I've been around."

The captain glanced over at Duff, then up at the first sergeant. After a moment he looked back at Jimmy, but he said nothing.

"Sir," Jimmy said, "if Coleridge doesn't go, I don't want to go. Can't you call their CO and see if he'll change his mind? I'm telling you, Duff's more than ready."

Shipley nodded. "Okay, men, I'll shoot straight with you," he said. "I didn't recommend him because I think he's too inexperienced."

"Well, with all due respect, sir, you're wrong."

Shipley's face flushed, but he grinned and nodded. "Okay, Specialist Nobles, you've been here for over a year. Let me ask you a simple question."

He paused and made direct eye contact with each man, before settling on Jimmy.

"You guys are obviously good buddies, but would you trust this man's experience if the enemy had your ass in a bind?"

Jimmy nodded. "Yes sir, I would, and it's not that he's been here all that long, but that he just does the right things naturally."

"Okay, men, step outside and wait for the first sergeant to call you. I'll see what I can do."

Duff and Jimmy walked across the road to a sandbagged bunker, where Jimmy squatted in the shade and lit a cigarette.

"Did you mean what you said in there?" Duff asked.

Jimmy looked up with a flat grin. "Yeah, I meant it, but don't let it go to your head. You've still got a lot to learn."

After nearly thirty minutes, the first sergeant came to the door and called out to them. "The CO wants to see you, men."

Shipley sat behind a field table stacked with reports, while Jimmy stood shifting from one foot to the other. Duff stood beside him.

"Okay, men, I spoke with Captain Meadors. Seems this war is producing more opportunities than we have experienced men to cover them at the moment. You can both pack your gear for the recon platoon."

"Thank you, sir," Jimmy said.

"Both of you need to understand you'll have to successfully complete training before they accept you, which means one or both of you could be kicked back down here to the line company. Coleridge, you better expect they're going to push you a whole lot harder than most. You better be ready."

"I will, sir," Duff said.

"Good luck, men. Any questions?"

"Only one, sir," Duff said.

"What's that, Coleridge?" the CO asked.

"Who was the Pickett that the operation was named for?"

Shipley wrinkled his brow and gave him a dubious smile. "Confederate General George Pickett, why?"

"Just wondering, sir," Duff said.

"He was a hell of general," the captain said. "Made that charge at Gettysburg when ordered, even when he knew it was a mistake."

Duff nodded. That was the issue. They had just spent a month in the field thrashing about in the jungle and fighting an almost invisible enemy with little to show for it. Worse, the old heads said that the day the brigade climbed aboard the choppers and left the area, the enemy returned. With his initial confidence already becoming eroded, Duff wondered if, like Pickett's charge, this entire war was a mistake.

* * *

One good thing about the LRRP platoon was they always knew before anyone else what was coming down the pike. Duff was no longer a blind pawn going about his duties. Pawns always got screwed. He remembered the summer when Lacey decided to become chess master of the world. After she beat him three games in a row, he learned to use his pawns as a screen. The pawns were always the ones that got sacrificed while you positioned the knights and bishops. And that was another good thing about the LRRP platoon, he was beginning to feel more like a knight, albeit one dressed in rip-stop jungle fatigues and whose trusty steed was a Huey helicopter.

The LRRP unit received new orders and moved north to I-Corps to help the Marines. Word was that this was going to be the new AO for the entire First Brigade of the 101st, as they joined a multi-unit force called Task Force Oregon. In the meantime, Duff faced the intense training regimen required to join the LRRP platoon. This included more indoctrination about the people of Vietnam, their history, and the politics of the country. It was something the training officer said was important. "The more you know about your enemy," he said, "the better you become at predicting his movements."

The first day began with an hour-long orientation, then a class which was led by a beautiful young woman of mixed blood. She was introduced by the training officer as Ms. Bouchet, a representative of the government of Vietnam and a liaison for a civic action center in Da Nang. Dressed in khakis with a white blouse, she wore her hair in a bun, and appeared to be in her early twenties. Although she had the looks of a fashion model, she was all business.

Duff, Jimmy, and their teammates were ogle-eyed as Ms. Bouchet explained their responsibility to respect the villagers they were brought here to protect. Despite her exotic accent, the woman spoke perfect English as she described the difficulties they would face in villages with Communist infiltrators, the enemy's tactics of intimidation and brutality, and how it would be easy to misinterpret the actions of frightened villagers. She spoke for nearly thirty minutes, describing the country's recent political history, its various factions, and the myriad problems its leaders faced. When she was done, she asked if there were any questions.

Jimmy elbowed Duff. "Ask her a question. Don't let her go. I think I'm in love."

Duff raised his hand.

"Yes," the woman said. "What is your question?"

Duff cleared his throat as he stalled for time, but it was useless. He could think of nothing to ask.

"I suppose I don't really have one, but my friend here," he motioned toward Jimmy, "said he wanted me to ask one so you would stay longer."

There came a riffle of laughter from the class, and the woman smiled. She had glistening white teeth and the crimson lips of a goddess.

"Thank your friend for his compliment," she said. "And what is your name, sir?"

Duff felt his face flush with embarrassment.

"Specialist 4th Class, Duff Coleridge, ma'am. Sorry, uh, I didn't mean to—"

"No apology needed, Specialist. Your honesty will serve you well in this war. Your accent is unusual."

"So is yours," Duff said.

The young woman smiled as she cocked her head to one side. "Touché, young paratrooper."

"We call it 'hillbilly' back home," Jimmy said.

Duff turned. "You ain't got much room to talk, partner, with your *jaw-ja* accent."

The woman let out a gasp of laughter.

"Both of you make your language much more interesting."

The class ended, and later Duff and Jimmy watched as Ms. Bouchet climbed aboard a chopper and was swept away, back to Da Nang and forever out of their lives.

"As Jesus is my witness, Coleridge, in all my life I have never seen a woman that beautiful. She was prettier than Susie Riley, our homecoming queen. And your dumb ass couldn't come up with a question."

Duff laughed. "What's wrong with your asker?"

"You two clowns better get your heads back in the war," someone said.

They turned. Following them up the dirt path was their new team leader, First Sergeant Ederson.

"You better forget about that woman and get your asses in gear," he said as he passed. "We'll be back in the field in ten days, and you've got a lot of training to do."

* * *

The first time they handed him the M-14 sniper rifle, Duff caressed it with a certain familiarity. It didn't have the black plastic-like frame of the M-16. They called the material on the M-16 frame "composite," but the M-14 frame was oiled wood, like his thirty-aught-six back home. And its 7.62 millimeter round, though smaller than the aught-six, was not nearly as tiny as the M-16 round. Putting the rifle to his shoulder, Duff peered through the three-by-nine Unertl scope. He smiled. This was a rifle he could like.

"The range officer down at Phan Rang said you're pretty handy with a rifle," the team leader said.

First Sergeant Tom Ederson, a thin and wiry vet who'd already fought in the Korean War, was on his second tour in this one.

"We're going to get you a little training with that M-14," Ederson said. "Nobles will train too, but he's primarily going to act as your spotter."

Duff nodded. And though he knew a lot instinctively, the trainers took his natural marksmanship abilities and honed them with lessons in range-estimation, wind-drift, and vertical angle calculations as well as camouflage and escape-and-evasion. This graduated into another week of conditioning and training, including advanced map reading, rappelling and a variety of skills the new job required.

He and Jimmy, the two least experienced men in the platoon, were paired as sniper and spotter, and word of their first mission came down the day they finished training. Ederson's team was headed inland to the Song Con River Valley, a mountainous area southwest of Da Nang. Duff and Jimmy were additions to what was normally a five-man team, and told to consider this their final test. After a thorough briefing on every detail of the patrol, Ederson told them to get some rest.

* * *

The single Huey flew beneath a sodden sky that day, hopping misty ridges as they made two false insertions south and east of the true LZ. Twice the chopper descended into the treetops where it hovered for a few seconds then climbed noisily skyward. This hopefully kept the enemy guessing and unable to determine when the LRRP team actually exited the chopper at its true destination, the opposite side of a high mountain ridge just south of the Song Con River Valley. The mission was to hump over the ridge and into the Song Con Valley, where they were to pull recon on a road paralleling the river.

On the third approach the chopper hovered several feet above a steep mountain hillside while the men dropped their gear and leapt from the skids. All seven were safely on the ground within seconds, and the chopper made a slow ascent until it cleared the jungle. Once above the trees, it pitched nose-down, shooting across the treetops, and down the valley, where it disappeared in the mist. Then it was quiet. The only sound was a faint shuffling as the men retrieved their gear. First Sergeant Ederson studied his compass. Duff looked down at his M-14. The scope was set on the lowest power, in case of close contact.

"Let's go," Ederson whispered. "Move out."

The lurps moved single file, climbing through rain-soaked vegetation as they made their way up the mountain. Everything metallic was wrapped with green tape to prevent the telltale clicks of metal to metal. The only sound was the gentle rustle of the evergreens and vines as the men quickly but quietly wove their way through the mountain jungle. Total camouflage and total stealth with complete silence blended the lurp team seamlessly with their jungle environment. And this was the reason Duff had volunteered. He had become the hunter instead of the hunted.

CHAPTER FIVE

The Snow Storm
February 1967

Brady looked out the window at the road in front of the house. Duff had been gone for two months. Hunting season was over, and nearly four months of school remained until graduation. Outside, the roads were clear, but the icy remnants of last week's snow hung in the shadows of the trees and houses. He waited and watched for Lacey. She had taken the pickup into town to get some groceries. For a moment his thoughts went to Duff, but quickly returned to Lacey.

She was still shaky with the manual transmission, and he thought of his promise to Duff to watch over her. She was overdue. He should have gone along with her, or at least tried to coach her more before she departed, but she was as stubbornly independent as she was beautiful.

Brady was thinking of calling the grocery store when the old GMC finally appeared. The pickup slowed as Lacey made the turn off the highway.

She didn't down-shift to match her speed, and the old truck chugged along in third gear as it labored up the hill. Lacey turned into the drive, and the pickup lunged to a stop. Not realizing she was being watched, she gave herself a firm "mission accomplished" nod. Brady smiled and walked out to help her with the bags.

"You know they're calling for more snow tomorrow night, don't you?"

"Yeah," she said. "Why?"

"Did you forget about the singing tomorrow night?"

He held the front door open as she walked inside.

"No, why?"

The singing was at the VFW in Cleveland, Tennessee, the nearest big town to Melody Hill. Between were more than thirty miles of twisting mountain highways.

"Driving home on a snow-covered road in the dark isn't my idea of a good time?"

Lacey set a bag of groceries on the kitchen table.

"Well, it's not supposed to start snowing until tomorrow night. We should be on our way home before it gets bad. Besides, the snow hasn't ever kept you from going hunting."

"That's because it's not but a mile or two around to Mr. Brister's place," Brady said. "I can walk home from there."

"Well, the roads are clear. They're having a big fund-raiser, and I promised them we would be there."

Brady shook his head in resignation. They hadn't played for an audience since Duff left for Basic last year, and it wouldn't be the same without him on bass, but Lacey was right. The VFW was depending on them, and the pay usually wasn't bad either.

* * *

By late Saturday afternoon Brady had gassed up the truck and loaded the instruments, speakers, and other sound equipment under a tarp in the bed. Lacey kissed her mother goodbye, while Brady pushed a large plastic bag beneath the tarp. Lacey ran out to the truck, and opened her door.

"What was in the bag?" she asked.

"Life insurance."

"Huh?"

Brady glanced off the mountain to the west where a sodden gray sky squatted on the horizon.

"It's one of Mama Emma's goose down quilts."

As they headed down Highway Thirty, the radio announcer said snow was expected by morning, and heavy accumulations were possible. Brady glanced over at Lacey. She smiled. "Don't worry, we'll be back home before it gets too bad."

"You better hope so. There aren't any hotels once we get out of Cleveland."

* * *

It was after midnight when they left Cleveland that night. The VFW had paid them well, and the old World War Two and Korean War vets were so infatuated with Lacey's fabulous voice they had given her twenty more dollars in tips. It had been a good night—so far. The first dots of frozen moisture hit the windshield as Brady headed back up the Old Copper Road. The highway was dark, except for the narrow tunnel illuminated by the headlights where the first snowflakes darted about. Lacey put her head on his shoulder, and after a few minutes she breathed heavily as she slept. Brady felt the warmth of her breath on his neck.

There was so much responsibility when you had to look after someone, and he owed a lot to this family—his family. They'd given him a new mother, a big brother who had become his best friend, and then there was Lacey. Duff said it was a crush, but she was the girl with whom Brady hoped to spend the rest of his life. And now that Duff was away, there was so much more to consider. Brady found himself second-guessing his decision to drive to Cleveland. He should never have let Lacey talk him into it. He should have stood up and refused, but it was too late now. If only they could make it back to Melody Hill before it got really bad, he would be happy.

The snowfall graduated to heavy clots of white flakes sticking to the windshield, further obscuring the roadway. Brady slowed the truck, barely going twenty miles per hour as the highway followed the banks of Ocoee Lake. He searched for the Highway 30 turn-off. The road disappeared no more than fifteen yards into the black tunnel where the headlights reflected against a wall of whiteness. Despite the defroster fan blasting against the windshield and the wipers struggling to slue away the snow, telltale accumulations began forming on the windows. It was a wet snow, the type that would make an icy sheet before it built up on the already frozen road.

Despite his slow speed, the Highway 30 junction sign sprang out of the darkness. Brady braked and turned the wheel, but the truck skidded. He turned into the skid. It seemed almost slow motion as the truck inexorably continued toward a huge roadside ravine, and only when the tires struck the gravel shoulder did the truck stop. With his heart thumping in his chest, Brady straightened the wheel and accelerated back onto the road, heading up Highway 30. They were still better than twenty miles from Melody Hill. Thankfully, Lacey remained sleeping soundly against his shoulder.

The downhill curves were the most dangerous, and Brady found he could drive with the right-side tires on the shoulder to gain better traction. Before long he realized with the near white-out conditions he'd lost track of where he was. He had traveled this way often, but he was now disoriented, and unsure how far they'd come. The tires began spinning again as he climbed yet another steep incline. Down-shifting, he searched for a place to pull off the highway.

Lacey raised her head and grasped his arm. "Where are we?" There was fear in her voice as she squinted at the windshield.

"Somewhere south of Reliance."

"I can't see anything. What are we going to do?"

"There's some houses along here somewhere, but I'm not sure exactly where we are."

"You mean find a house?"

"No choice. We can't keep going. Look for lights. If we don't stop and ask somebody to stay the night, we're going to end up running off the road."

A narrow snow-covered lane appeared in the headlights. Brady braked and eased off the highway. He started down what he hoped was a driveway, but after only a few yards he stopped.

"What is it?" Lacey asked.

"Did you see a mailbox back there?"

Lacey shook her head. "I don't know. I can't see anything."

Brady eased the truck ahead. The snow was getting deeper, but they were apparently on gravel, and it offered better traction. Tall pines lined the narrow drive. It certainly looked like a drive, but they had gone barely a hundred feet when a metal gate appeared in the headlights.

"Damn it," Brady muttered. "It's just a pasture."

After turning off the heater fan and stopping the wiper blades, he rolled down his window. Peering into the darkness, he sounded the truck's horn, then listened. If there was a house nearby he hoped to hear a dog barking, but the sound of the horn was instantly muted by the falling snow. The cold flakes stuck to his face, and the silence was broken only by the soft puttering of the truck's exhaust. He wiped the side mirror.

"There's a spot right beside the road that looks pretty flat. I'm gonna back up there and turn around."

Hooking the steering wheel, Brady pulled the transmission into reverse and backed slowly. The rear of the truck sagged with a thump.

"Shit."

"What is it?" Lacey asked.

Brady shifted into first and let out on the clutch. The wheels spun.

"I backed us into a ditch. We're stuck."

Brady opened the door and stepped out. The snow was already ankle deep.

"Where are you going?"

"To get the quilt. It's going to be a cold night."

It was an awkward but not totally unpleasant arrangement as Lacey lay atop him and buried her head against his shoulder. Brady pulled the goose down quilt around them like a cocoon. With their legs intertwined, the heat of Lacey's body was better than he had ever imagined. Holding her head close, he caressed her hair, and his thoughts took him back to that day at the bus stop when he had given Duff his word. It was going to take some special will power to make it through this night.

"This isn't so bad," Lacey whispered.

"I can crank the motor every hour or so to warm us up, but it's still gonna be a long night."

Lacey kissed his cheek, but Brady turned away. "Let's try to sleep," he said.

She sighed.

"It's got to be this way," Brady said.

"Why?"

"We owe it to Duff."

She kissed his neck. "I love you, Brady."

"I love you, too. Now, let's try to sleep."

She sighed again, but after a few minutes she was again breathing heavily with sleep. Brady was glad because the bulge in his pants throbbed until he was certain it would burst. He lay wide awake, knowing all he had to do was massage her back and she would awaken. The cold wind outside the truck moaned and the windows were sealed with an opaque coating of frozen vapor.

Brady jerked awake. He had been asleep, but for how long he didn't know. Lacey was still sprawled on top of him, her head hanging between his shoulder and the seat. His feet had come out from under the quilt and felt like blocks of ice. He pushed his hand beneath Lacey's shirt and began rubbing her back. She moaned softly and began to stir.

"You make a really lumpy mattress, boy, but the massage feels good."

Brady pulled his hand from beneath her shirt.

"Why'd you stop?"

"Are you getting cold?"

"A little," she said.

"Let's sit up for a while and run the motor."

Brady opened the window slightly while the motor ran and the cab heated. After a few minutes, he shut off the engine. They remained sitting upright, curled in the quilt as they dozed again. Only when the gray light of dawn shone through the snow-covered windows did he again begin gently caressing her head. He was still sitting upright, but Lacey had curled up on the seat with her head in his lap. Her eyes opened, deep brown eyes, and they looked up into his. It had indeed been the longest night of his life, but he'd made it without breaking his promise.

* * *

It was ten a.m. and the sunlight sparkled on a foot of new snow as Brady stood beside the highway. He'd been there since first light, and not a single vehicle had passed. Highway 30 was a totally trackless blanket of snow. Overhead the sky was cloudless and brilliant blue. A momentary breeze sent sparkles of snow drifting from the pines. Were he not worried about being marooned another night, it would have been a magnificently beautiful day. Turning, he was about to walk back to the truck to warm up when there came a muffled sound in the distance. He paused and listened. It sounded like an engine puttering softly somewhere nearby.

After a few moments the sound faded, and Brady was again about to return to the truck when a wrecker appeared at the top of the hill. Bright yellow lights flashed atop its cab, reflecting against the snowy landscape. Stepping out in the road Brady waved his arms over his head. The driver flashed his headlights, and a few moments later stopped beside him.

The man rolled down his window. "You Brady Nash?" His vaporized breath whipped away in the cold mountain breeze.

"Yeah. We're stuck back there about thirty yards off the road."

"Lacey with you?"

"Yeah, she's in the truck."

"I ain't believin' y'all ain't froze to death by now. Your step-mama done called Sheriff Harvey, and she's 'bout worried herself sick."

"We were tryin' to find a house last night, but turns out it was just an old pasture road and we got stuck."

"Get in," the driver said. "We'll see what we can do."

* * *

By midafternoon they were back home. A teary-eyed Mama Emma met them at the door. The exhausted travelers told her of their adventures as they took off their jackets, gloves, and scarfs and sat on the couch. When they were done with their story, a look of concern remained on Mama Emma's.

"What's wrong?" Brady asked.

"So y'all slept all night in the truck?"

Brady realized her concern, but he didn't know what to say. "Yes'm, with this quilt. It kept us warm."

"Don't worry, Mama," Lacey said, wrapping her arm around Brady's neck. "This boy was an absolute gentleman. I think Duff made him take an oath or something."

Mama Emma looked at Brady. There was a new tear in her eye. She nodded. "Or maybe he just has a lot of respect for both of you," she said.

Brady felt his face flushing as he looked down. "I'm starving," he said.

Lacey kissed his cheek. "Always the romantic."

* * *

Brady thought about Duff constantly, and he worried. He was trying to write another letter that evening, but he was at a loss. Duff had always presented a stalwart image as an older brother, but Brady couldn't help but wonder if he was really making it okay in Vietnam. What could he say? He wanted to write and ask him, but he knew it was a waste of time. Duff was as hardheaded as Lacey.

Brady pushed the paper away and stared at the framed photo on the desk. It was one of Duff wearing his football uniform, standing tall with the ball under his arm, but his eyes were what stood out.

They were deep brown, calm, steady eyes that mirrored his quiet determination and independence.

With the tragedies hurled into their early lives, both of them had, as Sheriff Harvey said, 'become men before their time.' They saw things their classmates often overlooked because of youthful exuberance and innocence. Brady realized that both he and Duff had their weaknesses, but Duff's were far and away less troubling than his own. He had always been unsure of himself, while Duff was so much the opposite. Brady wanted to stay in Melody Hill, while Duff fearlessly departed. It was for this reason he was determined to prove his loyalty to him. He had to measure up, and show Duff he was worthy as a brother. The question was: how?

CHAPTER SIX

The Song Con River Valley
February, 1967

Duff and Jimmy were in the middle of the little column as the patrol crested the mountain and began descending toward a place where they could view the valley below. After a few minutes Ederson brought them to a stop on a moss-covered rock outcropping. Below spread the misty Song Con River Valley. On a distant mountainside to the north a few stray sunbeams managed to penetrate the overcast sky. It was a panorama of almost uninterrupted green, except for the silver metallic reflection of the serpentine Song Con winding its way back toward the coastal plain along the South China Sea.

The jungles of the Central Highlands were high, wet, and cool, and Duff had barely broken a sweat all morning. He sat watching as Jimmy studied the valley with his binoculars. Next to them, Ederson and Harrison studied the map and took a compass reading.

"What do you think, about a fifteen degree azimuth?" Ederson asked.

Harrison nodded. The mood was tense. This was bad-guy country and one misstep could prove costly, but the way Duff figured, it was a hell of a lot better than stomping around like a herd of water buffalo with the line company. Jimmy had stopped scanning back and forth with his binoculars and seemed fixed on some distant object.

"You see something?" Duff asked.

"Yeah. Looks like a village *way* down there." He pointed down the valley. "There's also a smaller hamlet up this way, just the other side of the river."

"That's right," Ederson whispered. "And there's a road that runs between them. I thought we could see it from here. At least that was the plan, but there's no way. We have to get closer."

Ederson was old school army. Terse with his directives and explanations, a hard smile crossed his leathery face only on rare occasions. He turned to Riley, the RTO.

"Contact the operations center and tell them the OP we saw from the chopper yesterday won't work. We're going down into the valley and get closer to the road. Ask if we can get a fly-over every couple hours, because I expect we're going to lose radio contact down there."

Riley whispered into the radio, and Duff could barely hear the scratch of static from the handset. After a few moments Riley looked up. "They roger," he said.

Ederson nodded. "Let's move out."

With Harrison on point, the patrol worked its way single file down the steep slope to the valley floor, then a short distance along the river until Ederson again brought them to a halt. A few meters below, the river rippled over shallow shoals of rock and gravel.

He looked at his map and motioned with his head toward the river. "We'll cross here," he said. "The road should be over there about three hundred meters."

A cold misty rain was falling and nightfall was rapidly approaching by the time the LRPP team reached the road. They turned and paralleled it until the point man found a small rise off to one side. Ederson knelt with the assistant team leader Harrison, as they whispered into one another's ears. After a minute or so, Harrison signaled Riley to pass the radio to Ederson. Riley and Harrison had first watch atop the little knoll. The jungle was thick, and the OP had to be on the slight rise no more than twenty meters from the road. Even with his total lack of experience, Duff recognized it as a risky move.

"The rest of us will form an NDP thirty meters behind the rise," Ederson said. "We'll do four hours on. Bright and Lopez will take the second watch. Coleridge, you and Nobles will have the third."

Their night defensive position was little more than a tight circle, where they lay in the wet grass. Darkness enveloped them, and the men huddled beneath their ponchos, shivering and trying to catch snatches of sleep as the misty rain continued falling. After a few hours Duff heard Ederson whispering as he sent Bright and Lopez forward to relieve the first watch. A few minutes later Riley and Harrison crawled back into the little huddle.

"What'd you see?" Ederson whispered.

Harrison, an E-6, was second in command and another experienced NCO whose laconic responses normally matched Ederson's.

"It's more like 'What didn't we see?'" he said. "Twenty-five to thirty VC all moving east. It's so damned dark we lost count. There were at least three crew-served weapons, including a machine gun and two mortars. They all had weapons, looked like mostly AKs and SKSs. They were also pulling a pretty big two-wheel cart. Rice and ammo for the mortars, I figure."

"I think we counted at least four RPGs, too," Riley added.

"How accurate do you think you are with your numbers?" Ederson asked.

"It's a SWAG, Tom," Harrison said. "Like I said, it was awful dark, but I think we're pretty close."

Duff heard the scratch of Ederson's pencil as he apparently made some notes.

"Okay, get some sleep," Ederson said.

Jimmy poked Duff. "Did you hear that shit?"

"Yeah," Duff said.

"You new guys better get some sleep," Ederson said. "You're up in four hours."

Sleeping within a rock-toss of thirty enemy troops didn't seem possible, but Duff had actually managed to doze off when someone grasped his arm.

"You're up," Ederson whispered.

Duff nudged Jimmy.

"I heard him," he said.

"All right, listen up," Ederson said. "You two ease back down here at oh-six hundred. That knoll is too damned close to the road, and we're going to un-ass this AO before daylight. We'll relocate to a better OP as soon as you get back, so don't waste any time."

Duff found himself shivering as he crawled up the rise through the wet vegetation. The rain had ended, and a slight breeze had begun blowing. After a few moments he realized the clouds had broken and the first stars were peeking through overhead.

His hand touched something. A boot. He froze. Ever so slowly the boot rose off the ground in front of his face. The boot's owner slowly rolled to one side and bent back his way.

"We think there's someone out there on the road," Lopez said in a barely audible whisper.

Several minutes passed. Lopez pressed his mouth against Duff's ear. "We think it's just one man, a trail watcher, maybe."

Duff pushed his mouth close to Lopez's ear. "Do you want to try to get back to the NDP?"

"Yes. We got to tell Ederson. We saw twenty more men going east toward the village."

Moving inches at a time, Duff and Jimmy crawled past their two comrades as Bright and Lopez slid backward down the rise. After a few minutes, Duff realized the two men had made a totally silent departure. And as the clouds scattered further, Duff spotted the strange shadow on the far side of the road, no more than twenty meters away. Unlike the shadows of the vegetation moving with the night breeze, this one was rock still.

He watched. Jimmy watched. They were focused, locked like setters on point, moving not so much as a muscle. The odor of the mud on the road filled their nostrils, and the night sounds of insects and the wind filled their ears. Duff found the adrenaline had his ears ringing again. Adrenaline was, as Jimmy so aptly described, the preferred drug of combat veterans.

Nearly a half-hour had passed when the shadow suddenly moved. The movement added new dimensions as it grew and seemed to unfold. The form of a man became visible. His feet squished in the mud as he walked one way on the road, then the other. He had a weapon strapped across his shoulder. After a few minutes he stopped and morphed back into the same motionless shadow. He seemed to be waiting for someone. Duff no longer felt the stinging bite of the mosquitoes, nor the damp cold vegetation. His every nerve was focused on the enemy soldier only a few meters to his front.

The minutes turned into hours, and Duff angled his wrist as he held his watch toward the night sky. He studied it for the time. As best he could tell, it was 0545 hours. He had no sooner lowered his arm than the shadow made a sudden move. The man stood up and moved to the center of the road. From the west came a splashing sound, followed by that of feet squishing in the mud as more men came up the road. They were moving fast.

"Chào ban!" the man on the road shouted.

His voice pierced the silence, sending tingles down Duff's spine. Jimmy eased his M-16 to his shoulder. Duff held up his hand.

"Wait," he whispered.

A flood of men sloshed to a stop around the man standing in the road. Their voices came as plain as if they were all standing in the same room, nasally sharp voices talking excitedly in the predawn darkness. Duff could scarcely breathe. He cut his eyes to Jimmy. Jimmy was frozen. Neither dared speak. They waited, still as stalking cats while the minutes passed, but the men on the road continued milling about.

Duff raised his eyes skyward. The first gray light of dawn had dimmed the stars. Someone moved only a few feet away. A man had come off the road and was standing directly in front of him and Jimmy. From the corner of his eye, Duff watched Jimmy's thumb roll the selector switch on his M-16 from semi to auto. A moment later there came a distinctive sound and then an odor. The man was urinating.

After a moment or two, the man turned and walked back out to the road. Duff looked at his watch. It was 0610 hours.

"It's getting light. We've got to get out of here," he whispered to Jimmy.

"You go first," Jimmy said. "I'll cover you."

This was no time to argue, and Duff began inching backward. He had moved less than six feet when it grew suddenly quiet on the road. He stopped.

A whisper came from behind, "Hey, numb nuts."

It was Ederson. "Have you fuckers been sleeping?"

Duff dared not move, nor answer. The only sound was that of the breeze filtering through the trees above. Two men stepped toward them from the road and stopped. Staring directly at the knoll, the two VC stood with their AK-47s at chest level. They were less than ten meters from where Jimmy lay. Duff was directly behind him, and Ederson was behind Duff. The sky was rapidly turning a lighter gray, but it was still dark in the undergrowth. Duff slowly pulled a frag from his belt. One of the VC took several more steps. He was now less than three meters from Jimmy.

Ederson's and Jimmy's rifles fired simultaneously and Duff pulled the pin on the frag and threw it out on the road. He yanked a second frag from his web gear, pulled the pin and threw it. Jimmy emptied his first magazine and retreated past him in a low crouch.

"Let's go," Ederson said. "Fast."

The three men sprinted back to the NDP.

"We have to get back across the river," Ederson hissed. "Don't stop. Nobles, Coleridge, grab your gear."

The seven-man patrol sprinted single file. So far, the enemy on the road had returned only sporadic small arms fire. The lurp team reached the river within minutes, colliding with one another as Ederson stopped at the front of the column. He eased down the bank and looked up and down the river. Turning, he pointed at Duff and motioned for him to come ahead.

"You and Nobles cross first. Set up over there and cover the rest of us."

He slapped Duff's rucksack. "Go!"

Splashing and churning in the loose bottom gravel, Duff crossed the river in waist-deep water. Jimmy followed. Dawn was breaking as a white mist drifted above the water. Duff crawled up the bank and turned to face the river. Jimmy was panting as he reached the bank. Duff reached down to pull him up the bank.

"I cannot believe I let you talk me into this shit, Coleridge," Jimmy said.

"Sshh," Duff said.

Jimmy scanned up and down the river with his binoculars, while Duff checked his riflescope to ensure it was clear. A moment later the next man started across the river. It was Sergeant Harrison. Then came Riley, Bright, and Lopez. Splashing noisily across the shoals, they climbed up the bank and ran past Duff and Jimmy. Duff continued scanning up and down the river. After the others had climbed the bank and disappeared, Ederson came sloshing and splashing across the river.

Ederson had cleared the water, but had twenty meters of gravel bar to cross when two, then three figures came down the far bank behind him. Jimmy had his binoculars focused upstream, but Duff spotted them immediately and raised the M-14. His first shot sent one of the VC reeling, but the other two opened fire. Tracers and ricochets cracked everywhere around him as he found the next man in his scope. His second shot was center-mass, and he quickly found the third enemy soldier and sent a single round through his chest. It was over in seconds, but when Duff pulled his eye from the scope, his heart sank. Ederson was squirming in agony on the gravel bar below.

"Spray the bank over there with a burst, then cover me," Duff said.

He slid down the bank and ran to the team leader. Enemy rounds zipped and whined as they struck the rocks. Grabbing Ederson, Duff pulled him over his shoulders and trudged back up the bank. Jimmy was bug-eyed as he helped Duff lay the team leader on the ground.

Ederson lay face down, squirming in silent agony. Duff found the wound in the back of his right thigh and quickly applied his field dressing. He rolled Ederson over on his back to tie the bandage in place, only to discover an even larger exit wound on the front side of his leg. Duff grabbed the field dressing from Ederson's web gear, stripped the wrapping and pressed it against the wound.

"What are we going to do?" Jimmy asked.

"We gotta get some plasma in him, but we can't do it here. Carry him up the hill and find the rest of the guys. I'm going to keep these fuckers from crossing the river till you guys get some distance on them. Tell Sergeant Harrison, I'll try to catch up with y'all."

"But—"

"Just go!" Duff said. "No, wait! Give me those frags off his belt."

Jimmy stripped the frags from Ederson's web gear and gave them to Duff.

"Now, go."

"Leave me here," Ederson muttered. "Give me a weapon, and get the fuck out of here."

Jimmy hesitated.

"Ignore him," Duff said. "Go!"

Jimmy had the wiry little first sergeant draped over his shoulders as he disappeared up the hill. Duff turned to face the river. The mist over the water had increased until the far bank was barely visible. He pulled the pin on one of the grenades, wrapped it with a strap and pushed it carefully beneath Ederson's rucksack. Pressing it gently, he held it until he was certain the weight of the rucksack held the grenade's spoon in place.

Several minutes passed before a single shadowy figure appeared on the far bank. It was another VC guerilla. He knelt, studying the thick cover on the bank where Duff lay. After a few moments, he slid down the riverbank and knelt amongst his dead comrades, examining each of them. His shadowy outline came and went in the misty fog rising from the water. Several more enemy soldiers appeared on the far side. Duff waited.

The lead guerilla rose to his feet and began wading across the river. He was nearly halfway before the next man came down the far bank, followed by another, then another. By the time the first soldier was climbing the bank directly in front of Duff, seven more were strung out across the river. The first man's head and shoulders appeared above the bank and Duff squeezed the trigger of the M-14 at point-blank range. Quickly, moving to the next target, Duff found another guerilla in the scope and fired, then a second and a third. Some ran back toward the opposite bank, but two squatted in the river with their AK-47s and sprayed the bank where he lay.

Their rounds cracked inches from his head as leaves and small limbs fell from the surrounding trees. Duff found the first one in his scope, then the second and within moments the water around them turned crimson as their bodies floated downstream. Two more soldiers scrambled up the far bank, and Duff centered his cross-hairs on the one nearly to the top and fired a round. The guerilla pitched forward and slid back down the bank. The last enemy soldier reached the top and escaped into the jungle.

With all eight VC dead or running, Duff came to his feet and swapped magazines in his rifle. He turned to run, but noticed something moving far down the river. An enemy soldier was crossing at a bend in the river almost three hundred meters downstream. The river was much deeper there, and the soldier was up to his shoulders in the water, holding his haversack and rifle over his head. Another appeared behind him. They were barely visible in the drifting fog. Another enemy patrol was crossing in an effort to flank the LRRP team.

Duff wound his scope to nine-power and braced the rifle against a large sapling. He searched through the fog with the scope as the man's head became visible then disappeared. He waited. The man's head came into view again. Duff pulled the crosshair slightly in front of him and squeezed the trigger. The round's extended hiss and crack echoed down the river, and Duff saw a splash as the fog again shrouded the distant riverbend. He caught sight of another soldier quickly returning to the far bank, but there was no time for another shot. He turned and ran up the mountain to catch up with the team.

* * *

Duff had trotted straight up the mountainside for nearly five minutes without finding a sign of his comrades. He paused to catch his breath. Tall trees and thick undergrowth prevented him from seeing more than fifteen or twenty meters in any direction. He had to keep his head. The team wouldn't return to the river valley. Too damned much enemy activity down there and no LZ. Besides, they had no radio contact with the TOC unless they climbed the mountain. It came to him.

The last place they'd been able to make contact with the operations center was from the original planned OP, the rock outcropping where they'd stopped the evening before. It was also the only place on this side of the mountain that might make a possible extraction point. That was where they were going, and it had to be fairly close.

He started trotting again, straight up the mountain, but there came the *karooomph* of an explosion down near the river.

Duff stopped. From below came the screams of the wounded. Had he not been so stressed, he might have smiled. There was something deeply satisfying with giving the enemy a dose of their own medicine, and whoever had picked up Sergeant Ederson's rucksack had gotten just that. By the sounds of the screams, it was several somebodies. But there was no time for celebration. He had to find that outcropping and the team or else wind up as an MIA feeding jungle rats with his bones.

CHAPTER SEVEN

The Hog's Tooth
March, 1967

The rock outcropping had to be somewhere close, but the jungle was thick, and Duff was uncertain. He stopped again, searching what little of the slope above he could see through the trees. A few hundred feet to his right appeared a particularly steep part of the mountain. He began angling up that way but soon lost sight of it as he climbed the nearly vertical slope. Sweat dripped into his eyes and he stopped again to listen.

Panic and fear were easy options, but he refused to let them to cloud his judgment. He kept his head and continued listening. From somewhere to his right came a sound, the wind perhaps, except it was repetitive—more like an animal breathing heavily. Carefully, he eased through the trees. He heard it again. Something was exhaling sharply every few seconds. Duff had heard the old heads talk about tigers in the mountains. It would be hell to come all the way to Vietnam to be eaten by a tiger.

He went to his hands and knees as he crawled through the undergrowth. The sound grew louder. He had moved only a few meters, when he suddenly realized he was above the rock outcropping. Below he made out the forms of at least two of his teammates lying motionless in the bushes. Two more, Sergeant Harrison and Jimmy, were lying prone on the rocks scanning the river valley with their binoculars. The breathing had to be Sergeant Ederson laboring from the pain of his shattered thigh.

Duff found a pebble and threw down into their mist. One of the men jerked, then slowly raised his head as he gazed up the mountain. It was Riley, and a smile broke slowly across his camo-blackened face as he saw Duff waving back at him. Riley signaled the others, and Duff crawled down amongst them. Jimmy clenched his hand and nodded in silence. His face was creased and taut.

"I reckon you knew what you were talking about," Harrison said. He was looking at Jimmy as he spoke.

Duff looked at the assistant team leader. Harrison smiled. "Nobles said not to worry because you would find us."

"You're a motherfucker with that fourteen," Riley said.

"How do you know?" Duff asked. "I might have missed."

"We watched through the binoculars from here," Jimmy said. "We saw those fuckers trying to cross the river. You got at least six of them."

Duff nodded. "There were eight," he said. "I got seven."

"What was that last shot?" Ederson muttered.

The old team leader had opened his eyes for the first time since Duff's arrival.

"Yeah," Harrison said. "Sounded like you were shootin' down the river."

"Some more of them tried to cross about three hundred meters downstream, near that bend in the river. I'm not sure, but I think I got the point man, and the others turned back."

"Okay," Harrison said. "The chopper should be here soon. We already called for extraction, and they're sending a couple of gunships in, too, for cover."

Within minutes the distant thump of rotors came from the east as the choppers approached. The extraction from the outcropping was tricky, and took nearly ten minutes, but it was successful. Climbing above the ridge the chopper headed east. A medic replaced Ederson's now empty albumin bag with a fresh one, and a few minutes later a warm wind buffeted them as the chopper cleared the mountains and crossed the coastal plain. The salt odor of the South China Sea actually smelled good for once. Duff finally exhaled.

* * *

The S-2 debriefing lasted two hours. The team sat around a table in a hooch fighting to stay awake as they answered questions. What size was the mortar tube? How many carried rucksacks? Were any uniformed NVA seen? The questions seemed to go on endlessly, but sadly there were few definitive answers. It was simply too dark. The obvious conclusion, given the unusual amount of night movements, was that something major was occurring. Was it simply a relocation of forces closer to the coast, or was the enemy planning some type of offensive?

Duff only wanted to sleep, and he was finally allowed to return to his hooch where he slept the rest of the afternoon and through the night. He awoke the next morning when Sergeant Harrison poked his head through the door.

"Wake up, dude. They're flying Sergeant Ederson to a hospital on Okinawa," he said. "He probably won't ever walk without a cane again, but the good news is they think he's going to keep his leg."

Duff sat up, rubbing his eyes. Harrison stepped inside and sat on an empty cot across from him.

"Coleridge, I don't think I've ever seen a new guy perform like you did out there. I just want to tell you that you did a damned good job. Also, the last thing Ederson said before they medevac'd him was to see that you got a medal for hanging back that way and covering our rear. He also told me to give you this."

It was an enemy 7.63mm bullet on a leather lanyard.

"Ederson bailed a wounded marine out of a tough situation a few months back. The marine gave it to him. It's called a Hog's Tooth, kind of a sniper tradition."

Duff took it and put it around his neck.

"I think you deserve it," Harrison said. "I also pushed the medal up to Top. He's taking my after action report to the CO. I think they'll award you the Silver Star, but just for the record, I have to say this, too. You know staying behind like that is not SOP. We can't afford to get separated on an op. I don't want that to happen again. You understand?"

Duff nodded. "No problem, Sarge, but just so you know: with us carrying Sergeant Ederson up that mountain, the VC would have been all over us in a matter of minutes."

Harrison smiled. "It worked out this time," he said. "So, we'll say it was a good call. Just don't scare the shit out of me like that anymore. Okay? I'd rather we took our chances together."

Duff nodded. "You got it, Sarge."

* * *

The first thing Duff noticed in the next few days, was that he was no longer referred to as a new guy. And as word spread, even a couple of the old heads came around and struck up conversations, but the glory was short-lived. It was 10:00 hours that morning when Harrison called them together. They were going back into the highlands that evening.

"We already have two teams working the area where the Song Con flows into the Song Vu Gia southwest of here. One team is in the hills north of the river," Harrison explained. "The other is south of the river. We spotted at least eighty of the enemy on our last op, but we still don't know what they're up to or where they were going. We're not sure if they're using Highway 4 or if they crossed the river and are using the trails on the south side, but we're pretty sure they're moving toward the coast. Riley and I did a fly-over this morning, and we found a couple good LZs in the hills north of the river. We'll be about four klicks east of Sergeant Booker's team.

"The problem we face in this area is it's a hell of lot more populated. There are villages all up and down both sides of the river and along the highway. We shouldn't have the communication problems we had last week, but there'll be a lot more opportunity for contact. The team will consist of me, Riley, Lopez, Coleridge, and Nobles. Riley will walk point, Lopez slack. I'll be behind them. Coleridge will be behind me and Nobles will walk drag. We'll meet back here at 14:00 hours. I'll give you the radio frequencies and shack code, and we'll look at the map. After that we board the chopper. Any questions?"

No one said a word.

"Okay, make sure your gear is all taped, and try to get a nap."

* * *

The nap had been impossible, and Duff still felt a mild adrenaline rush as the team sat at the LZ rubbing camo paint on their faces and the backs of their hands. The chopper pilot already had the Huey rotors turning at a fast idle as he went through his preflight checklist with the co-pilot. Harrison motioned to the team, and they stooped beneath the rotors as they boarded the chopper. A few moments later the chopper lurched skyward, and Duff watched as the base disappeared in the distance. They were on their way again, back to the enemy's home turf.

The sun was sitting low atop the hills when the men jumped from the skids of the chopper. Moving quickly into cover, they didn't stop as they moved swiftly through scrub palms, putting distance between themselves and the LZ. It was nearly dusk when Riley slowed and motioned Sergeant Harrison up to the front of the column. Jimmy knelt facing the rear with Duff at his side. Off to the south were several villages along Highway 4, which was little more than a muddy road. Beyond that lay the tree-lined Song Vu Gia River.

Harrison motioned the team together.

"We're going to work our way a little higher up this slope and try to find some thicker cover for the NDP. Stay low. This is too open of an area, and we don't need to be spotted."

Fifteen minutes later it was too dark to continue. Harrison brought them together and the team hunkered down in a night defensive position just off the trail to wait for daylight. Covering his face with a towel, Duff dozed, only to awaken sometime in the night. He pulled the towel from his face and lay on his back staring at a night sky clotted with milky white stars too numerous to count. Around him, the team breathed heavily as they slept. He tried to focus his eyes on his wristwatch. As best as he could tell it was around 02:30 hours, another four hours till daylight.

Times like this were what he hated most—times when he could think about what he was doing. He never considered himself particularly bright or analytical, but what the fuck was he doing here? He remembered something he had read about another war in World History class back at Polk County High. It was about Napoleon Bonaparte and his defeat in Russia, the gist of which was not getting involved in a ground war in Asia. He had to believe America knew what it was doing—surely.

He lay there knowing he had to get some sleep, but his gut feeling was that he was part of a futile madness. It wouldn't let him go. He had no choice but to fight on, yet nothing made sense. How could the United States leaders not see what he saw, or was it that they saw so much more? Perhaps, he was the stupid one. Perhaps they had some grand plan that would lead them out of this mess. He thought of Melody Hill the morning when he left for Nam. He saw the steeple of the church, and the brilliant morning sun over the Tennessee hills. It now seemed like a faraway oasis.

There came a sound and Duff's mind cleared as he reverted to the instinctive animal he'd become, sharp and alert. He listened. He waited. The night breeze was all but stilled, and there was nothing but the sounds of his team lying around him, breathing heavily in sleep. Another sound came, and he would have thought it was one of his team members rolling over, or moving an arm, but it came from only a few meters to his front, outside the NDP.

Duff grabbed a frag and locked his finger in the ring, but held it. Whatever, whoever it was, was close, real close. It wouldn't be necessary to throw the grenade, but only to toss it a few feet into the brush to his front. He waited, and he listened. Perhaps it was a snake or just a rat. If he threw the grenade and it was nothing, Harrison and the others would be pissed. It would be a "cherry" mistake. So far, he'd been lucky and avoided making a fool of himself.

There came the slightest hint of something, a sound or maybe it was his imagination. Duff pulled the pin and held it. With his free hand, he pulled another frag from his pocket and bit down on the ends of the cotter pin with his teeth, trying to straighten it. It was useless. Pulling grenade pins with your teeth was a John Wayne move. His instinct took over. He'd rather be branded a dumb-ass cherry than let his team be overrun by the enemy. Tossing the first grenade, he reached and snatched the pin on the second, throwing it beyond the opposite side of the NDP. Grabbing his M-14, he pointed into the darkness, but held his fire so as not to give away his position.

The two grenades thundered, showering them with dirt and leaves. The other team members rolled onto their bellies, momentarily disoriented as they held weapons at the ready, but no one fired. Duff saw movement only feet away and fired several rapid shots into the brush.

It was suddenly quiet. No one said anything. The silence was as eerily disrupting as were the explosions of the grenades moments before. Several seconds passed. There came a slight sound, a scratch, almost as if someone were striking a match. Duff raised his rifle, wondering if he should shoot in the direction of the sound, but he was beginning to realize that he had made a mistake. Paranoia had gotten the better of him, and shooting his rifle had given away their position.

Something, a rock perhaps, probably thrown by one of his team members, struck his head. Whatever it was nearly addled him before tumbling into his lap. Duff felt for it in the darkness, and no more than a fraction of a second passed before the realization of what it was sent a jolt of adrenaline through his body. It was an enemy grenade. He fumbled in the darkness to find it.

* * *

The last Duff remembered hearing was his team leader, Sergeant Harrison saying "Who the fuck got flaky on us?" Grasping the enemy grenade, Duff had clumsily thrown it into the brush to his front. That's when everything went black.

When he opened his eyes, it was daylight, the wind was roaring through the chopper and Jimmy was above him, tears in his eyes as he held a plasma bag and yelled at him. Duff wasn't sure what his partner was saying, but he looked up at him and saw he was in a state of near panic.

"Shut the fuck up," Duff said. "I'm trying to sleep."

Jimmy's eyes widened, but he seemed suddenly calm.

"Duff?"

Duff closed his eyes again.

"Hey. No. You can't sleep. Stay awake."

The steady whine of the Huey's engines and the thud of the rotors made him realize he was back in the world again, but he was tired and wanted to sleep.

"Come on. Open your eyes."

Duff decided it was useless trying to sleep, and tried to sit up, but Jimmy held him back.

"No. Lay back. It's okay. We're heading in."

It began dawning on him. He'd been wounded.

"How bad is it?" Duff asked.

"Not bad. Not bad at all," Jimmy said. "You're gonna be just fine."

Duff's eyes popped open, and he looked up at Jimmy.

"Okay, dumbass, stop bullshitting and give me the straight dope. Where am I hit?"

Jimmy's eyes grew wide. "Huh?"

"You heard me. I want to know. Tell me."

Harrison's face appeared above him.

"Take it easy, dude. I think you're going to be fine. Just some shrapnel and a concussion from the grenade."

"What happened?' Duff asked.

"Hell, Coleridge," Harrison said, "You tell us. We found three dead gooks and a couple blood trails, but we never saw nothing."

"Later," Duff said, and he closed his eyes.

He felt someone grasp his chin.

"No! Stay awake, you sorry fucker. We don't sleep, so nobody sleeps. You hear me?"

He opened his eyes. It was Jimmy.

"You are one worrisome fucker, Nobles, you know?"

* * *

Turned out Duff's worst wound was the concussion from the blast. The shrapnel wounds from the grenade were mostly superficial, and he was back with the unit a few days later. The team remained on a week-long stand-down and was taking it easy when one of the old-head NCOs came by and asked Duff to go for a walk. The old sergeant said he wanted to talk privately. It was Sergeant Lowe. He didn't have a team. He was one of the interviewers with S-2 intelligence who did the debriefing whenever the teams came off a mission.

"Do you know why we took you on and trained you as a sniper?" he asked.

Duff shook his head. "Other than the obvious reasons, I reckon not."

"In the past we've seen some pretty high level NVA officers out there, usually at long distances. We pulled a lot of ambushes, but we seldom got any of them." Lowe poked a cigarette in his mouth and

114 | RICK DESTEFANIS

flipped open his Zippo. Cupping his hands, he lit the cigarette. He held out the pack. "Have one?

"No thanks," Duff said.

"Anyway, the idea was that if we got some snipers on board, we might be able to take some of those pricks out."

They walked down past the helicopter pad where several green Hueys sat idle, their rotors drooping.

"So far it hasn't worked. We don't have enough snipers to assign one to every team, and we've already promoted several of them to team leaders."

"Yeah?" Duff said.

"Look, Coleridge. Bottom line is this: I know a diamond in the rough when I see one. You act like a man twice your age."

Lowe looked over at him as if he expected a response.

"My father got killed in a mine accident when I was six. Same accident killed my foster brother's dad, too. His mama died six months later, and he came to live with us. Me and him had to grow up fast. We worked every summer since we were twelve, mucking stalls, hauling firewood, anything to make a buck. Reckon we had to hustle."

"Explains a lot," Lowe said.

"So, what's this about?" Duff asked.

"Coleridge, I don't normally like to see men as good as you leave us, but I have a proposal for you. Just don't tell anyone around here that I had anything to do with it."

Duff continued walking with Lowe until they stopped in the shadow of a watchtower near the main gate. The scent of a brine-laden breeze came from the South China Sea in the east, and he pulled off his boonie hat to wipe the sweat from his face. The cottony white clouds overhead had not yet begun piling atop one another for the usual afternoon rains. Sergeant Lowe propped his foot on the row of sandbags surrounding the base of the tower and gazed out beyond the wire.

"I was a member of a MACV SOG team working out of Da Nang before they sent me down here to work S-2. That team is detached to a special unit up there run by the spooks. They take on some pretty tough gigs, but it's not like most of the SOG outfits. They never go outside the fence, and they live like kings. Top-notch individual air-conditioned billets, hot food every day and they don't pull ops near as often as we do. They pretty much have the run of Da Nang. There are men in this man's army who would give their left nut to be a member of that group.

"Anyway, their team leader is a friend of mine. He called me yesterday. Said he was looking for another sniper or two. Their old one rotated out, and they have another man on sick leave. MACV is trying to get them some replacements, but I told him I had someone in mind. Thought you might be interested. How about it?"

"I don't know. How long do I have to make up my mind?"

"I don't want to rush you," Lowe said, "but I told them I'd let them know by tomorrow."

"You said they might want two snipers, right?"

"Yeah, why?"

"Do you think they would take Jimmy Nobles, too?"

"Here's my question for you. Would you trust Nobles with your life in a really tight situation?"

Duff looked off at the hazy green mountains in the distance.

"Yeah, I would."

"Tell you what," Lowe said. "Sleep on it, and drop by the S-2 bunker around noon tomorrow with your answer. I'll check to see if they'll take you both."

CHAPTER EIGHT

Special Operations Group
1967

S partan sat with his feet propped on his desk at the back of the Intelligence Operations Coordination Center near Da Nang City. It was quiet around the IOCC that afternoon, nothing much going on. Payday had come, and after getting their money the Special Police and PRU were in town blowing it on whores, hooch and heroin. It was time to relax. Spartan's biggest worry was running out of beer as he thumbed through the latest issue of Playboy. He pulled out the center-fold and took a deep breath. The girl had the finest tits and ass air-brushed photography could offer.

There was nothing like that in Nam, except for Lynn Dai Bouchet, and she always played 'hard-to-get.' Other matters, though, were looking up. A new replacement, a sniper, was being sent up from a lurp unit for an interview, and he'd finally made contact with a buyer on the black market. If the sale went as planned in the next few weeks he'd have the first major installment on his retirement, a pre-sold packet of uncut heroin worth nearly a quarter-million dollars. That was payment for the weapons. All he had to do was get it to the buyer. The buyer for the heroin, a Frenchman in Saigon, had guaranteed him payment in American dollars, enough money to buy more pussy than he could ever want.

Selling the weapons had been somewhat problematic. No one in Vietnam had a quarter million lying around. It took some back and forth, but his man with the Special Police had finally come up with the deal for the heroin. All he had to do was produce the goods. With a deuce-and-a-half and several able-bodied men from the PRU to load the weapons, he was nearly ready. He had only two more details to work out, a payoff for the Nùng guards at the warehouse and someone to provide security during the exchange—someone he could really trust, an American.

A couple deals like this one and he wouldn't have to worry about a permanent job with the company. Graduating from a contract employee to a full-time analyst back at Langley would guarantee a nice supplemental income, but it wouldn't be required. He smiled as he tossed the magazine on the desk. There was more than one way to launder a half million. Just the same, his operation was getting a reputation with the Ivy Leaguers as one of the best. He had turned up more VC spies than any of them, making a job offer all but inevitable.

* * *

Duff didn't want to miss this opportunity. It was even more exciting than being a lurp. Only a few weeks ago he had been a cherry humping the bush with a line company. A certified cherry, they had called him, but now things were moving way too fast. All of a sudden, he had this opportunity to jump from the lurps to a SOG outfit. He had heard men talk about Special Operations Groups like they were mysterious warrior gods, and the only ones who got to join them were those with multiple tours, men who were Army Rangers, Special Forces, Navy SEALs, or Marine Recon. It seemed Captain Shipley was right. This war produced lots of job opportunity.

He found Jimmy fresh back from the showers, sitting on his cot. He was drying his head with a towel. Duff sat across from him.

"Where have you been?" Jimmy asked.

"Talking with Lowe."

"The Master Sergeant from S-2?"

"Yeah."

"More questions?"

"Only one."

Jimmy raised his eyebrows and looked at him expectantly.

"You can't mention this to anyone, but he wanted to know if I wanted to go to a Special Operations Group in Da Nang."

"You're fucking kidding me."

"No, I'm not."

"SOG, for real?"

"Yeah. I suppose the next question is: Are you interested in going with me?"

Jimmy's eyes widened with the appearance of a man who'd been asked if he wanted to skinny dip with crocodiles.

"What? Are you crazy?"

Duff shrugged. "He said it's a pretty good gig."

Jimmy shook his head. "Hell no. No way. Not now, not ever. This boy's mama didn't raise no fool."

"I'll take that as a 'no'," Duff said.

"So, you're really going?"

"You know, when I was growing up in Tennessee, my younger brother and I did some really crazythings, like the time we got this cheap little inflatable raft and ran the rapids in Reliance Gorge. They said some French kayakers came all the way from Europe one time to do it, but after seeing it first hand, changed their minds. I reckon we were lucky we both weren't killed, but it was just something we had to do, just to see if we could. You know?"

Jimmy sat staring at him.

"I always wondered how I'd stack up in the real world," Duff said. "And so far it seems I'm doing okay, but this is a chance to *really* do something different."

Duff recalled his father before he died, holding him and Lacey in the big rocker. With his arms wrapped around them, he read from an old history book about the men who fought at Kings Mountain during the American Revolution. These were his people, men from the backwoods of North Carolina, Tennessee, Georgia and Virginia, men whom King George had allowed to taste the sweet honey of freedom. They shot deer and turkey for their families without worry that they might be the King's deer, or that they might be violating some aristocratic lord's private hunting ground. They were men who had found their way free of the monarchy's shackles and were willing to defend that newfound freedom.

These mountain men answered the call and went to Kings Mountain where they crawled through the roots of giant oaks and tulip poplars with their squirrel rifles. And each time after the British Major Ferguson and his loyalist militia showered the trees overhead with a rain of musketry, the mountain men rose up and carefully picked their targets. And when the loyalists charged with fixed bayonets, the patriots gave way, only to return again with their rifles.

The Overmountain Men of Tennessee were called 'mongrels' by Ferguson, but they made him pay for his arrogance with his life. And Thomas Jefferson said it was this decisive victory by the mountain men that was the turning point of the American Revolution. Duff's only wish was to extend that legacy, not with some heroic death wish, but by simply doing his part and making a good accounting of himself. Jimmy looked down at the floor and shook his head.

"Well, partner, I let you talk me into this lurp thing, and frankly, it's not a bad gig. I kind of like it. But I'll be damned if I'm going to follow you to some SOG unit. Go for it, but count me out."

Duff pressed his lips together in neither a smile nor a frown, and nodded.

"Let's stay in touch," he said.

* * *

Master Sergeant Lowe came to him the next day. SOG wanted Duff, but not Jimmy, which Duff explained was no problem. Lowe said it would take a few days to get orders through MACV, and those wouldn't be finalized until he passed an interview with the team in Da Nang. Lowe departed, and it wasn't long before Sergeant Harrison dropped by the hooch. The sergeant had the look of a high school teacher catching his student smoking a cigarette.

"Word is you're going up to Da Nang to interview with a SOG outfit," he said.

Harrison sounded none too excited.

"How'd you hear about it?" Duff asked.

"Someone from MACV in Saigon sent the CO a message for you to fly up to Da Nang to meet with those people."

Duff nodded.

"I just hope you know what you're doing," Harrison said. "SOG can be a big feather in your cap, but I've heard those fellas in Da Nang are working for the spooks. That's a bad scene. Heard a lot of bad rumors about them, and I was looking forward to keeping you on my team."

Duff remained silent, and Harrison nodded.

"Well, I suppose you've got to do what you want. I don't blame you. Go ahead and pack up your personal things and turn in the rest of your gear at the supply tent. There's a Chinook coming through on a supply run sometime this afternoon. You can catch a ride on it."

* * *

It was midafternoon when Duff arrived at the huge airbase at Da Nang. A sprawling complex, the base was clamoring with activity as he made his way across the tarmac. Fuel trucks streaming diesel fumes roared down the ramp, and a row of helicopters churned the hot afternoon air with their rotors as they prepared to take off. To the north, plumes of black smoke rose from the city, and a couple Sky Raiders circled in the sky above.

A shout came from the surrounding din, and Duff saw a man wearing tiger-stripe fatigues motioning him over to where he sat in a jeep. He was about to speak when several F-4 Phantoms took off on a nearby runway, drowning out all else with their thundering roar. Their bomb racks were loaded.

As the roar faded the man spoke, "Coleridge?"

"Yes…uh…sir?"

The man wore no insignia on his fatigues.

Grinning, the soldier stuck out his hand. "Name's Sam Roland. We don't wear rank or insignia, but I'm army, a staff sergeant. Climb in."

Roland was lean and rangy-looking with a sharp glint in his eyes and a raw Vietnam tan. His jungle fatigues were clean but well-worn with evidence of carefully stitched rips and tears.

Duff motioned with his chin toward the city. "What the hell's going on up there?"

"A coup. You haven't heard?"

"Huh?"

Roland's jaw was set hard, his mouth turned down at the corners. "Yeah, some of the local boys are dukin' it out."

"The South Vietnamese?"

"Yeah, Nguyen Cao Ky arrested their general up here when he got wind he was planning on takin' his job. The Buddhists are in on it now. They took over the radio station."

"No shit?"

"Get in," Roland said again.

Duff tossed his duffel bag into the back of the jeep.

"So how the hell are we supposed to fight this war if these people can't stop fighting amongst themselves?"

"We work with the Vietnamese Special Police, and they're still loyal to Ky. So it's business as usual for us."

Roland steered the jeep out through the buildings and down the road to a sandbagged gate laced with concertina and manned by Air Force police with M-16s. There was also a squad of Marines lounging around a nearby bunker.

"Our barracks are back there on the base," Roland said, "but we're heading over to the Embassy House to meet with our boss and the rest of the team."

The streets of Da Nang City were filled with ARVN soldiers, and several buildings were guarded by squads of U.S. Marines, squatting behind sandbagged barriers.

"Is it safe out here?" Duff asked.

"It's about as safe as anywhere in Nam, but we're sticking to the part of town where they know us."

He looked over at Duff and smiled. There came the distant crackle of small arms fire, and Duff realized he didn't have a weapon. Roland was packing only a .45. Eventually they stopped in what appeared to be a residential area. Roland parked the Jeep and jumped out, motioning for him to follow. They made their way on foot through a maze of houses.

Along the way there stood several guards, Chinese-looking men whose uniforms also lacked insignia. They acknowledged Roland with nods as the two passed. Roland trotted up to the door of what appeared to be a large mansion and walked inside. Although ornately decorated with furniture and plants, the building appeared to have been converted for other use. Roland turned down a side hallway to another room. Inside, two men in tiger-stripe fatigues sat at a table with open cans of beer.

"This is our new man," Roland said. "Where's the boss?"

The man closest to the door stood up. "The Bouchet girl came in a little while ago. I think he's back there hittin' on her," he said. He turned to Duff and extended his hand. "John Spencer."

Duff shook Spencer's hand as the man on the opposite side of table also stood and extended his.

"John Dibrell," he said.

Dibrell had a skull and dagger tattoo on his forearm.

"Have a seat," Roland said, "while I go find the boss man."

Spencer reached into an ice chest on the floor and retrieved a can of 33. He tossed it to Duff. "Have a beer and relax."

A few moments later Roland returned, followed by a man who also wore the same tiger-striped fatigues, except he also sported a shoulder holster with a forty-five automatic. Only now did Duff realize all four men wore side arms, but the others were all in standard military belt holsters around their waists.

"This is Spartan," Roland said. "We're detached to his command."

Duff stood and extended his hand, but Spartan turned to Roland instead. "Let's get started," he said.

Spartan took a beer from the ice chest and walked down to the far end, where he took a chair and propped his feet on the table.

"Let's begin with your military experience," Roland said.

Duff began explaining his arrival in Nam in early December and how he started with a line company with the 1st Brigade of the 101st. He'd been talking less than thirty seconds when Spartan dropped his feet to the floor and sat up.

"Whoa, whoa, wait a minute! Just a *damned* minute. Are you saying this is your first tour, and you just got here in December?"

Duff nodded. "That's right."

"What the fuck?" Spartan said. He turned to Roland. "What kind of shit is Lowe trying to pull, sending us a fucking cherry?"

Spartan had a fresh purple scar running the length of his jaw, and it seemed to glow as his face flushed and the veins popped out on his neck.

"Maybe you should hear us out before you jump to any conclusions," Roland said. "This man has built a pretty good resumé in the last four months."

"I don't give a shit about his fucking *resumé*. You tell Lowe if he can't find people with real combat experience don't send anyone."

He glanced over at Duff. "And you can send this cub scout back where he came from."

"MACV is saying it could be weeks before they get us replacements," Roland said. "We at least need some dependable bodies to carry gear, and like I said, this guy has already shown he's capable."

Spartan leaned back in his chair and tipped up his beer, drinking long and hard for several seconds. He set the can back on the table and looked directly at Duff while talking to Roland. "All right, go ahead. Let me hear what this peach fuzz has done that's so special."

After nearly thirty minutes the questions stopped, and they sent him out of the room. He waited outside a few minutes before the door opened again and Roland motioned him back inside.

"Okay, Coleridge. We're taking you on. You'll be paired with me until you get a little more experience. That means you're in my hip pocket twenty-four/seven. You don't shit without checking with me first. Spartan is going to review some procedures with you right now, and then we'll head back to the base for supper and get you moved in."

Spartan stood and placed his hands flat on the table as he leaned toward Duff.

"I want to make it perfectly clear that this is going to be strictly a temporary assignment. In the meantime you need to understand our rules. Standard operating procedure here is we talk to no one outside of this room about anything having to do with our operations. Your orders come directly from me or one of the men in this room, no one else. You will sign papers swearing you to secrecy and be given a secret clearance.

"All outgoing mail must be posted through me, and me only, and I promise you, it will be read. If you should hear a name or see something in writing while in the performance of your duties, you will forget it when the operation is complete. A shackle, that is code, will be used for all communication. When in the presence of others outside of this room, you will use the following names only: I am Spartan, Roland is Rocky, Spencer is Speed and Dibrell is Dibbs. Your new tag is—"

He turned to Roland. "What?"

"Dusty," Roland said.

Spartan turned back to Duff. "You got any questions?"

"No sir," Duff said.

"Okay, I want you to remember three things. I call them Spartan's rules of war. Number one is: Never underestimate your enemy, because when you do that sonofabitch will put you in a body bag. Number two: nothing and no one is more important than the end-game. We play to win in this business. Number three is there are no rules. We play to win."

As he walked to the door, Spartan spoke without looking back. "All right, enjoy life. Hang out with these guys, and we'll meet later in the week to get those papers signed."

* * *

Duff's first impression of his new boss was that he was all business, more than a little arrogant and kind of crazy, but he dared not share this with his new teammates. They returned to the base where a big cookout was in progress. Duff was given another beer when he arrived. This one was a Miller High Life. As he tipped up the gold can and took the first long drink, he was certain that if every sip tasted like that first one, he would be a hopeless alcoholic. Biding his time, he remained silent and let his new team members start the conversations. For the moment they were too busy grabbing knives, forks, and plates.

The savory aroma of meat cooking on the charcoal grill wafted through the mob. Some were Air Force, some Army, some Marine, but all were crowded around the smoky grill. Roland, who was standing in front of Duff, turned his way and dropped a huge porterhouse steak on his plate. Duff nearly dropped his plate. It was the biggest and thickest steak he'd ever seen, and it was still sizzling.

"Come on," Roland said.

He walked over to another grill and grabbed a couple foil-wrapped potatoes. Duff's steak hung over the sides of the plate as he followed Roland behind a nearby building, where they found an unoccupied table under a tree.

"So, what do you think?" Roland asked. He wiped the juice from his chin.

"I could get used to this," Duff said.

"Don't let that asshole, Spartan, get on your nerves. He just likes to play the hardass."

Roland was either a mind-reader, or else he, too, saw the boss in the same light as Duff.

"He gets his nut trying to be super-spy."

"Is he army?" Duff asked.

Roland looked around to see who was nearby.

"No," he said in a lower voice. "He's a civilian contract worker for the CIA. Besides our SOG team, he advises several indigenous outfits, including a Vietnamese Special Police Unit, a provincial recon unit and some other Ruff-Puffs."

"Ruff-Puffs?"

"Local boys who assist the Special Police. Popular forces. Some PRU, some RDF, some detached ARVN. Kind of a militia outfit."

"What's our primary mission?" Duff asked.

"Varies some, but mostly we shake the trees and see what kind of nuts fall out."

If a meal could make amends for months eating C-rations, this one was coming close. Duff forked another juicy cut as he looked across at Rocky. The sergeant had a hard smile, one no doubt forged by the daily realities of war.

"The Special Police and the others mostly run missions to search out specific NLF cadres, spies and other VC low-lifes. Mostly, we assist, but occasionally we'll run our own ops to go after a big wig they've located."

"How long do you think it will be before we run our next mission?"

"Probably, not long," Roland said, "but first we've got to get you some gear. I'd like for you to carry another M-14 with a scope, if you don't mind. We need to have that long-range capability. I'll also have Spartan issue you a .45 for a side arm, a rucksack, smoke, frags, star-burst, whatever else you want. We usually travel pretty light, but Spartan's people have a helluva stockpile of weapons in a warehouse near here."

"Works for me," Duff said. "So, what did you do before you joined SOG?"

Roland finished chewing another bite of steak.

"I was a lurp like you, except I was with the 173rd Airborne down at LZ English."

"What about Dibbs?"

"He's a Navy SEAL. Did a tour down in the Mekong, then came up here to Da Nang. We caught wind of him and recruited him a couple months back. Good man. Busts his ass, and he's pretty sharp in the field."

"And Speed?"

"He's been with SOG the longest. Came to us from another team. He's Special Forces, specialties are language and commo, but he can do most anything. He's another good one. Pulled a lot of duty with an A-team across the fence, up on the DMZ.

"So, now, you tell me something," Roland said. "Where did you learn to shoot?"

Duff laughed then took another swallow of beer.

"You know, my little brother and I grew up in the hills back in Tennessee, and my mother bought us both single-shot .22 rifles when we were ten. I was eleven the year a trick shooter came to Trade Day in a town down in the valley near where we live. That guy could make shots with a rifle I didn't think were possible, and every day after that, we tried to shoot like him. I wouldn't tell my little brother this, but fact is, he's actually a better shot than me."

Roland laughed.

"Where'd you get the Hog's Tooth?" he asked.

Duff looked down. The bullet Sergeant Ederson had given him was dangling outside his shirt.

"My first team leader with the lurps gave it to me."

"He must have been wounded pretty bad," Roland said.

Duff stopped chewing and looked across the table at Roland. "How did you know that?"

"A man doesn't give away his Hog's Tooth unless he's pretty sure he won't be going back into combat. It's kind of a sniper's talisman, you know? Keeps him from getting the one with his name on it."

Duff nodded. "That explains why the wounded Marine gave it to Ederson," he said.

"So, what happened between you and Ederson?"

"Like I said, he was my team leader. He got hit, and I pulled him up out of the Song Bo while we were running from a bunch of VC trying to smoke our asses."

Roland set his fork aside and held out his hand. They shook, and he smiled.

"Yeah, I heard you're up for a Silver Star for that one. I think you'll fit in good around here."

"Thanks," Duff said.

"Just one word of caution," Roland said. "Don't let Spartan trip your trigger. He gets a little crazy sometimes, and he can't stand to be challenged. Let me run interference and take the flak for you."

Duff nodded. He was supposed to meet with his new boss again in a few days. Hopefully, Roland would be around, because boss or not, Spartan wasn't going to walk over him.

CHAPTER NINE

Fixing a Flat
April, 1967

B rady and Lacey were on their way home from school that afternoon, when the steering wheel began pulling to one side. He slowed the old GMC as the front left side of the truck began to sag.

"Flat tire," he said.

He pulled to the side of the road and got out. The red buds of March had burst with the first emerald growth of April, and he was thankful for the improving weather.

"Want some help?" Lacey asked.

"Sure. Get out and make sure nobody comes along and runs over me."

Brady tossed his jacket on the hood and began rolling his sleeves.

"What's that?" Lacey asked.

A letter from Duff had fallen from the jacket pocket. Lacey reached for it, but Brady snatched it up and stuffed it in his shirt pocket.

"Why did you do that?"

"It's just an old letter from Duff."

"When did you get it?"

Brady had shared most of his letters with Lacey, but not this one.

"A while back."

"Have I read it?"

"Not this one."

"Can I?"

Brady pulled the spare from the bed of the truck, bounced it on the pavement and rolled it to the front.

"Duff wrote that he didn't want me to share this one with you or Mama Emma."

Lacey looked at his breast pocket as if she could somehow read the letter.

"What's it about?"

Brady pushed the jack beneath the truck.

"Just some crap about his friends and a Vietnamese prostitute."

Lacey gasped with an open-mouth smile. "My big brother with a prostitute?"

"No, he wasn't. It was some buddies, and he just wrote about it."

With one hand on her hip, Lacey held out the other. "I want to read it."

"No. He said you can't."

"I'm not a baby. I want to read it."

She reached for his pocket, but Brady dropped the tire iron and wrapped his fist around the shirt pocket. Lacey tried to pull his fingers apart, but was no match for Brady's grip. Their eyes met. Lacey's lips were set hard, and her jaw flexed.

"No," Brady said softly.

"It's not about a prostitute, is it?"

It was more accusation than question. Brady shook his head as he began loosening the lug nuts. "No, it's not."

"What's it about? Is he okay?"

"He's okay."

First there came the phone call from a man who identified himself as an officer with the One Hundred and First Airborne at Fort Campbell, Kentucky. He had asked for Emma Coleridge, but Brady explained she was not at home. Mama Emma and Lacey had walked over to the neighbor's house. The officer explained that Duff had been wounded in action, but his wounds were not serious and he had already rejoined his unit. Brady was going to tell them when the time was right, but decided to wait, and a few days later the letter arrived from Duff.

March, 1967

Dear Brady,

If the army hasn't notified Mama, please try to keep this from her and Lacey. I am at a medical unit because I got hit with some shrapnel last night. I'm okay and the doctor said

I can go back to my unit in a couple days. If they already know, just tell them it's really not that bad here, but the truth is it's totally fucked up. The reason I'm telling you this is because whatever you do, you have to keep from getting drafted. I'd tell you to go to Canada like the draft dodgers, but I know you won't do that. Sign up for the National Guard. They aren't sending hardly any NG outfits over here. That's probably the safest thing, or go to college. I know you're not really gung ho about going to school four more years, but you could do that for a while, till this war is over. Whatever you do, believe me when I tell you that coming here would be the biggest mistake of your life. I've seen some very bad stuff. And this war is so crazy it's hard to explain it all. One good thing is I've been able to move up fast and get out of the line company. I am in a recon platoon now, and mostly what we do is sit and watch. That's what we were doing last night, but it was a heavily populated area around some villages, and the VC must have spotted us. They snuck up and threw a grenade in our night defensive position. I caught a little shrapnel. It came through my boonie hat and made me bleed like a stuck hog since it was in my scalp, but it wasn't anything serious. Everyone else is okay. Try to keep this stuff from Mama and Lacey, and take good care of them. I love you all.
Duff

Brady tossed the flat into the bed of the truck and wiped his hands with a rag.

"It's bad over there, isn't it," Lacey said. "I mean, that's what he wrote in the letter, right?"

Brady cranked the engine and pulled back onto the road.

"Yeah. He said I should join the National Guard or go to college."

"What do you want?" Lacey asked.

"What do you mean?"

"What do you want to do with your life?"

"I don't really know."

Lacey said nothing, but it was obvious she wasn't going to let him leave it at that. And even though it wasn't what she wanted to hear, it was probably best to just tell her the truth.

"I reckon I want to get a place somewhere around here, build a house, have some kids someday, you know?"

"That's it?"

"What's so wrong with that?"

"Don't you want to get away from here, maybe move to a big town, try to do something different, go to college or find something you really love to do?"

Brady remembered those few weeks after his mother died, when he'd stayed with Preacher Webb and his wife. He'd overheard them talking of sending him to a children's home in Knoxville if someone didn't take him in. The fear and doubt of those few weeks were forever branded into his psyche, and leaving the comfort and security of Melody Hill never occurred to him.

"I reckon, but it seems so much is happening right now that I need to wait and see before I decide."

"What do you mean? What's happening that makes you need to wait?"

"Everything, Duff being in Vietnam, you hell-bent to go to Nashville. Mama Emma being left here all alone."

"I don't think I've seen Mama mad more than once or twice in my life, but you say something like that to her and she'll set you straight. She can take care of herself, and she'll tell you as much."

"What about you?" Brady asked.

"What about me?"

"Someone needs to look out for you too."

"So, go to Nashville with me."

"You mean live together?"

"Why not?" Lacey said.

"Cause your mama wouldn't like that at all, and Duff, well, you already know how he feels."

"So we get married," she said.

Brady turned and looked at her. She gave him one of her cocky little smirks. Lacey was probably one of the best-looking women in all of Polk County. She was also smarter than most and had a stubborn independence that only increased her attractiveness.

"Did you just ask me to marry you?" he asked.

"No. I just suggested that as a way to keep my brother from killing you. Asking is up to you."

"Hey, maybe he can give you away and be my best man, too." Brady said.

"So, are you asking?"

Brady looked straight ahead up the highway.

"Lacey, I think you know full well I want to marry you someday, but I don't think I want to leave home, at least not as soon as we graduate."

Lacey's face reddened and she turned away.

"Don't be mad," Brady said. "Let me think about it. We still have three months till graduation."

CHAPTER TEN

A Spy in Their Midst
April, 1967

D uff's first meeting with Spartan was at the Embassy House. It was short and to the point. He signed several documents stamped with big red letters that read, "SE-CRET." Afterward he held up his right hand to take the oath. There was no small-talk or explanations, and the entire process took only minutes. Spartan seemed preoccupied the entire time. Apparently the next mission was imminent, and the boss was busy planning the details with the Special Police and PRU leaders.

The next evening Duff rode with Roland and the rest of the team out to a place they called the IOCC. The Intelligence Operations Coordination Center was on the outskirts of Da Nang City. The heat of the day had dissipated to a point where it was almost tolerable as they drove in the open jeep up Doc Lap Street. A clutter of pedi-cabs and cyclos slowed their progress. As daylight faded, the sky overhead turned a deep purple, and neon lights, blue, red, and green flickered to life. Vietnamese prostitutes strutted along in red vinyl mini-skirts, waving as the team passed.

"I lo' you too many," one shouted.

"What's she saying?" Duff asked.

"She wants to fuck you," Dibbs said.

"Yeah, if you've got twenty bucks and don't mind dipping your pecker in the equivalent of a public toilet," Harrison said.

"She's saying 'I love you too many'," Roland added. "You'll have to make your own translation."

The city lights burned bright until Roland abruptly turned the jeep down a darkened side road. It was a back street, one beyond the lights and the main streets. It was unpaved and lined with shacks and clumps of palms. There were no people here, at least none that could be seen—only shadows. Working for the spooks was spooky. Duff smiled inwardly at the thought.

They drove up and stopped at a huge steel gate. The headlights reflected off the solid barrier of sheet-metal. Sandbagged watch towers stood on either side as their occupants, mere shadows, looked down at them. The gate began moving, ponderously at first, creaking metal against metal as guards opened it from the inside. Roland gunned the engine and gave them a casual salute as he drove inside and parked the jeep. A cluster of cinder-block buildings with corrugated steel reinforced roofs, was protected by the high concrete walls, the tops of which were lined with sandbags and rolls of concertina. Back in the shadows, another watch tower rose above the back wall behind the largest building.

Duff followed the other men as they entered the main building and walked into a room crowded with radios and maps. A thick haze of cigarette smoke hung in the air, and several uniformed Special Police sat along the wall monitoring the radios. Others lounged around a table where Spartan sat with a large topographical map.

The briefing was relatively detailed. A village on the north side of the Song Thu Bon River was home to some suspected VC cadre, and the Special Police planned a cordon and search mission there. Duff and Roland would be inserted on the opposite side of the river south of the village, while Spartan, Dibbs, and Speed set up an ambush to cover a trail leading westward out of the village along the other side of the river. Duff and Roland would take on any boats attempting to escape. The Special Police, the PRU and the others would approach from the north, forming a cordon.

"Like shooting fish in a barrel," Dibbs said.

* * *

Just after first light the following day Duff and Roland slipped into position on a high bank across the river from the village. On the other side of the river, Spartan, Dibbs, and Speed were doing the same west of the village. Duff scanned the village with his binoculars. With the early morning fog, only the boats moored on the far bank and the thatched roofs were visible.

"It's usually pretty routine," Roland whispered. "The Special Police go in, arrest a few likely suspects and take them back to the

IOCC for interrogation. We'll sit tight here and watch for people trying to sneak out the back way. We'll probably be back at the base in time for supper."

Duff nodded as he continued scanning the far bank. Because there were no roads nearby, the river was a lifeline. The Song Thu Bon flowed out of the highlands, and though warm, muddy, and quiet at this point, it could no doubt tell stories about an undercurrent of activity back in the mountains—stories of a determined enemy, people who persisted despite the napalm and other lethal armaments the Americans brought to bear. Duff had quickly grown to realize they were fighting an enemy that would never surrender.

Sergeant Harrison had told him as much, explaining how the lurp patrols observed dozens, sometimes scores of enemy combatants walking valley trails, inhabiting hidden jungle villages, tunnel complexes, and bunkers. Harrison said almost every time his lurp team was inserted he saw the enemy. They occupied the hills and valleys by the thousands, and he wasn't sure there was a strategy that could defeat them. After all, the Chinese had tried, the Japanese and the French as well. Why should the Americans be any different?

"If we *do* spot someone, and they come down to the boats," Roland whispered, "wait till I give you the word."

Duff lowered the binoculars and nodded, but as he did, he noticed several black forms on the other side of the river running toward the village. He threw the binoculars up again.

"We've got trouble," he said, still gazing through the binoculars. "There's at least ten VC over there across the river, maybe more."

"What the…?"

Roland sat upright and pulled the radio handset from his pocket. Duff dropped the binoculars and raised his rifle, focusing on the shadowy figures running through the trees. They were headed toward the village on the same trail where Spartan, Dibbs, and Speed were supposed to be.

"Sampson One, this is Two," Roland whispered into the handset. "You've got Victor Charlies coming up on your six. Over."

"Sampson One, do you roger? Over."

Duff took aim at the pajama-clad guerillas.

"What about it?" he asked.

"Light 'em up," Roland said.

Duff opened fire, maintaining a steady and accurate staccato of suppressing fire. It worked. The guerrillas dove to the ground. And as Duff fired his last round, Roland opened up with his AR-15. Duff swapped magazines.

"Take it," Roland said.

Duff opened up again with a steadily paced fire as he searched for targets through the scope. He found none, but green tracers were now streaking back at them from across the river. Roland again grabbed the handset on the PRC-25.

"Sampson One, this is Sampson Two, Over."

Finally Speed's voice answered. "What the fuck is going on?"

"We've got a squad of Victor Charlies pinned down seventy-five mikes to your whiskey. Over."

Duff fired his last round and quickly swapped magazines again, but the pause allowed the enemy to gain the advantage as their rounds began clipping tree limbs all around.

"We've got to move," Roland said.

He didn't wait for a response as he scrambled back into the bushes. Duff followed, and they made their way up the river to another vantage point. Just as they reached a place where the village was again visible, huge clouds of pot-metal gray smoke blossomed above the thatched roofs on the far side of the village. A moment later the thundering booms of the explosions reached them, followed by the rattle of automatic weapons.

"Holy shit," Roland muttered. "They're hitting the Special Police and PRU from behind."

Duff searched the trees across the river for the guerrillas—nothing. They were still not moving.

"Hold your fire a minute," Roland said.

He grabbed the radio handset.

"Sampson One, this is Two, over."

"This is One, go." Speed's voice was calm but tense.

"Tranh's people just got hit from behind on the other side of the 'ville," Roland said. "You've got to move on these guys behind you quick, Speed."

"Roger. Try to draw their attention. We're coming," Speed said.

Roland looked over at Duff. "Okay, you ready?"

"Yeah," Duff said as he peered through his scope.

A pajama-clad guerrilla had come to his feet on the far side of the river and was motioning for the others to follow. Duff carefully aligned the crosshairs and squeezed off the first round. The guerrilla fell, and Duff continued a steady suppressing fire as the others again took cover. A few moments later the blasts of several hand grenades erupted, followed by more small arms fire. Speed and company had apparently caught the enemy by surprise.

The remaining guerrillas bolted back down the trail, quickly disappearing into the jungle.

Smoke drifted through the trees and down the river bank on the far side. In the distance the drumming of helicopter rotors echoed, and on the other side of the village the firefight slackened to a staccato of small arms fire. The VC had heard the choppers coming and were pulling back. The radio lying between Duff and Roland crackled as Speed answered calls from the inbound chopper pilots.

"Roger, Sky-Saber One, this is Sampson One. We have multiple enemy sampans on the bank of the blue line adjacent to the 'ville." Simultaneously, in the background, Spartan's shrill voice could be heard, "Tell them to sink those fuckers."

Duff turned his binoculars to the boats moored along the river bank near the village. There were several old men and women sitting about on them, villagers who threatened no one. The boats were also floating high in the water, making it obvious there was no hidden cargo on board. A moment later the first chopper appeared. Streaking up the river, it unleashed a salvo of rockets.

* * *

The firefight dissipated quickly after the arrival of the two Cobra gunships that morning, and by late afternoon the team was back at the operations center, waiting in Spartan's cramped office. A rusty ceiling fan did little more than stir the dank air as they lounged about still wearing their muddy fatigues. Spartan was down the hall meeting with the head of the Vietnamese Special Police detachment, Colonel Tranh. Tranh and his men had entered the village and escaped the ambush relatively unscathed, but Captain Truc's PRU and the Regional Defense Force troops out on the cordon had been badly mangled.

Even though Spartan was at the far end of the hallway with the door closed to Tranh's office, Duff could hear him shouting. "Someone is either running their mouth when they shouldn't, or we have a spy."

Tranh's barely audible voice answered, but the words were unintelligible to the men in Spartan's office.

"Well, they're under your command, so I expect you better figure it out quick, before we all get killed," Spartan shouted.

A moment later the door slammed, and the beat of Spartan's boots sounded as he stomped back down the hallway. Walking into the office, he brushed past Duff and Spencer and tossed his hat on the desk. Dibrell, who'd been sitting behind the desk cleaning his fingernails with a Ka-Bar, stood and stepped aside. Spartan sat down and looked over at Roland.

"You know, I thought it was awful damned fishy when we hit that village up north last month and the sonofabitch we were after wasn't there. He'd been seen every damned day for a month, and the day we moved on him, poof, he just disappeared, and he hasn't been seen since. Now, put that together with the shit that happened today. Those damned gooks knew we were coming. Stop and think about it. We've had several missions the last few months that were duds. What do you think?"

"I think somewhere in the PRU or the Special Police there's an An Ninh agent," Roland said.

"I take it Tranh doesn't have any ideas who the culprit might be," Spencer said.

"Hell no," Spartan said. "He thinks there's a spy in the PRU or the regional defense force. I told him he's a fucking genius."

"So, tell him to check and see if any of them didn't go on the op this morning," Roland said. "If our boy knew about that ambush, he probably didn't go."

Spartan nodded. "Not a bad idea. Okay, stand down for the rest of the day. We'll meet again tomorrow to get our ducks in a row. Apparently, someone already contacted Naval Claims about the boats we had the Cobras smoke on the river this morning.

"The Bouchet girl with Naval Claims wants to ask us some questions. I told her we'd meet with her at the Embassy House."

"Why all of us?" Roland asked.

"Well, first she wanted to talk with each of us separately, but I nixed that."

"So, who says we have to talk to her at all?" Roland asked.

"All I know is that the woman has some pull somewhere. My people say we have to meet with her."

Duff watched and listened as the men discussed the attack. It was Spartan who ordered Spencer to call in the Cobras on the boats moored along the river that morning. He later claimed there were VC hiding on them, attempting to escape. The only people Duff had seen were four or five old men and women lounging around in plain sight, and they weren't trying to hide or escape. The choppers fired salvos of rockets, shattering the wooden boats and scattering the remnants into a confetti of wood scraps, straw and fishnets on the water. When the attack ended, the bodies of the old villagers floated amongst the debris as it drifted downstream.

The sounds of the exploding rockets still echoed in his mind, and Duff told himself that he didn't have enough experience to question his new boss, but he had been there. He had been as much a part of destroying the boats and the people on them as anyone. The one fact of which he was certain was that the four or five old men and women posed no immediate threat, and theirs were the only bodies he saw floating in the river that morning.

* * *

The meeting with the claims investigator at the Embassy House was about to begin. She introduced herself to Spartan and the SOG team as Lynn Dai Bouchet. She was a liaison from the government of Vietnam who worked with Naval Claims and aided with the investigation of claims against the American government for accidental property damage and the injury or death of innocent civilians.

Their eyes met for only a moment, but Duff recognized her immediately. She was the same remarkably attractive woman he'd met back in January when he first joined the LRRP platoon. Lynn Dai Bouchet was obviously of mixed blood and stood somewhat taller than most Vietnamese women. Her hair was rolled and pinned behind her head, and she wore a very western white blouse with a plaid skirt. Speaking with the same perfect English, she assured the men that her investigation was strictly routine and was to be standard procedure for all such future claims.

When the meeting was done, Spartan had solidified his lie by claiming his eye-witness account of several guerrillas climbing aboard the boats in an attempt to escape. Duff had remained mostly silent and felt fortunate he hadn't been asked to give his account. He wasn't about to lie, but Spartan and Roland explained that he was much too busy with the firefight to have noticed the VC hiding on the boats.

* * *

Details, details, too many to cover by himself. Spartan needed another man, someone he could trust, an American. He left the Embassy House that day impressed with the new man, Coleridge. As he drove back to the IOCC he mulled it over. Coleridge didn't seem overly bright, but he was bright enough to keep his mouth shut during the investigation, and Roland said he'd performed like a seasoned professional during the operation. He might be just the person he needed to provide security for the arms exchange—an American who could be trusted. He would watch him awhile before deciding. If the new guy seemed okay, he'd have to approach him in a way that if he declined, the arms deal wouldn't be revealed.

In the meantime, Spartan was onto another opportunity. The PRU leader, Captain Truc, had brought him some new intelligence, and it wasn't simply hearsay. Truc had taken several of his men out and verified it. There was an NVA colonel coming and going in a village up on the Cu De River. Truc had personally observed him arriving at night, shedding his uniform, and moving about the village during the day. He was apparently directing some type of training in the village and the building of tunnels.

For Spartan, capturing an NVA colonel could be the coup that finally garnered him the respect he deserved if he pulled this one off. Even the big-shots in Saigon would know him by name. The plan was to cordon the main village, then search the tunnels until they flushed their boy out in the open. He would put Roland and the SOG team at key points outside the village in case the colonel somehow slipped out. He'd still be a prize catch, even dead.

* * *

Most of Da Nang city was off limits to military personnel, but Duff soon learned SOG had its privileges, as the team roamed freely. They sat on the veranda at the White Elephant restaurant, drinking beer and waiting for their food. Dibbs had ordered shrimp, and Speed was giving him grief about being a squid and eating shrimp. Dibbs laughed and told him it was better than being a green beanie.

"At least we don't eat our cousins," Speed said.

"No, you just fuck them," Dibbs shot back.

The men laughed, but Dibbs stopped laughing and glared at Duff. "What the fuck are you laughing at? You hillbillies fuck your cousins, don't you?"

Duff smiled. "That's just a rumor perpetuated by you dumb Yankees," he said.

"He got you, Dibbs," Speed said.

"Tell the truth," Roland said, turning to Duff. "Did you even own a pair of shoes before you went into the army?"

"Yeah," Duff said, "but Mama only let me wear them on Sunday." They all laughed again.

"So, what do you think about our business so far?" Roland asked.

Duff paused. His daddy had said something to a man one time when he was selling an old pickup. Duff was five years old, but he still remembered it. "A man who won't tell the truth and stand by his word, won't stand by anything," his father had said. Duff had to speak his mind.

"The only thing I have a problem with is those boats."

Spencer's face flushed, and Dibbs looked off to one side. Roland squinched his lips sideways as he looked down and rolled his beer can between his thumb and fingers.

"Yeah," Roland said. "I think we all do, but you've got to understand how this works. Spartan has absolute authority. He's also privy to a whole lot more intelligence coming from several different agencies. He doesn't always share it with us, but like those boats for instance. He told me the PRU witnessed the VC using them to move rice and weapons up and down the river."

"Why doesn't he tell all of us those kinds of things?" Duff asked.

"Do you remember how I told you he thinks he's some kind of super spy?" Roland asked.

Duff nodded.

"Well, I think that's just part of the persona, so to speak. He's got a big ego, and he doesn't want us to know everything he knows. We've already asked some of the same kinds of questions, and our superiors at MACV..." Roland paused and looked around. "Our superiors," he said in a whisper, "made it clear he has the authority to make those calls, and we're to obey him. Simple as that."

"Makes better sense, now," Duff said.

The waiter arrived with their food.

"Let's eat," Roland said. "We've got another op to talk about later."

CHAPTER ELEVEN

The Cu De River Op
April, 1967

"We're headed north tomorrow," Roland said. The team was gathered at the operations center, waiting for Spartan.

"The PRU claim they spotted an NVA colonel near a village south of the Cu De River," Roland explained. "Since he's fucking with the NVA, Spartan has us tagging along for extra security. We'll be hanging back somewhere just outside of the village, simply putting more eyes on the area. We don't need to get caught flat-footed out there by a bunch of NVA regulars. Spartan is going in with the Special Police to interrogate some of the locals and gather intel. Right now, they're trying to figure out when they'll inform the Ruff-Puffs."

"Still worried about the spy thing?" Dibbs asked.

"Yeah, they told them to prepare for an op, but they're not telling them where until tomorrow morning."

"Sounds like the way to do it," Speed said. "Whoever it is won't be able to warn his buddies we're coming."

Roland raised his eyebrows and pressed his lips together with what Duff was beginning to realize was his favorite expression, one that was neither smile nor frown, but an invitation for more input from his other SOG members. No one spoke.

"I agree with you, Spencer," Roland said, "but the fucking province chief that runs the Ruff-Puffs is having a fit over it."

"Tough shit," Dibbs said.

Roland nodded. "That's what I said, but Spartan and his people are meeting with the fucker over at the Embassy House right now, trying to appease him. I think they'll fold rather than lose his support."

* * *

The next morning the team made an insertion from a Huey landing several klicks from the suspect village. A relatively flat area with numerous villages and hamlets, it was a broad plain of rice paddies threaded with palm-shrouded streams. The team couldn't remain totally unseen, so Roland led them in a circle, taking an indirect approach to the village, something he hoped would throw off any observers. Roland was a sharp team leader, but Duff worried. How could they provide security with no high ground to observe the village? The terrain was flat and covered with rice paddies and scrub palms.

The Vietnamese Special Police were coming up Highway One in trucks and jeeps along with the PRU and Regional Defense forces. Working with so many different units was one of the things he was growing to dislike about Spartan's version of special operations. Communications were difficult at best, and the Vietnamese RDF and PRU were called Ruff-Puffs by the American soldiers for good reason. Despite the swagger they displayed with all their fancy new American weapons and fatigues, the Ruff-Puffs often tended to melt away when the bullets began flying. The army had a great name for what was often the result. They called it a *cluster-fuck*.

The column coming up Highway One was supposed to arrive by late morning, and time was drawing near as the SOG team knelt just outside the village. They lit cigarettes and checked one another for leeches while they waited. It was quiet, and the sun was a hazy white disk, nearly hidden by a light overcast. Having passed several farmers in the rice fields and some kids playing near a dike, Roland had led the team the last half-kilometer down the middle of a small stream so their approach would be hidden from view.

"Okay," Roland said, "Speed, you and Dibbs move straight in from here and get as close to the village as you can. Coleridge and I will go around the other way near where the Special Police are coming in from the road. We'll crawl up to where we can see the main opening at the front of the village. Stay low, and watch your back. This place gives me the creeps."

Duff followed Roland as they inched forward on their bellies through the grass. A few hundred feet away, the Special Police convoy had just arrived and their muted voices filtered through the trees as the men jumped from the vehicles and rushed toward the village. From less than seventy meters away, Duff had a clear view as the Special Police officers directed their people into the village. Spartan was there with Colonel Tranh, standing in a cloud of dust stirred by the troops as they ran past. After a few minutes, several PRU returned, escorting an old man.

"I figure that's the village chief," Roland whispered.

He couldn't hear their voices, but Duff watched as the chieftain motioned for Spartan and Tranh to come with him further into the village. Tranh waved his hand and Spartan shook his head, both refusing to go. Spartan turned and said something to Tranh, who then pointed back into the village as he spoke. The old man shook his ahead, and turned, also pointing into the village. He seemed insistent that they go with him.

"What's going on?" Duff whispered.

"I don't know," Roland said, "but be ready. I smell a rat."

Roland pulled the radio handset from inside his fatigue shirt and keyed the mike. "Something's not right," he whispered.

That was all he said.

"Roger," Speed's barely audible voice came from the handset.

Tranh, who was holding the old man's identification papers, motioned with them to Spartan and walked back out to the road where his jeep was parked.

"Tranh's going to radio someone about the old man's papers," Roland whispered. "Keep an eye on those huts closest to Spartan and the old man. I don't like the way this is going down."

The only ones remaining in the open area at the front of the village were Spartan and the two PRU guards holding the old man. The remaining PRU and other soldiers had disappeared amongst the hooches. Duff studied the nearby thatch-roofed huts. He caught a shadow of movement through the open door of one on the far side of the village. Peering through the rifle scope he looked inside.

"I have movement inside that open door across the way," he whispered.

As he continued watching through the scope, he saw what appeared to be a reed matt as it was tipped upward. A head appeared to rise out of the floor. It was a man with a rifle.

"We've got trouble," Duff whispered. "I think someone just came out of a tunnel over there in that hooch."

"You sure?" Roland said.

"He's got an AK."

"Okay," Roland said, "On my word, fire up that hut, then move to the next one. I'll take the ones on this side of the road."

"Ready, now!"

Duff fired several rounds through the open doorway, then redirected to the next hooch as he perforated it with more shots. The open area where Spartan and the other three men stood became a beehive of clashing red and green tracers as one of the PRU guards fell, then the village chief. Spartan and the other guard fell to the ground scratching and clawing first one way then another as geysers of dust shot up all around them.

The back of a man's head appeared above the grass only a few feet in front of Duff. Springing to his feet, Duff shot down into the hole. It was a tunnel. Snatching a grenade, he pulled the pin and dropped it into the opening. More fire was coming from the hooch to his immediate front. Duff bolted toward it. Spartan writhed in the dirt like a man being stung by a thousand hornets. Pulling the pin on a second grenade, Duff shoved it through the wall of the hooch and dove back as the explosion sent a shower of sticks and straw into the air.

Sporadic shots continued spitting up streaks of dust around Spartan as Duff rose to his feet and ran toward him. He didn't hesitate as he ran past, grabbing Spartan's collar and dragging him like a rag doll clear of the open ground. Roland sprinted across the open area and tossed grenades into several huts on the far side. A few moments later Speed and Dibbs showed up, and more PRU troops arrived from deeper inside the village. It was over in seconds.

"Call for a dust-off," Duff yelled at Speed.

He snatched his field dressing open and rolled Spartan on his back. His boss's face was white, as much from the panic as the dust.

"Where are you hit?" Duff asked.

Trembling, Spartan's mouth opened wide as if he were screaming, but nothing came out. Duff ripped open his fatigue shirt. Nothing there. Spartan's mouth continued opening and closing, until he finally managed a loud but pitiful moan that was more that of a trapped animal than one of pain. His eyes bulged from their sockets. Duff jerked him over onto his belly and examined his back and legs. There were no signs of wounds anywhere.

The rest of the team gathered around, along with several of the Special Police. Speed had picked up Spartan's weapon, a Swedish-K. It hadn't been fired.

"I've got a dust-off coming," Speed said. "Where's he hit?"

Duff pulled Spartan upright, and opened his canteen. "Here, drink some water."

He put the canteen to Spartan's lips and looked up at Speed. "I can't believe it, but I don't think he has a scratch."

"Okay," Roland said. "I don't think he believes it either. He's not going to be much use the rest of the day. We'll medevac him out with that wounded PRU."

Roland motioned with his head toward the two bodies lying out in the open. "That other guy and the village chief are toast."

He turned to Colonel Tranh. "Colonel, sir, I suggest you reorganize and have these men search out the village for more tunnels. I suspect they'll find a pretty big network under our feet. You might even flush out your NVA colonel."

Tranh nodded. "Thank you, Sergeant. Be assured my men are already well into their search."

Duff pulled Spartan to his feet, and Speed handed him his weapon as two of the Special Police escorted several detainees to the front of the village. Three young men, naked but for shorts and sandals, had their hands bound behind their backs. The Vietnamese policemen pushed the prisoners forward with their gun barrels. Spartan still seemed dazed and disoriented, watching as the captives were shoved to the ground at his feet. None was more than thirteen or fourteen years old.

"Two of these," Colonel Tranh explained, "are grandsons of the village chief." He motioned toward the old man's body lying in a dusty heap nearby. "They say he was being forced by the VC to help them, and that they were being held as hostages."

"Do you believe them?" Roland asked.

"The PRU found them in a tunnel with their hands and feet tied, but I will investigate further," Tranh said.

Spartan stepped forward and without warning pointed his machine gun down at the prisoners and opened fire. On full automatic, the weapon spewed empty brass as he swept it back and forth. The Special Police and PRU scrambled for cover, as the three young men writhed and twisted in the dust. Roland lunged forward and wrestled the weapon from Spartan's hands, but it was too late. Dark crimson blood pooled around the young men's bodies before being quickly blotted by the thick dust.

"What the fuck?" Roland said.

He was red-faced as he glared at Spartan who stood staring down at the bodies with slack-jawed indifference. After a few moments Spartan turned and without speaking, walked back out to the road.

Roland turned to Tranh. "Colonel, apparently my boss still felt threatened by these VC. Maybe you can find more to interrogate hiding in the tunnels."

Tranh didn't respond, and Roland turned away. Roland looked at Duff, and they stared wide-eyed at one another for a brief moment, each seeing into the other's mind. Duff realized his team leader was attempting the barest facade of an alibi for Spartan, a lie Roland apparently found repugnant, but one he had to tell. And Roland's eyes revealed that he knew Duff understood what he had just done. Duff cut his eyes over to the bodies lying in the dust then back at Roland. Despite the old sergeant's toughness, he looked beaten. He simply turned and walked out to the road.

* * *

The next day, Roland came by Duff's room. Duff was lying on his bunk re-running the mission in his head. Was it paranoia, or had this op also been compromised? It seemed oddly coincidental that Spartan had somehow been left standing alone in the open with the two PRU soldiers and the village chief. If the spy was a member of the PRU, he just as easily could have put himself in jeopardy, but surely it wasn't one of the Special Police. Those hard-core bastards seemed to take pleasure in killing the Communists. None of it made sense.

"Hey, you lazy fucker," Roland said. He was grinning and the spark had returned to his eyes. "You gonna sleep all day?"

Duff sat up on the side of his bunk. "No, I was thinking about going out for some breakfast."

Roland leaned against the wall. "Ballsy move, yesterday," he said. "I think you made a friend out of our boy, Spartan."

"Really," Duff said. "I didn't think he allowed himself that pleasure."

"Well, don't let it go to your head. That SOB is about as predictable as a pet hyena. Tomorrow he's liable to turn on you and rip your head off."

Duff stood up. "That's comforting."

"Just saying, you know? He wants to meet with you over at the IOCC. You can take the jeep. I don't think we're going to need it for a few hours."

"What's he want?"

Roland shrugged. "Hell, I don't know. Maybe he wants to thank you for saving his bacon. Just keep in mind what I said. Keep your distance and don't trust him. Let me know if he says anything about the three VC he shot yesterday."

"VC?" Duff said.

Their eyes met, and Roland looked away.

"Leave it alone for now. If he says they were VC, just nod. Don't argue with him. We'll talk later. Hell, maybe you'll get lucky, and he'll tell you how his friends killed Kennedy."

Duff was in the process of laying out clean clothes, but stopped and looked around at Roland. "His friends did what?"

"I kid you not. The crazy fucker claims it was the CIA that arranged Kennedy's assassination in Dallas because he was going to end their presence here in Nam after the election. He says they were already pissed off at him because he didn't back them at the Bay of Pigs. Sonofabitch just loves LBJ. Says he's a president who knows how to fight a war."

"So, what about it? Do you believe him?"

"Don't know. Guy's a nut-case, but he knows some pretty high-level spooks. Thing is, if it were true, I don't think he'd be talking about it."

"I can't believe I'm in the middle of this shit," Duff said.

Roland laughed. "Beats hell out of bustin' your hump in the boonies."

"That's what I thought, too, but now I'm not so sure."

* * *

Spartan sat behind his desk sipping a breakfast beer as he contemplated his next move. It looked like Coleridge was going to be a good fit with his plans. He was definitely a risk taker, and seemed willing to follow orders without question. The arrangements were complete for the arms sale. The Nungs agreed to disappear when given the word, and he'd figured a way to get Coleridge to participate. All he needed was to wait for the right time and conditions.

When the time came he'd post Coleridge at the end of the street with orders to stop anyone from coming near the warehouse. Coleridge would be none the wiser about what was going on down the street, and when the buyers arrived with the heroin, their truck would back inside the warehouse. The exchange would be made and the truck loaded with crates of AKs, SKSs, M-16s, claymores, grenades, mortars, LAWs and enough shells and ammunition to supply an entire battalion. All he had to do was call the Frenchman in Saigon the next morning, and he'd fly up with a satchel full of American greenbacks to purchase the heroin. It was an air-tight plan.

* * *

Duff drove through the gate at the IOCC late that morning. He found Spartan in his office in the ops center building.

"Come on in, dude. Grab a beer from the fridge."

Spartan motioned with his head toward a once white but now rusted Frigidaire. He sat smiling with his feet propped on the desk while the old ceiling fan barely stirred the air. His tiger-stripes were custom-tailored, brand new rip-stop fabric, and he had a new addition to his ensemble, a tiger-stripe camo silk scarf wrapped around his neck and tucked into the front of his fatigue shirt. Duff's first thought was 'true cornpone,' something they called bad jokes in the Overhill. Normally part of the Vietnamese dress uniform, the silk scarf around his boss's neck had the effect of a dictator's chest full of tin medals.

"It's a little early, yet," Duff said. "I'll pass on the beer."

"Have a seat. Relax."

Spartan dropped his feet to the floor and rested his arms on the desk as he leaned forward. "Look, Coleridge, I asked them to send you over here today so I could thank you. That was a damned bold move, coming out in the open like that to help me get to cover."

Duff nodded. "Glad I was there," he said.

"You and me both," Spartan said. "I can't say it didn't rattle the shit out of me, getting caught in that crossfire. Hell, I thought I was dead."

"Yeah, me too," Duff said. "I reckon you were lucky."

Spartan held up his can of beer.

"Best breakfast there is after a rough op."

"Reckon so," Duff said.

"You know, you're a pretty laid back kind of dude, Coleridge. You don't say much. I like that. When people are calm, they don't make as many mistakes, and now that I know what kind of man I have on my team, I want to get you more involved. You deserve some of the extra benefits we get out of this job. So, let me ask you a question."

Spartan lowered his head and cut his eyes upward, squinting as he looked at him. "What do you want out of this war?"

His voice was suddenly low and clandestine.

"Nothing," Duff said, "except for it to end."

"Yeah, that's a pretty standard reaction once people get a taste of it. It's a nasty business, but make no mistake, it can be a profitable one, too. There can be some pretty good rewards. Hell, a couple years ago, I was a fucking uniform patrolman in Detroit making grunt pay, when a professor from Michigan State told me about this program. He said he came over here in the fifties to train the Vietnamese Police, and found there were lots of opportunities for those willing to take the risk.

"I figured he was talking about jobs and promotions, but those are only a part of what you can get here in Nam. Hell, you can get rich if you play your cards right. I'm on my second contract extension with the company. Yeah, they give me all the dirty work they don't want their Ivy League buddies doing, but I give them what they want, and they leave me alone.

"In another year or so, I'll have enough money that even if I don't get on as a full-time analyst, I won't ever have to work again."

"Is it legal, the way you make the money?"

Spartan looked at him with a crooked smile.

"Ah, from the mouths of babes. You've got to understand how things work. It's neither legal nor illegal. It's what the company expects us to do. We supply guns, drugs, money and whatever else they say to the Vietnamese. It might be simple aid or a bribe or hush money, or whatever, and when we take a small cut of the proceeds nobody gives a shit as long as they get what they want."

Roland was right about keeping his distance and not trusting Spartan.

"Look," Spartan said. "You can think on it, but remember, these gooks were fighting long before we got here, and they'll be fighting after we leave. You need to look out for number one.

"Now, let's talk about our next op. We're going to catch the sonofabitch that tried to take me out in that village yesterday. Tranh's men interrogated some more VC they caught in the tunnels, and it seems someone had tipped them off before our visit. Some of the villagers said that NVA colonel told the VC to set up the ambush. That old village chief was supposed to lead me into the 'ville where they were going to nail me, but we outsmarted them. And now I'm going back and find that goddamned NVA colonel.

"The PRU went back out there today, except they've moved up river about eight or ten kilometers into the highlands where the villagers said there's an NVA base camp. If our people can locate it and find the trails they're using, you and the SOG team are going out and nail that bastard. Hell, I might go with you."

"Messing around with an NVA base camp is like poking a hornet nest. Why not just call in an airstrike when they find it?"

Spartan's face flushed crimson.

"I want that bastard, and I'm going to show him that two can play his game. He tried to bush us, so I'm going to bush his ass. Besides, the Marines and everybody else have been all over that area, and none of them have been able to root them out. I'm going to get him."

* * *

Four days passed before Spartan sent word. The SOG team was going up the Cu De River Valley. The PRU had spotted a number of NVA soldiers moving back and forth on trails leading to the coastal plains, and Spartan told Roland he was coming along, because it was personal.

Late that afternoon, the team sat in the door of a chopper as it crossed over the river valley and turned westward behind the mountains bordering the river. After the insertion, they humped southward up the mountain, crossing over into the river valley. Dusk had already settled when they crawled into the heavy undergrowth on the mountainside to spend the night. Roland said it was a stupid risk they were taking, just to satisfy Spartan's ego. The team had no direct American military support on standby, only that of the Special Police back at the tactical operations center, and they wouldn't risk their necks attempting an extraction under fire this deep in the mountains.

Daylight came the next morning as the men mixed water with their lurp rations and ate breakfast. The mountain mist began clearing, revealing the Cu De River in the valley below. Paralleling it on the other side there appeared to be a major road. Twelve hundred meters down the mountain, between Duff and the river, the relatively open valley had a well-defined trail running east and west. He scanned its length with the binoculars.

Almost immediately he spotted three men ambling along the trail where it emerged from a patch of trees. They were uniformed NVA carrying AK-47s, but they were totally relaxed, seemingly unaware of the team's presence. He poked Roland and pointed out the enemy soldiers. Roland nodded and pointed them out to the others.

"They're well over a thousand meters," he whispered. "We need to move closer."

Within minutes they were on their way down the mountain, Roland on point, Dibbs walking slack, Speed with the radio, then

Spartan, and finally, Duff walking drag. After nearly an hour moving slowly and methodically down toward the valley they broke into a small clearing. They were four hundred meters above the valley floor but still nearly six hundred meters from the trail. Roland looked past the others at Duff.

"What do you think?"

A steady coastal breeze had begun blowing up the valley as the grasses swayed and the leaves trembled. With a new Redfield scope, his M-14 was pretty much accurate out to five-hundred meters. It had been worked over by an armorer, but even with a fully tooled sniper rifle, glass-bedded with a tuned trigger, the shot would be a tough one under these circumstances.

"I'd like to get down to four or five hundred meters for the shot," Duff said.

Roland nodded and turned back toward the valley just as several more soldiers appeared on the trail below.

Duff raised his binoculars and immediately realized he was looking at NVA officers. Two men out front carried AK-47s as did the two in the rear, but the two in the center of the column walked side by side and wore only side arms. One carried a small map case.

Everyone on the team simultaneously went to one knee, as Roland turned to Duff.

"What do you think?" he asked. "It might be our only chance."

"No promises, but I can try," Duff said.

Spartan crawled up beside them. "Are you going to take a shot from here?"

"I think we should," Roland said. "We might not see another officer for weeks."

"Give me your rucksacks," Duff said as he watched the little column of soldiers making their way up the valley.

He had no more than a minute or two before they would reach the next copse of trees. After that, the trail was no longer visible.

He handed the binoculars to Roland. "Here, spot for me. Let me know if you can tell where the round hits."

Stacking the rucksacks, Duff made a rest for the rifle and hunkered down. He cranked the Redfield up to nine-power and peered at the targets. He was north of them and they were moving east to west. A breeze bent the grasses on the hillside slightly to the right, and Duff watched the heat waves shimmering from the valley floor. They drifted in the same direction. He estimated the targets had maybe a ten-mile-an-hour wind at their backs. With little better than two and a half minutes of angle accuracy, it was going to be a SWAG any way he figured it. Lining the men head to foot on the mil-dots in the scope, he estimated the range. It was just under six hundred meters.

They were walking, not fast, not slow, maybe two and half miles per hour left to right, which meant in the second it took the bullet to travel to the target the men would travel maybe three feet, but the wind would also drive the bullet about thirty-two inches to the right as well. It was damned near a break-even. With the match-grade 173 grain, 7.62mm bullet zeroed at three hundred meters, he held above and slightly in front of the closest officer's head. He began a slow squeeze on the trigger.

A second later, not the first NVA officer, but the second, pitched forward as he fell to the ground. The others dove for cover. The enemy soldiers apparently thought they were hidden from view, lying in the grass below, but they were still in plain sight. The remaining officer pointed to the trees at the base of the mountain. The officer that Duff's bullet had hit was sprawled face-down and unmoving. It was either a head or spine shot. Duff lined up on the original target and squeezed off another round.

"You're right almost three feet with that one," Roland said. "Elevation is good."

"Shit, I forgot to re-adjust," Duff muttered. "He's not walking now."

Duff lined up again, this time holding nearly three feet to the left of the remaining NVA officer. The rifle was well braced. He exhaled and began a careful squeeze of the trigger. The officer jerked and rolled, then came to his feet, running back down the trail. Duff followed him in the scope, but another round wasn't necessary. The enemy officer tumbled to the ground and lay shaking. Two of the NVA soldiers closest to him scrambled toward their fallen leader and began dragging him back east toward the trees. Duff squeezed off another round.

"I couldn't tell where that one went," Roland said, "but you didn't hit any of them."

The NVA soldiers were rapidly pulling their officer back down the trail, getting closer to the cover of the trees. He'd only led them three feet. Duff pulled ahead of them five and a half feet, and squeezed off another round. Another soldier fell. Duff quickly squeezed off two more rounds and the second one fell as well. He swung over to the remaining two enemy soldiers who, by now, were sprinting in the opposite direction toward the trees nearly four hundred meters to the west. He watched them through the scope as they ran like men possessed.

"Shoot," Spartan said.

"Not yet," Duff muttered. He watched and waited, and he remembered a frosty November morning back in the Overhill when Brady had taught him something about the nature of a fleeing animal.

As they crept along the base of a rocky bluff that morning, a huge whitetail buck sprang from a cattail thicket, going into a nearly vertical climb up the face of the bluff. The magnificent ten-point's muscles rippled in the amber morning sun as it climbed the mountain, sprinting and dodging, in an effortless display of animal stamina. It was Brady's turn that day to carry the rifle, and he hesitated. The deer seemed to be getting away.

"Shoot!" Duff shouted.

Brady raised the rifle. Holding it atop his shoulder, he placed his eye to the scope and aimed up the mountain at the buck. The big deer was now over one hundred and fifty yards away and only fifty yards from the top. It was nearly a vertical shot, and the big deer was still climbing like a mountain goat, bouncing and dodging.

"Better take him," Duff said. "He's gonna get away."

It was the biggest deer they had ever seen. His heavy antlers spread beyond his hindquarters and were at least eighteen inches above his head.

It was only when Brady flicked the safety off with his thumb that Duff believed he was actually going to shoot, but his little brother hesitated instead.

"He's fixin' to get away," Duff said.

Brady held steady. The buck made a final lunge atop the last visible rock outcropping, and Duff grabbed the bill of his cap, ready to throw it to the ground and stomp on it, but something peculiar happened. The big buck stopped atop the outcropping and stared back down the mountain at them. His vaporized breath coming in panting bursts, the magnificent animal stood, his antlers glistening in the morning sun, only a step or two from getting away.

The thirty-aught-six thundered in the thin mountain air, its report echoing down the valley. The deer reared and disappeared from view. Brady lowered the rifle and turned to him.

"You *do* know we're gonna have to do a lot of climbing to get to that deer, don't you?"

Duff continued following the fleeing enemy soldiers in his scope.

"Fire them up," Spartan all but screamed. "They're getting away."

"Sit tight, boss," Duff said. "This is my department."

The first soldier ran into the trees, but stopped and turned to look back. He was only partially visible. Duff exhaled and timed his heartbeats as he squeezed off the round. A moment later the enemy soldier looked as if an invisible fist had knocked him to the ground.

"Five out of six at this distance ain't bad," Roland said.

"You're a shootin' motherfucker," Dibbs said.

"Where'd you learn to shoot that way?" Spartan asked.

Duff shrugged.

"My younger brother and me had a Remington thirty-aught-six we hunted with when we were in high school. We had to share it, so we mostly hunted together. Sometimes we'd see deer four or five hundred yards away on the side of a mountain. We just learned what it took to shoot them."

"What I want to know," Speed said, "is how you knew that last dink was going to stop?"

"That was something I actually picked up from my brother. Sometimes, we'd miss, and I always kept shooting, trying to hit 'em on the run, but he wouldn't. If he missed, or a deer jumped up and ran, he'd wait, and sure enough, better than half the time, that deer would stop somewhere out there and look back. Then he'd pop him. If you want to see a real badass with a rifle, you should see my little brother."

"Let's get a move on, back over the mountain," Roland said. "That base camp is somewhere close by, and I'm sure these dudes have friends that are coming to look for us. We'll relocate and call for extraction."

"We need to go down and check the bodies for intel," Spartan said. "Besides, I have some trophies to collect."

Roland slowly turned and looked at him.

"And, I want to see if one of them is our boy, the colonel."

Duff looked first at Spencer then back at Roland, but the team leader had raised the binoculars and was again studying the valley below. Surely he wasn't considering going down there. The valley was too open, and they'd already seen nine NVA soldiers in the last fifteen minutes.

"Go ahead," Roland said, still gazing through the binoculars. "We'll wait here. And while you're down there, ask his buddies over there in the trees if they won't mind us using the valley floor for an LZ?"

Duff looked up the valley where Roland seemed to be focused. There was nothing readily visible, but as he studied the swaying grass and palms he found the first one, an NVA soldier, probably an officer, studying the mountainside with binoculars. After a few moments, more became visible, squatted along the tree line, weapons at the ready. There were at least a dozen.

"I don't see anybody," Spartan said.

Roland handed him the binoculars and turned to the other men. "We need to move fast to put some distance between us and that patrol. Get your rucksacks. Dibbs, you take point. I'll walk slack for you. Duff, drop back to drag, but you gotta keep your eyes open."

He turned to Spartan. "You find them?"

"Yeah. Do you think they know where we are?"

"They know we're up here somewhere, but I don't think they've pinpointed us yet. We'll stick to the heavy cover. It'll slow us down some, but they'll have a harder time finding us. Let's move out. We gotta go fast."

The team moved rapidly up the mountain. Duff continually searched the back-trail for signs of the enemy. Several times he heard suspicious sounds coming from down the mountain, sticks breaking, muted voices, but after nearly two hours they crested the mountain. As they moved down the opposite slope, Spencer cradled the radio handset to his ear as he called for extraction. Duff knew scores of NVA regulars had to be streaming up the far slope after them, and it reinforced just how risky and stupid this mission was from its very inception.

He wanted to charge ahead and kick his boss in the ass. For someone on a second tour, and with the tremendous responsibilities of an American advisor, Spartan had again shown incredibly poor judgment. If it weren't for the experience of his team, he'd probably have been killed by now, and they weren't entirely out of the woods on this one.

CHAPTER TWELVE

The Marionettist
April, 1967

The chopper arrived at the extraction point within minutes that afternoon, and Duff scrambled aboard with the rest of the team. Sweat-soaked, briar-torn, and exhausted, the men lay against the bulkheads panting as the chopper cleared the treetops. Roland punched Duff and pointed out a column of enemy soldiers in the distance. They were coming down the far slope behind them. Had there been the slightest hitch, a sprained ankle, unexpected terrain, anything, the team would have been overtaken within minutes and slaughtered.

It was all much too risky, and what had they accomplished besides a few kills? They didn't call for airstrikes or artillery against the enemy, Roland later explained, because they didn't have time.

They had nearly sprinted up one side of the mountain and down the other just to escape. It was a close call, and the entire mission was simply a result of Spartan's personal vendetta against the NVA colonel. Duff came to realize that his boss was a reckless idiot.

* * *

A few days after the Cu De River Op, Spartan told Duff to come by the Embassy House that evening for drinks, said he wanted him to meet someone there. Large social gatherings weren't Duff's favorite thing, and he was still angry over the last mission, but he couldn't refuse him. He donned clean fatigues, and the team dropped him off on their way to a nearby market.

Duff hesitated at the door. He would rather have gone with the team to shop for a camera, but after a few minutes he took a deep breath and walked inside. The people at the Embassy House— both Vietnamese and American, men and women—all seemed in various stages of inebriation. Some were in uniform, but most weren't. Several navy nurses with bright eyes and China Beach tans sat together, and they smiled at him, their faces glowing in the soft light of the chandelier. Duff drew the essence of their perfumed bodies deeply through his nostrils.

Percy Faith's *Theme From a Summer Place* played over a sound system that rivaled live music, and Spartan walked up smiling like a griffin. Motioning for Duff to follow, he led him through a large opening into an open side-room where a group of men were gathered around a table. Expensive bottles of Glenlivet mingled with glasses and a silver ice bowl at the center of the table. There were no mixers for this group, and the smoke from their expensive cigars hung heavy in the air.

"Gentlemen, this is the young man, I told you about, Duff Coleridge."

"Hear, hear," someone said. "A toast to the newest member of the family."

Glasses collided at the center of the table as a man pushed his chair back and stood. He walked around to Duff and extended his hand. Clean and trim with a white shirt, red suspenders, and pressed khaki trousers, he stood apart from the others. He also wore small wire-rimmed spectacles and had the erect posture of a nobleman.

"Crandall Reeves," he said.

They shook hands.

"Duff Coleridge."

"My pleasure, Specialist Coleridge. Mr. ah—Spartan," He shot a quick wink at Spartan, "speaks highly of you. Says you're quite the marksman."

Duff nodded. Although his fatigues were clean and pressed, he wished he had worn something better. The man spoke with a distinct accent, one Duff had heard before. It was perhaps that of someone from New England. He also seemed educated, but he wore a strange ring. It was gold, capped with what looked like a pirate Jolly Roger, a skull and cross-bones inscribed with the numbers 322. The skull had diamonds for eyes.

"Mr. Reeves is my boss," Spartan said. "He's the man who signs our checks."

He gave Duff a sideways glance that said there was a lot more intended meaning to his cliché about signing the checks.

"So, make yourself at home," Reeves said, "and enjoy the evening." With that he turned and went back to the table.

"Head out there to the bar, and get yourself a drink," Spartan said. "I'll see you in a few minutes."

Duff turned, and across the room he spotted Lynn Dai Bouchet. For a moment his eyes locked with hers. They were dark brown eyes, somewhat almond shaped, but neither occidental nor totally Asian, rather an alluring combination of both. It was only a brief moment before she turned away, but not before Duff felt her hesitation. A Roy Orbison song, *Only the Lonely*, began playing as he made his way over to the bar and asked for Jack Daniels over ice. An old, brown-skinned Vietnamese man with thinning hair and a burgundy jacket filled the glass to the top. Duff turned and again found Lynn Dai Bouchet standing beneath a palm tree in a huge planter. She was talking with several men in uniform, an American and two Vietnamese.

Duff sipped his Jack Daniels, but after several minutes became restless. Leaning against a wall just wasn't something he felt comfortable doing. He ambled across the room. Two of the men talking with Bouchet wore Vietnamese Special Police uniforms, starched camouflage with black berets. The other was a tall American, a marine colonel. Duff watched from the corner of his eye, and Bouchet again glanced his way before turning back to those in her group. It was another look—brief but definitely a look.

He saw a familiar hallway. It was where the SOG team's meeting room was located. Down the hall a light shone from beneath the door, and voices came from inside. Duff stopped and listened. The voices were familiar. He pushed open the door. Roland, Spencer, and Dibbs looked up at him.

"Hey, guys."

"Well, looka here," Dibbs said. "It's Spartan's drinking buddy."

"Oh, screw you," Duff said. "I thought y'all were going over to the market."

"Nobody there this late," Spencer said.

Duff pulled up a chair.

"So, did you meet his boss?" Roland asked.

"Yeah. An interesting sort of guy. I think Spartan's still out there talking with him."

"Super-spy works overtime sucking up for a full-time job with the company," Dibbs said.

"The company?" Duff said.

"The company, the CIA," Dibbs said, his voice dropping.

"Oh, yeah," Duff said. "I noticed he actually acted somewhat civil when he was around the guy."

"I'm telling you, baby brother, watch your step," Dibbs said. "That motherfucker is a total whack-job, and when he's done with you, he'll toss your ass out with the rest of the trash."

"So, why *wouldn't* they give him a job?"

"You know," Roland said, "you may be a country boy, but you know the right questions to ask."

"He's trying to say you ain't as dumb as you look," Spencer said with a grin.

"Give my boy a break," Roland said.

Duff grinned. "Yeah, give me a break," he said.

"Most of the CIA people," Roland said, "are either Ivy Leaguers or ex-military with damn good credentials. Spartan sort of snuck in the back door, and he's been overcompensating ever since."

"Yeah," Dibbs said, "pulling shady deals and selling shit on the black market."

"So, why don't they run his ass off?"

"Because," Roland said, "he's their resident sleaze-ball. They keep him around to do the dirtiest of their dirty work. And if he totally fucks up, his extracurricular activities provide them with enough insulation for a plausible denial."

"And us?" Duff said. "I guess we're just pawns?"

"That's why I'm telling you to keep your distance," Roland said.

The door hinge creaked as it swung open. It was Spartan.

"Man, I bring you in to meet my boss and some of the higher-ups, and you're back here hanging out with this bunch of derelicts. What's with that?"

"Sorry, boss. I just felt out of place with all those officers and such."

"You should hang with us," Spartan said. "There'll be some more round-eye nurses coming over from China Beach later. We'll push back the couches and play a little slow music."

Spartan disappeared, and the men relaxed. Duff hadn't danced since high school, and he couldn't imagine actually dancing with an American woman in Vietnam. It seemed like an impossible dream. After all, he was supposed to be fighting a war. This SOG business was surreal, an oasis in the middle of a world of insanity.

Duff turned to the others. "Are any of you guys going out there later?"

"We might," Roland said. "Hell, you should go. You might get lucky."

* * *

Roland's cautionary statements preyed on Duff's mind, and he didn't return to the party that night. Instead, he rode back to the base with the other team members. From what he had observed of Spartan's schizophrenic personality, he figured their warnings were well founded. The less he had to do with him, the better. There was, however, one regret. He wished he had gone back and spoken with Lynn Dai Bouchet. She possessed a mysterious attraction that went beyond her beautiful figure and super good looks, something Duff sensed more than observed.

The next afternoon the rains began, and it rained straight through the night and into the next day. It rained without let-up, heavy shimmering sheets of rain running off the roof as Duff lounged gloriously in his dry bunk, reading and napping. He thought back to that first night in the field with Jimmy Nobles and the misery of sitting in the foxhole with muddy water up to his armpits. The SOG life was almost too good to be true.

Nightfall came, and he heard a jeep pull up outside the barracks. He figured it was the other team members returning from the mess hall. Stepping over to the door, he looked down the hallway toward the screened front door. The rain continued spilling off the roof like Niagara Falls, and a jeep was sitting sideways outside the door, its engine idling. Someone inside peeled back the side window cover from the canvas top. It was Spartan.

"Get your poncho and side arm, and get in," he said. "I need your help."

Duff strapped the forty-five to his hip and pulled the poncho over his head. Within minutes they passed through the base main gate and were winding through the back streets of Da Nang City. Duff tried to see out the windshield. The wiper blades beat a mad rhythm, but a solid gray rain obliterated everything outside.

"How the hell can you tell where you're going?"

"I know this city like the back of my hand. We're almost there. I want you to pull sentry duty for me. We're transferring some weapons to a regional defense force truck, and we don't want anyone sneaking up on us. I'm dropping you off right here."

He came to a stop, and pointed to a doorway.

"Stand over there under the stoop on those steps. There's a truck coming in here in a few minutes. Let it pass, but if any other vehicles or anyone on foot comes around, challenge them. Show them your ID, and tell them you've been instructed to keep anyone from going down this road."

Pulling the hood of his poncho over his head, Duff trotted over and stood beneath the stoop. A few minutes later a deuce and a half with a canvas cover pulled past. There were two men in the cab, but he couldn't see their faces. They had no sooner gone down the road than a black car slowly rounded the corner coming from the same direction. It stopped a couple hundred feet up the road. A European make, it was obviously following the truck, but the driver had apparently spotted him.

Try as he might, Duff couldn't make out the driver, but his impression was that it was a woman. The car began backing until it reached a place to turn around. Duff glanced back down the road where the truck had backed through a large cargo door into a building. The men had closed the door behind them. He turned back in time to see the car's taillights disappear around the corner. It was leaving faster than it had come.

Roland's warning was ringing in his ears. This whole setup smelled of something bad, and he had let Spartan pull him right into the middle of it. Had it been legit, they wouldn't be out here in the rain after dark. And why was that car following the truck, only to back up and speed away once the driver saw him?

Nearly an hour passed before he heard the truck's diesel engine whining as it came back up the road. It was followed by Spartan's jeep. The truck kept going, but Spartan stopped, and Duff crawled inside to escape the rain. A few minutes later they passed through the main gates at the base and were back at the barracks. Spartan reached in his pocket and came out with a wad of bills, all hundreds, American. He peeled three off and shoved them into Duff's hand.

"What's this?"

Spartan winked. "It's a little tip for helping me out on a shitty night. Thanks."

"Where'd it come from?"

"Don't worry. We're good. It's company money. They supply it for me to pay the locals when they help us."

Duff wasn't a MENSA candidate, but there was no doubt he was being fed a line of shit. Refusing the cash, though, might create another problem, because he was certain it was bribe money. Folding it in his fist, he stepped from the jeep, and without a word closed the door and went inside. The door to Roland's room was open, and Duff walked down the hall and peeked inside. The team leader was sitting on his bunk, wearing army issue olive drab boxers.

He looked up. "Where the hell have you been?"

Duff pulled the dripping wet poncho over his head and dropped it in the hallway.

"You won't believe what just happened," he said.

"Try me," Roland replied. Even in his skivvies the wiry old sergeant had a presence that demanded respect.

While Roland sat quietly, Duff related the sequence of events from the last two hours. When he finished he tossed the money on the bed beside Roland.

"That low-life sonofabitch sucked you in, didn't he?"

"So you're pretty certain it wasn't what he said it was?"

"He's selling those weapons to black market dealers. Hell, they're probably going straight to the VC."

Duff grabbed the money off the bed and turned toward the door.

"Where are you going?"

Duff stopped in the doorway. "I'm going to shove this money up his ass."

"Whoa, whoa. Calm down. Bad move."

"Why? What would you do?"

Roland rested his elbows on his knees and held his head in his hands. "I'd let it go."

"Like hell I will."

"Look, Duff, I know you're pissed, but be smart about it. Just wait. Let that asshole think he put one over on you. If you go back and confront him now, he'll get spooked, and there's no telling what he might do. At the very least he'll make your life miserable.

Bide your time, but don't let him get you any more involved than you already are."

* * *

The next morning the sun came out, and Duff borrowed the jeep to go into Da Nang City. He had to get away and try to think. Finding an open-air market, he parked and walked. The deep blue sky had returned and a few scudding clouds were all that remained of the three-day rain. The odors of fresh flowers mixed with that of rice cooking, and he caught a whiff of the pungent fish sauce the Vietnamese called mouc nam. Children played while dim-eyed old men sat in silence and raisin-faced old women sold every sort of food imaginable, including exotic fruit, vegetables, live chickens, C-rations, fish heads, and rice. On the periphery, young cowboys in Ray-Bans strutted about pimping their sisters.

"Number one, fucky, sucky girl for GI, twenty dollar."

The Vietnamese cowboys stole the beauty of the day, but Duff was preoccupied with thought. What to do next? That was the question. He had opened the door and let the snake crawl inside. Now, he had to deal with it. Perhaps Roland was right. He needed to wait, but that also gave Spartan the advantage of making the next move. Duff looked down at an old woman squatted beside a large basket of rice. She smiled with betel-nut-blackened teeth as she waved her hand over the rice in an offering gesture. Duff looked again. The rice seemed to move.

Roland had told him about the "living rice." He said he never ate rice in the local restaurants, because it was difficult to tell what part of it was rice and what part was maggots. If Melody Hill was heaven, this place was pretty close to hell. He longed for home, the crisp mountain air, the evening chimes from the church drifting through the trees, but most of all he missed his friends and family. If only he could find one honest person in Nam it would be a godsend.

"Specialist Coleridge?" The voice behind him was that of a woman.

Duff turned. It was Lynn Dai Bouchet. She wore a white blouse with khaki trousers. Hanging from her shoulder and clutched tightly under her arm was a brown leather purse.

"How did you find me?"

Bouchet smiled. "I have the impression that telling you anything less than the truth will be a waste of time," she said.

She fixed him with the same brown eyes that had found him across the room that night at the Embassy House—curious eyes, mysterious yet honest eyes. With high cheekbones and flowing dark hair, what little makeup she wore she hardly needed.

"The question still stands," Duff said.

"I have people who work within the same organization as I. They assist me."

"And what organization is that?"

"Come walk with me," she said. "The market has many ears."

They walked from the market, and he saw a car. It was the same one he'd seen the night before while standing sentry for Spartan's arms theft. Bouchet walked to it and opened the door.

"Please," she said. "Come with me."

He got in, and she started the engine. They drove through the streets, and Duff recognized the road that led to the IOCC. Bouchet drove past, continuing until the houses thinned and they were at the farthest outskirts of the city.

"That was you I saw last night when it was raining," Duff said.

"Yes."

"Why were you there?"

"I was following men who are associated with the National Liberation Front."

"National Liberation Front—the VC?"

"Yes, those were the people buying the weapons your leader sold."

"How do you know all this?"

"I feel I have revealed more than I should. I have no choice but to beg your trust."

"Who are you?" Duff asked. "I mean, who do you work for?"

"I will explain, if you will give me your word to share with no one anything I say. To reveal who I work for could endanger not only my life, but yours and those of others."

Duff nodded.

"First, I must tell you that the man for whom you are working is a ruthless anarchist."

"Anarchist?"

"Did he not sell weapons to the enemy for his personal gain?"

Duff nodded.

"Did he not slay those men in the village that day with no knowledge of their allegiances?"

Lynn Dai turned the car down a narrow road just beyond the last houses at the edge of what appeared to be open country. She stopped in front of an old mansion where bougainvillea climbed the aging stucco walls, and scrub palms mixed with flowers grew along the walks. Behind the house rose a steep, jungle-shrouded ridge. To the west, across rice paddies and tree-lined streams, the mountains rose up, a hazy blue-green mass, almost ogre-like giants dominating the horizon. Duff stood beside the car gazing at them.

"They are called the Annamese Cordillera. The French call them Chaîne Annamitique, and the Vietnamese Giai Truong Son," Lynn Dai said.

She turned toward the house. "This was my father's home. He and my mother were slain by NLF guerrillas, the Vietcong, you call them."

"So why are you trusting me with this information?"

"I trust you because I saw your eyes when your leader lied the day I questioned him. Your eyes tell me you are an honest man. That was why I chose not to question you in his presence."

Duff followed her up the steps into the house. Once inside, she walked up a wide sweeping stairway to the second floor. The mansion was in disrepair, its plaster walls cracked and yellowed with the patina of age. The high ceiling in the main room was one of tarnished copper squares stamped with the fleur-de-lis. At one time it had been a place of grandeur, but was now irrevocably surrendering to the surrounding jungle.

"Is it safe here?"

"Safety is an illusion in my country. No place is safe. I only hope that someday a fair wind will blow once again, leaving us so that we might live here in peace."

"So, why did you bring me here?"

"I brought you here for two reasons. My first is to recruit your assistance."

"For what?"

Lynn Dai walked down an open-sided hallway overlooking the room below. She entered a bedroom. Inside was a dresser with a large mirror and a large four-poster bed draped with mosquito netting.

"There is an An Ninh agent in your midst. That is to say, he is somewhere in one of the organizations over which your Mr. Spartan maintains influence as an American advisor. I believe this spy has Mr. Spartan's confidence and thus influences his decisions. He is also responsible for revealing many of your plans to the enemy before they can be enacted."

"I agree that someone is compromising our missions, but I can't see anyone influencing that horse's ass, Spartan."

Lynn Dai laughed.

"An apt description, Specialist Coleridge—"

"You can call me Duff if you want."

She smiled and nodded.

"Duff, you must also remember he is ruthless and headstrong, and it is such men who are easily influenced. He is a very bad person, but he is protected by the people for whom he works."

"What exactly am I supposed to do?"

"Simply share with me information—the things you see and hear."

"Like what?"

"Did anyone besides the Special Police know in advance about your last mission?"

"I think the province chief in charge of the RDF was told the night before. Who do you work for?"

"My official role is as a civil claims investigator working in conjunction—"

"What's your other job?"

Lynn Dai did not blink but remained clear-eyed as she looked back at him.

"I work for my government's intelligence service. My mission is simple. I must identify this spy, but it must be done unobtrusively and without interference with the American advisor, the Special Police field forces, or their operations."

"How do I know you aren't an enemy spy using me to get information?"

She slowly nodded. "You are wise to ask such a question. I will never ask you questions pertaining to your missions in advance, nor any that may cause you to reveal information that could in some way be used against your government or mine. And I do not want you to volunteer such information."

Lynn Dai opened a set of French doors and stepped out onto a second-story balcony. Small red and yellow birds flitted about in the trees on a steep hillside less than fifty meters away. It was a nearly vertical jungle wall, and Duff's eyes followed the steep hill upward to where the white clouds climbed away into a blue sky. He turned and made eye contact with Lynn Dai.

"You said your first purpose for bringing me here was to talk."

"The other, should you accept the first, was to let you know that, should you need a temporary place to hide, this house is here for you."

"Why would I need to hide here?"

"Should you be discovered passing me information, those I am attempting to identify could be of danger to you. I come here only occasionally. My usual purpose is to pay those who maintain the building and grounds, and to provide the appearance that I am hiding nothing. Thus, the NLF and their spies believe I am of no danger to them, and they have nothing to fear."

"But you said they killed your mother and father. I don't understand how you think it's safe."

"I did not say it was safe, but the American Marines have a base just to the west. It is no guarantee of safety, but it does provide some protection. As for my parents, my father was of French descent, a professor at the university, and my mother was from a Vietnamese family in Hue. They were slain in front of this very house by the Viet Minh while I was still young. I also had an uncle who was an officer with the French paratroops. He was killed by the Viet Minh at Dien Bien Phu."

"So, the Vietcong have no idea that you are doing anything other than working as a liaison with Naval Claims?"

Lynn Dai nodded. "That is correct."

"What about Spartan?"

"No one in Da Nang or anywhere other than Saigon, except for you, knows of my real work."

Duff gazed into the woman's sad brown eyes. She could be no more than a year or two older than him, but she had already seen enough grief for a lifetime.

"I will help you if I can," he said.

"Thank you, Duff. I will honor your trust with my silence, and do nothing that may in some way bring harm to you or your friends."

"We can talk some more later," Duff said, "but I need to get back to the market to pick up my jeep. I've been gone too long already."

Duff found Lynn Dai Bouchet's eyes neither completely innocent nor naïve. They were magnificently beautiful eyes, infused with intelligence, and they revealed a woman of honesty and integrity, burdened with a sense of duty to a greater cause. He had never met such a complicated woman, one who seemed willing to walk the razor's edge, yet one who seemed so vulnerable.

He was somehow honored she had come to him, but he was now certain she only wanted him for whatever help he might provide. He only hoped he could live up to her expectations without violating his military oath. As they drove back into the city Duff tried to sort it all out in his mind. Matters had taken a turn for the surreal. He had actually been approached by a South Vietnamese spy, an incredibly beautiful one at that.

CHAPTER THIRTEEN

Driving Lessons
April, 1967

"Slow it down and push it up into second," Brady said. The old pickup was gaining speed as they rolled down the mountain, and he was trying to teach Lacey how to downshift the manual transmission. She pushed the clutch with her foot and shoved the gear shift lever upward on the steering column.

"Now, ease out on the clutch."

"But the engine is getting louder," she said.

"It's okay. You're using it to slow the truck, instead of burning your brakes up."

They were on their way to Chattanooga to shop for a new car for Lacey. Right or wrong, both he and Duff had driven the old pickup extensively, but Lacey hadn't. Always pushed to the center of the seat between them, she'd only been allowed to use the truck for occasional errands to the store. Brady was now answering for their sins, as Lacey fought the mountain curves, making numerous corrections with the steering wheel.

"Brake before you reach the curve, not in the middle of it, and hold the wheel steady. Stop fighting it."

She turned and looked at him. "If you and Duff had let me drive more, this wouldn't be so hard."

The truck veered into the opposing lane.

"Watch the road!"

Instinctively he grabbed the wheel, knowing she was about to over-correct.

"There you go," he said.

"Sorry."

"It's okay. You're learning. Just keep your eyes on the road."

By the time they reached the outskirts of Chattanooga, Lacey was handling the pickup like a seasoned pro. She fiddled with the radio.

"You're listening to WDOD, Chattanooga," the broadcaster announced.

"Pay attention to the road," Brady said.

Lacey looked up and smiled. "I got this."

"I think we should try to find something with an automatic transmission," he said.

"Why?"

"You can concentrate on your driving better if you don't have to mess with the clutch and shifting gears."

"You act like an *old* man."

"Pull in up there at that car lot."

A used car lot with big yellow and red signs sprawled across several acres along the highway. Lacey slowed and turned into the drive. A door on a house trailer at the back of the lot came open, and a man stepped outside. Walking down the steps, he met them with a big grin as they rolled to a stop. The cars on the lot had mysterious numbers chalked on the windshields, but no prices.

"Y'all get on out," the man said. "Take a look around. What kind of vehicle you lookin' for?"

"Something dependable for her to drive," Brady said.

"How much you lookin' to spend?"

"I have—"

"Ugh, excuse us just a minute," Brady said, cutting her off mid-sentence.

Lacey looked puzzled as he took her by the hand and led her out of hearing distance of the car salesman.

"Duff showed me a lot about bargaining with folks back when he bought that old truck. You don't want to tell him how much money you have," Brady said in a low voice.

"Well, how is he gonna know what we can afford?"

"You remember when we were playing cards how Duff said you were tipping your hand too much?"

Her lips were pursed with frustration, but she nodded.

"Yeah, well it's kind of the same when you're bargaining. Try to keep your feelings inside, and we'll talk with this man about what you like or don't like."

She nodded, and they walked back to the salesman.

"Y'all can't be having a lovers' spat. Buying a car is supposed to be fun."

"Nothing like that," Brady said. "We just had to decide how much we're going to spend."

"And how much is that?"

"Why don't you show us some of what you have and tell us what you can sell them for?"

Three car lots, two dealerships, and several hours later they were still trying to decide, when Lacey spotted a car at the back of the Chevy dealership.

"I want to look at that one," she said.

The salesman was an old man with thick glasses and a brown fedora, and he was the nicest and seemingly most honest person they'd dealt with.

"Oh no, honey. You don't want that car," he said.

"Why not?"

Brady shook his head and shrugged as he and the old man followed Lacey toward the car. What she did for a pair of jeans was almost scary. The car wasn't bad either. It was a magnificent, deep-water-blue Chevelle Malibu SS, with black mag wheels and red pinstripe detail on the tires and side panels. The grill was black with a red SS emblem. Brady glanced inside. It had black and red bucket seats, and on the center console was a T-handled shifter engraved with "Hurst."

The little old man glanced first at Brady then Lacey. "It's just way too much car, little lady. It has a three hundred and ninety-six cubic inch V-8 with a four-barrel Holley carburetor and ram air induction. It's a customized demo. We used it as a pace car up at the big race at Bristol last fall."

"Is there something wrong with it?"

"No ma'am. It's in pristine condition, belonged to our owner. He's the one had it customized."

"You really don't need this car," Brady said.

"You and Duff have treated me like a baby long enough."

She turned to the old car salesman. "Can we drive it?"

The old man looked at Brady.

Shaking his head in resignation, Brady turned to Lacey. "Okay, but maybe I better drive it first, so you can get an idea of the power this car has."

"Fine," Lacey answered. There was a troubling smirk on her face.

While the old man went for the key, Brady removed the two chrome hood pins and raised the hood. He let out a low whistle.

"What is it?"

Lacey bent over and looked under the hood.

"What's all that shiny stuff?"

"Chromed ram air induction and valve covers."

"What does it do?"

"The chrome is just for looks, but the ram air makes it run like a scalded dog."

He dropped the hood, replaced the hood pins and went around to sit in the driver's seat. The old man returned with the key. "I'll sit in the back," he said. "You sit up front, little lady."

Brady twisted the key, and the engine rumbled to life as the car seemed to come up on its hind legs and sway with each tap of the accelerator.

"It's loud," Lacey said.

"Dual glass packs," Brady replied.

Lacey smiled. "I like it."

"Mama Emma will not be happy if you buy this thing. We probably need to go home and talk to her about it. Besides, I'm sure it has to be put through the shop first."

"Oh, no," the old man said. "It's been serviced. It's ready to go."

Brady rolled his eyes as he looked in the rear view mirror.

"Oh," the old man said. He shook his head. "I mean it might need a wash, or—"

Brady eased out on the clutch. It was tight and responsive. The car lurched into motion, and he pulled onto the highway. Despite his caution, they were pushing sixty as he shifted into third gear and the tach hadn't broken two grand. The speedometer stopped at a hundred and forty.

Brady again glanced at the car salesman in the rearview mirror. "How fast do you reckon she'll go?"

The old man gripped the back of Lacey's seat with both hands. The skin on his knuckles was bone-white.

"I don't know, sir, but I certainly don't want to find out right now."

Brady laughed. "Don't worry. I'm not crazy."

They took the Malibu down the highway and back. Brady liked the feel. It was as if he sat on a thoroughbred in a holding pen. God only knew what it would do with the reins loosened, but there was no changing Lacey's mind. She was hell-bent, and after she purchased a cashier's check at the bank and signed the papers, the old salesman pulled the car to the end of the drive near the highway.

"I want to drive it home," Lacey said.

"No, we need to get out of town first—out on the open road," Brady said.

"It's my car."

"You have no idea—"

She jumped into the driver's seat. "I'll be careful."

"Okay, this thing is nothing like that old truck. You don't have to give it much gas, and the clutch is short and tight. Just barely ease out on it."

Lacey rolled her eyes. "Yes, Daddy. I got it. Go get in your old truck, and let's go."

Brady was at a loss. "Okay, take a left out of here, and—"

"I *know* how to find my way home."

Brady laughed. Lacey feared nothing, and she was growing fiercely independent, but these were only two of the things that set her apart from other girls.

"Go for it," he said.

He started back toward the truck, but the Malibu's engine roared and the tires screamed. White smoke billowed from beneath the car as it shot out of the drive and across the highway. Spinning sideways on the far shoulder, it sent a rooster tail of gravel skyward as Lacey fought the steering wheel. The engine continued roaring as the car shot back across the highway toward the dealership, and Brady was about to run when she got it straightened out. Rocketing past the drive, Lacey headed the wrong way back into town. Brady ran out to the road, and looked down the highway. Lacey had finally found the presence of mind to let off the accelerator. Slowing, she pulled the car to the side of the road.

Brady sprinted the hundred yards down the highway to where she'd stopped. When he arrived, she'd already turned off the ignition and sat white as a bucket of milk with both hands on the steering wheel. He tapped on the window. She turned and looked up at him, dazed and disoriented. He opened the door.

"Crawl over there in the other seat. You can drive the pickup, and I'll follow you."

Without hesitation she crawled over the console. He cranked the engine and made a U-turn.

"At least you didn't pee in your pants," he said as they turned back into the dealership.

She laughed and broke into tears. Brady stopped the car and pulled her close. "It's okay. We should have let you drive more before now. I'll stop out on the highway and give you some more driving lessons."

And he did. By the time they approached Melody Hill that afternoon, Lacey was running the gears like an old hand, and he could hardly keep up with her as he followed in the pickup.

* * *

It was warm and sunny that next Saturday, and they'd taken Lacey's new Chevy out to the bluff above the Hiwassee River. Always one of Duff's favorite hangouts, the overlook offered a panoramic view of the miles of forests and farms below. To the west in the haze above the valley red-tailed hawks soared on the spring thermals as they climbed walls of towering white nimbus. After spreading a blanket on the grass, Brady lay back and closed his eyes while Lacey opened a bottle of Coke and sat beside him. A quiet day, there was only the gentle whispering of the breeze in the pines. Duff had always said the Overhill was like heaven, and today it felt like it.

"Do you think something's wrong with Duff?" Lacey asked.

They hadn't gotten a letter from him in two weeks.

"I don't think so," Brady said. "His last letter said he was moving around a lot and staying busy."

"I wish he'd write."

"He will. Quit worrying. You need to focus on what you're gonna do when we graduate next month."

"You mean when I move to Nashville?"

Brady opened his eyes and looked over at her.

"I told you, Duff was right about Langston. That guy's a shyster, and I don't trust him. What if you get up to Nashville and he says he didn't get you an apartment to rent, or he couldn't find you a job?"

"Why don't you go with me? We can get an apartment together."

"And what happens when I get drafted or sign up for the guard? You know it's gonna happen."

"Go to college. You'll get a deferment."

"Go to college with what? It costs, you know? And what about Mama Emma? Who's going to look after her?"

"You're just making excuses," Lacey said.

She set her Coke aside in the grass and lay on the blanket beside him. Crossing her leg over his, she ran her fingers through his hair. He put his hand across her back and pulled her close as their lips met. Her mouth was wet and sweet, her tongue hot. Parting her legs, she pushed hard against his thigh. He grasped her head and rolled with her until he was looking down into her eyes. Pushing her blouse upward, Brady ran his hand under her bra. Her breast was soft and hot, her nipples instantly rigid. She moaned. His promise to Duff became a basket of dry leaves in a forest fire of passion.

Lacey reached for his belt buckle, and Brady began unbuttoning her blouse, but there came a sudden roar from overhead, and the two lovers parted instantly as they rolled onto their backs and stared skyward.

"What the he…?"

A small red Cessna had passed less than thirty feet above them as it shot down the river and out over the valley to the west. Glinting in the afternoon sun, it slowly turned and circled back toward them. Brady cupped his hand above his eyes. Lacey, still gasping both from the passion and the sudden fright, pulled her shirt down. On the engine cowling of the aircraft was the inscription "Miss Whippoorwill."

"That's Jesse Harper," Brady said.

"The guy that got back from Vietnam last month?" Lacey asked.

"Yeah. And they say he's a hell of a pilot."

The plane was coming straight back at them, the engine bawling as if it were wide open.

"What's he doing?" Lacey said.

"They say when he gets drunk he does stunts out there over the valley."

The plane again roared overhead before going into an almost vertical climb.

"It's just a little Cessna, but he did some modifications to the engine."

"Well, I wish he'd go away."

Jesse was a war hero, and Brady thought of Duff. He drew a deep breath, and only then did he realize some power other than his own waning will power was at work in his life. He came up on his knees and stood up. Taking Lacey by the hand, he pulled her to her feet.

"I think I'm gonna take up drinking like Jesse," he said.

"Why don't we take the blanket and go for a walk over there in the trees?" Lacey asked.

Brady picked up the blanket and threw it over his shoulder. "Why do you—?"

He paused, catching himself.

"Why do I what?" Lacey asked. "Why do I love you so much?"

It was a conversational minefield, one where he had to pick his words carefully. "Why can't we wait just a little longer? I gave Duff my word."

Lacey's jaw flexed as she folded her arms and gazed out across the valley. Jesse Harper's plane still buzzed in the distance. Otherwise, it was quiet.

"What is it?" Brady asked.

Lacey's stare remained fixed on the horizon. "I love you. What's so hard to understand about that?"

"Lacey."

She refused to look at him.

"Lacey."

"What?"

"We've grown up together. I know you. There's something else."

Brady took her hand, and they walked up the slope.

"You might as well tell me."

They made their way through the trees back toward the car.

Lacey drew a deep breath. "Do you remember Mr. Hubbard's history class last December when he talked about Pearl Harbor?" she asked.

"Sure."

"Do you remember how he said there were twenty-three sets of brothers that died when they sank the USS Arizona?"

"Yeah."

"Well, all I've thought about since that day was keeping you from going over there to Vietnam with Duff."

Brady wrapped his arm around her waist and pulled her close.

"Lacey, I love you more than anything in this world. And I want you more than you can even imagine, but you've got to realize if they draft me I have no choice but to go."

"But they won't draft you if you have a son or daughter, will they?"

"That doesn't make any difference. I'd still be drafted."

"Really? Even if we have a baby?"

"Look, we'll figure something out, but in the meantime you've got to realize I gave Duff my word, and I intend on keeping it till we graduate. After that, well...."

Brady hugged her tight, and Lacey laid her head against his chest.

"I love you, Brady Boy."

CHAPTER FOURTEEN

A Nest of Vipers
April, 1967

few days after his encounter with Lynn Dai, Duff received word about another meeting at the Embassy House. Lynn Dai had questions for Spartan and the team about the first Cu De River mission. She requested that the entire team be present, and the men gathered in the room shortly after noon that day. Lynn Dai laid a yellow legal pad on the table. Several pages were already filled with notes. She scribbled a date at the top of a clean sheet. The scratch of her pencil in the surrounding silence must have sent a clear message to Spartan as he shifted in his chair and lit a cigarette.

"Mr. Spartan, you killed three men that you described as enemy combatants. Were they armed at the time?"

"How the hell should I know? We were taking fire. We found them hiding in a tunnel, and I didn't want them to escape. Simple as that."

"Mr. Spartan, I am only following up on claims by their relatives for compensation. According to witnesses, the men had their arms bound and they possessed no weapons."

"So now we're going to pay for all the VC we shoot, right? Were any of your so-called 'witnesses' caught in the crossfire by those bastards? We already had two people down, and the village chief killed. I needed to get control of the situation."

"I simply need to understand the facts," she said.

"So, what's your point?"

"As a claims investigator, I must determine if they were or were not enemy combatants. If they were mistakenly killed and were not enemy combatants, your government owes their families reparations."

"Well, they were VC, no doubt about it."

"Your report said you felt they were forewarned of your arrival at the village, and the ropes were simply a ruse used when they were trapped. How do you feel they were warned in advance?"

"I think we have someone in one of our units talking to the enemy."

"In which of the units do you suspect there may be a spy?"

"I think we've narrowed it down to the PRU, but that's not definite. You know, I think I'd rather discuss this later, one-on-one, if that's okay."

"Why do you wish to do that?"

Spartan cocked his head and looked off to one side as he gave his best rendition of a condescending smile. He then raised his head and looked directly at her.

"Our organization operates on a need-to-know basis, little lady, and you're asking questions about matters I don't want to discuss openly. You come by my office at the IOCC later this evening, and I'll answer all your questions. After that maybe we can go by the Embassy House for a drink."

Bouchet agreed, and when she was gone Spartan propped his feet on the table. "Bitch can ask some tough questions, can't she?"

No one at the table replied.

"Don't worry. I'm going to fuck her brains out tonight. When I finish with her, she'll be purring like a kitten."

Unless Duff had badly miscalculated, he was certain Lynn Dai would have nothing to with Spartan, as much from personal disdain as from her position with the South Vietnamese government. Although somewhat naïve, she seemed a respectable person with good intentions bent on doing her duty. The problem was that the intelligence and security apparatuses of the American and South Vietnamese governments were tangled with that of the An Ninh and the Cuc Nghien Cuu like a nest of vipers. Anyone trying to match a snake's head with its body was almost guaranteed a snakebite. Hers was a battle he wouldn't take on for any reason.

The lights inside the Embassy House were turned down low and the Righteous Brothers were crooning *Unchained Melody* when Duff and Roland arrived that evening. Sparkling glasses flowed with liquor as everyone imagined themselves immersed in this exotic place called Vietnam, loathing and loving it at the same moment. Spartan's answers to Bouchet's questions that day had left Duff with a growing realization that this world of highbrow sophistication was a terrible mirage. It was one of exotic cities, sparkling rice paddies, and green palm trees becoming enveloped in a mushrooming napalm cloud of lies and deceit.

The two men walked across to the bar where the little Vietnamese man in the burgundy jacket set two glasses in front of them. He poured Jack Daniels in Duff's and cast a questioning glance at Roland. Roland studied the empty glass for a moment.

"Oh hell, pour me the same," he said, "but for god's sake put a little Coke in mine."

The men leaned against the wall and sipped their drinks. Duff glanced about at the nurses and other women clutched in the arms of the officers and Embassy House staffers. They shuffled and swayed with the music. *Unchained Melody* had ended, and The Honeydrippers were singing *Sea of Love,* when Duff felt a sudden pang of guilt.

He was standing here warm and dry with a glass of whiskey in hand, while somewhere not far away in the surrounding hills, his buddies were squatting in muddy makeshift bunkers. Their last meal had probably been a can of cold C-rations, their last drink from a canteen of warm, iodine-flavored water. Their feet were a mass of festering blisters, and they were swatting mosquitoes and listening for the sounds of the enemy beyond the wire. Some wouldn't live to see the morning sunrise.

"Man, I feel so out of place here," Duff said.

"I thought you wanted to come down here and dance with the nurses," Roland said.

"I really wanted to dance with Lynn Dai Bouchet."

"I'm afraid Spartan has other plans for her tonight."

"You know that prick won't get to first base with her," Duff said.

Roland smiled. "Do I hear the voice of jealousy?"

As if a silent prayer was answered that very moment, Lynn Dai came through the front door of the Embassy House. She paused, and they made eye contact across the room. Before now Duff had not seen her in a dress, nor with her hair down. She was even more beautiful, and it seemed the entire room took a momentary pause as she made her way toward him.

Duff elbowed Roland. "She's here," he said.

Roland nodded. "Well, hell, it looks like your wish just came true, lover boy."

Lynn Dai walked up and stood in front of Duff. "I hoped to see you here tonight."

"Me too," Duff said.

"He's a man of few words," Roland said.

Lynn Dai gazed down at the floor and smiled.

Roland elbowed Duff in the ribs. "You're up, boy."

"Uh, yeah," Duff said. He had never felt so uncomfortable around any girl. "Will you dance with me?"

"I would be honored," she said.

He took her hand in his and held her close. The scent of her perfume and the warmth of her body filled his senses as she rested her head against his shoulder. Never had he felt as he did at that moment, and it wasn't some hormonal rush, but a feeling that the woman he held in his arms had a mysterious yet vulnerable power, one she was trusting to him. *Sea of Love* ended, and Chad & Jeremy's *A Summer Song* began.

"I wish we were somewhere besides here," he said. "Someplace where we could talk."

Duff looked down into her brown eyes. Lynn Dai had the mixed beauty of both worlds, the French and the Vietnamese. He was mesmerized and pulled her closer. The lyrics seemed made for the moment:

Trees swayin' in the summer breeze
Showin' off their silver leaves
As we walked by
Soft kisses on a summer's day
Laughing all our cares away
Just you and I

When the song ended, they walked over to where Roland still stood.

"Why do you want to leave?" she asked.

"I feel out of place here with these people."

Lynn Dai smiled and nodded her head. "I thought perhaps—"

"How about this next dance?" someone asked.

Duff turned. It was a tall marine officer, and he had grasped Lynn Dai by her arm. The colonel wore dress greens, and had the physique of an oak. He stood at least six-foot-four, but his face was flushed from the effects of alcohol.

"I am so sorry, Colonel, but I regret that I must decline, for—"

He pulled her arm. "Aw heck, little lady, one dance is all I'm asking."

Duff hesitated as Lynn Dai attempted to pull away, but the officer's huge hand was locked like a steel shackle around her upper arm. Her eyes reflected the slightest hint of—was it fear?

"With respect, sir," Duff said. "I think she doesn't want to dance right now."

The big man turned to face him. He stood at least four inches taller than Duff and wore the grim mask of an ogre. His hand remained locked around Lynn Dai's upper arm.

"You know, specialist, when they introduced you at our table last week, I thought you were a pretty sharp kid, sharp enough at least not to challenge an officer, especially a—"

"Why, Jack, my friend, you must know we don't pull rank here on weekends."

Duff turned. It was Spartan's boss, Crandall Reeves. He was smiling, but his eyes were sharp and focused as he held the big man's stare. The colonel released Lynn Dai's arm.

"I'm sorry, sir," the colonel said. "It was just a misunderstanding."

He turned to Lynn Dai. "I hope you will forgive my lack of courtesy, ma'am." He then turned to Duff. "I apologize. I acted inappropriately."

Duff could not find the words to respond, and Reeves motioned the colonel to follow as he walked away. Duff grasped Lynn Dai's hand and pulled her between him and Roland at the bar. He looked over at Roland. "Did that guy just call a Marine colonel's hand?"

"They say he's got a lot of Juju in DC," Roland said.

Duff glanced back at the two men now taking seats at a table. "Damn. I reckon I'm gonna hear from that colonel later."

"I don't think so. You just made him a friend for life, or at least as long as Crandall Reeves is around."

* * *

It was near midnight when Duff met Lynn Dai at her car outside the Embassy House.

"What kind of car is this?" he asked.

"It is a Citroën," Lynn Dai said. "It was manufactured in France and belonged to my father."

They had driven no more than three minutes when she pulled into a small alcove.

"We are here," she said.

Duff looked around. He assumed she was taking him back to his quarters at the base, but they drove through a gate into a small courtyard.

"We are where?" he said.

"You said you wished to talk in private. I have an apartment here."

They went inside, and Lynn Dai bolted the door. The small apartment was decorated and furnished with a mixture of plush European and serene Vietnamese influences. A shrine with joss sticks and photographs sat on a small lacquered table against the far wall. Above it hung a crucifix with Jesus wearing the crown of thorns. Thankfully, the couch was of European descent with soft pillows, as Lynn Dai invited him to be seated. She went to a small turntable on a shelf and placed an LP record on it. The album's cover said it was the sound track from *Breakfast at Tiffany's*.

"I suppose American music is one of my greatest pleasures. Are you familiar with Henry Mancini?"

"This is *Moon River*," Duff said.

"Can I get you something to drink? I have a bottle of wine."

"That's fine."

Duff closed his eyes and listened: *Dream maker, you heart breaker*. Lynn Dai returned from the small kitchenette with the bottle, two glasses and a corkscrew.

"I am sorry, Duff, to keep you from your rest, but I, too, wanted someplace private so we could talk more about your boss."

Duff exhaled and nodded as he tried to avoid showing his feeling of disappointment. Nam had reared its ugly head and snuffed out his momentary dream of being seduced by this beautiful woman. She only wanted to talk business.

"Yeah, you met with him earlier this evening. How'd that go?"

She pressed her lips together and looked away.

"Not good, I take it."

She inhaled deeply, and paused before speaking. "I do not know how to explain, except to say that your boss is an animal."

Lynn Dai handed him the corkscrew. Duff looked at it, then at the bottle. He had never opened a bottle of wine.

"I questioned him about his actions, both destroying the villagers' boats and murdering the three boys. I also told him he had sold arms directly to the National Liberation Front. He became angered, called me a liar and other names, and then he…"

She hesitated.

"Did he hit you?" Duff asked.

"No. He tore my clothes and tried to rape me."

A tear trickled down her cheek.

"That sorry bastard," Duff muttered. "How did you get away?"

"I hit him in the eye with my fist and screamed. Then I ran away."

"Where were you?"

"At his suggestion, I met him in his office at the intelligence operations center. I thought it would be safe there, but none of the Special Police were present. We were alone."

"Are you okay now?"

He wiped the tear from her cheek with his thumb.

"Yes."

"That explains the look you gave that colonel back at the embassy house when he grabbed your arm, and why Spartan never showed up there tonight."

Duff finally fumbled through uncorking the wine and began pouring it into the glasses. Setting the bottle aside, he handed her a glass. "Drink this. It'll make you feel better."

"I am still worried about what he might do."

"Why?"

"He threatened me as I ran away."

"What did he say?"

Duff felt his heart in his chest, and his anger grew. He was tempted to gulp the wine, but forced himself to sip it slowly.

"He threatened to—I am unsure of the word he used, but essentially he said he would eviscerate me as he did a young Vietnamese girl last year."

"The VC prostitute?"

Roland had told him about Spartan's scar, and how a Vietcong woman masquerading as a prostitute had tried to murder him with his own knife.

"She was neither VC, nor was she a prostitute," Lynn Dai said. "We knew one another from the university. She was a young woman from a very good family who fought back when he raped her at the point of a knife. She took his knife away afterward, but made the mistake of slashing his face. He killed her for it."

"How do you know it happened that way?"

"Because he eviscerated her and left her to die. Her mother found her, and she lived long enough to tell her about it."

"My god," Duff whispered. "He *is* an animal."

"I fear I am failing my mission and my country. The An Ninh agent for whom I am searching is even more evil than your boss, and I have perhaps asked too many questions. I am afraid he will discover my true purpose."

Duff refilled the glasses. "What are you going to do?"

"I will go to Saigon and talk with those for whom I am working."

"I am sorry for what he did to you," Duff said.

The red wine glowed with a dark luminescence in the dim light of the apartment as Lynn Dai raised the glass to her lips. Afterward she set the glass aside and looked into his eyes.

"Thank you."

She bent forward, and their lips met. Her hair held the delicate scent of shampoo and the subtle hint of her perfume. After a soft kiss, she laid her head against his chest and closed her eyes.

"I feel safe and comforted with you, Duff."

Duff held her close and lay back, closing his eyes. If all she wanted was to be held, he understood.

* * *

Awakening sometime in the night, Duff realized Lynn Dai had curled on the couch beside him and lay with her head in his lap. The couch was lined with pillows, and he grasped one. Gently lifting her head, he slid the pillow in place. She stirred, and her eyes opened. She smiled.

"Sorry," Duff said. "I didn't mean to wake you."

Lynn Dai sat up. "You must be uncomfortable. Please, lie down beside me."

He hesitated. "Are you sure?"

"Yes," Lynn Dai said. "I need for you to hold me."

They lay together on the couch, and she pressed hard against him. He kissed her softly. Given the trauma she'd been through earlier in the evening, his every instinct said to move slowly, and he tried, but he felt the warmth of her tongue as she thrust it between his lips. The hot rush of the moment was inescapable and overpowering. She tugged at his belt, and he pushed her dress above her hips then carefully pulled her panties downward. She kicked them free.

Duff grasped his belt, but Lynn Dai suddenly planted her hand against his chest and pushed him away. "Please," she said. She was breathless as she spoke. "Wait."

Duff went cold with fear. He had moved too quickly. Sliding from beneath him, Lynn Dai stood. Her dress fell back into place, and she turned away. What had caused her to suddenly stop? Perhaps she was having second thoughts or worse, thinking again of Spartan's attempted rape.

She walked across the room to the small family shrine, where she turned the two pictures face down. As she returned to the couch, she loosened and dropped the dress to the floor, then peeled her bra straps from her shoulders. Duff felt he would burst from the pressure in his groin as he sat watching her. He quickly unbuttoned his shirt and shed his trousers.

She pulled him down and rolled her hips upward pressing her soft underside against him, and her eyes begged him not to wait. She was soft and already wet as he sank gently into her. Lynn Dai grasped his buttocks, pulling him deeper as she arched her back, moaned and trembled uncontrollably. The heat of her body was more than he could stand, and he instantly burst inside of her. It had lasted for only a moment and her body seemed to collapse in exhaustion. Afterward, they lay very still for nearly a minute, their bodies pressed closely together.

"I'm sorry," he said.

"For what?" she asked, still breathing heavily.

"For...well, for being so, uh, quick."

She drew a hard quivering breath, her brown eyes wide and bright as she smiled. "Don't be. I was quicker than you."

After a few minutes, Duff again felt himself growing aroused.

He wasn't sure how many times it happened that night, but sometime before morning he realized the relief she had brought him. And it wasn't necessarily the release of sexual tension, as much as a temporary reprieve from the cold reality of the war. He didn't want to move. He wanted stay there beside her forever. He drifted off to sleep again, and only when the gray light of dawn filtered across the courtyard outside her window did he finally sit up.

The tensions of his life until that moment had been erased. He had also found someone he was certain he could grow to love. Lynn Dai slept in a blissful and silent exhaustion, a slight smile on her lips. She breathed softly as he quietly stood buttoning his shirt.

* * *

It was midmorning when Lynn Dai drove him back to the base. She showed an ID card at the gate, one that the guard seemed to quickly recognize and approve without hesitation. Promising to contact him as soon as she returned from Saigon, she asked Duff not to confront Spartan. He agreed, as long as Spartan didn't try to lure him into another situation like the one the night of the weapons theft.

The April sunshine reflected brilliantly off the white buildings as they drove across the base, and Duff found the tensions of the war seeping back into his psyche. He glanced over at Lynn Dai. She smiled, and the wind scattered her hair across her face. He was at once the happiest and the most frightened he'd been in his entire life.

As she turned the car down the road toward the billets, Duff realized there was an extra jeep parked in front of the building. He raised his hand.

"Stop! Quick, stop right here."

Lynn Dai braked and pulled to the side of the road.

"What is it?" she asked.

"I'm not sure, but I think that's Spartan's jeep parked in front of our barracks."

They were still several hundred feet away, and there was no one in sight.

"Drop me off here, and turn around."

He bent over and kissed her gently.

"He will know we were together, and he will be jealous," she said. "Tell him we simply visited friends and played cards."

Duff nodded and stepped from the vehicle. After Lynn Dai's car disappeared back toward the main gate, he began walking toward the barracks. If it was Spartan's jeep, there could be only one reason he had come here.

CHAPTER FIFTEEN

The Temple Ruin
April, 1967

D uff walked inside the barracks to find Spartan leaning against the wall beside his room. His arms were folded across his chest, and he wore a silly smile, one that was no doubt a precursor to an irritating line of questioning. Duff took a deep breath as he walked down the hallway. The billet had the odor of stale liquor, dirty socks, and the men who lived there.

"Well, I *will* be damned, if it isn't our MIA lover boy dragging his tired ass back in here."

Duff stopped in front of Spartan, who had moved to block the door to the room. Spartan's left eye was bruised and bloodshot.

"Why is the door to my room open?" Duff asked.

Spartan pushed past him and walked back up the hallway to the outside door where he looked up and down the road. He turned to Duff.

"Hell, Coleridge, I thought maybe you were dead in there. I opened it to check on you. So, how the hell did you get here?"

"I walked."

"You walked? You walked all the way from that Bouchet bitch's place?"

Duff felt a twinge in his gut. He must have fallen hard for her, because he realized he would have broken the jaw of another man saying that, but he forced his anger inside. This one had to be played carefully.

"What makes you think I was with Bouchet?"

"What, you don't think I have friends at the Embassy House?"

"I danced with her, so?"

"Yes, and you acted like a fool with Colonel Greer. And according to people who know, they saw you get in the car with Bouchet outside the Embassy house."

Spartan cocked his head upward and to one side. His mouth hung open, his bottom lip tight across his teeth. He knew he had the advantage. "So, why don't we cut to the chase? What'd you do, bone her and stay the night?"

Duff wanted to hook an uppercut to the cocky bastard's jaw. Instead he forced his body to totally relax, and put his hands on his hips. He smiled. "No, actually she acted more like a nun. We went to a friend of hers' place, drank some wine, and I fell asleep on the couch while they played some kind of Vietnamese card game. So, what happened to your eye?"

Spartan's initial response was to reach toward his eye, but he caught himself and stopped. "Comes under the heading of, none of your fucking business," he said.

Duff turned and went into his room. Sitting on the bunk, he began removing his shoes.

"So, are you going to tell me how you got here?" Spartan asked.

"I walked from the main gate. That's where she dropped me off."

"Okay, I'm going to make this real clear," Spartan said. "You stay the fuck away from that bitch. You hear me? She's asking way too many questions—questions that are outside her venue of responsibility. If she comes around asking you anything else, I want to know. Understood?"

"What kind of questions is she asking?"

Spartan's face turned red and his lip curled. "I'm going to take care of her nosey ass. You just stay the fuck away from her. End of subject. You hear?"

Duff was disgusted with this sorry excuse for a human being, but he fought to hide the pressurized chamber of magma inside. He looked up at Spartan and smiled.

"Does this mean we're not friends anymore?"

"Don't fuck with me, you smart-ass bastard. You'll do as I say, or I'll bust your ass out of here."

Duff stood up, his nose inches from Spartan's. Spartan didn't flinch. "I'm not exactly sure who pissed in your drink this morning, boss, but I'm not the one who's been yelling and screaming. I didn't know I was breaking any rules by riding with Bouchet to her friend's house. And if you don't want me in your outfit, I'll be glad to go."

Duff had allowed a tiny bit of the fire inside to show, but he held the rest, and it apparently worked. Spartan seemed to relax.

"Okay, maybe I was a little out of line. Had a rough night last night."

He touched his eye gingerly with his fingertips. "Yeah, I got in a little scrape with a bunch of cowboys wanting to clip me for my forty-five last night. One of them got in a lucky punch, but I mopped the street with their little dink asses, all three of them."

Duff looked away for fear of revealing himself. The only thing Spartan could mop a street with was his own tired ass.

"Go ahead and get some sleep," Spartan said. "We have another op meeting tomorrow afternoon with the Special Police."

* * *

Duff had closed his door and heard Spartan's jeep leave, when someone knocked at his door.

"Yeah?" he said.

"It's Roland," came a low voice.

Duff opened the door and walked back to his bunk. Roland was wearing fatigue pants with a T-shirt and flip-flops. Duff sat on the bed.

"You've got big balls, my friend, fucking with him that way."

"You were here the whole time?" Duff asked.

"Yeah, asshole came beatin' on my door, but I was a little hung over. Didn't answer."

"So, you heard everything?"

Roland leaned against the door frame and lit a cigarette.

"Yeah, I did."

"Any suggestions?"

Roland exhaled a cloud of smoke toward the ceiling.

"Yeah. Get out."

"Get out?"

"Yeah, put in for a transfer back to your unit. I've already talked with the rest of the team about what's been happening. Dibbs wants to hang, but Spencer and me, we're leaving."

"You're not going to report that bastard or anything?"

"Not right now. Look, you've got to understand, Spartan is holding all the cards. Reeves needs him, so he sure as hell isn't going to step in, and Spartan knows it."

"Do you think Reeves knows about the weapons he stole, or the other shit he's done?"

"I doubt it, but he doesn't *want* to know. Don't you see? Even if he did, he might not do anything, because Spartan is his executioner. He's his way of keeping his own hands clean."

"I'm not sure I can just bail, especially now that Spartan says he's going after Lynn Dai."

Roland smiled, and Duff realized he'd shown his hand.

"I take it you and that girl hit it off pretty good?"

"I reckon so," Duff said.

"And you weren't at her friend's house all night, either, were you?"

Duff didn't answer.

"What did she tell you about her meeting with Spartan?"

"He tried to rape her."

Roland's mouth turned down slightly at the corners as he nodded. "I should have figured as much."

"Yeah, she had to fight him off and make a run for it," Duff said.

"And the black eye, that's how he got that, too, right?" Roland said.

"She said she hit him a pretty good lick."

"Did she say if they talked about any of the ops or other stuff that's been going on?"

"Yeah, she confronted him with all of it."

"The weapons theft, too?"

Duff nodded.

"That's not good," Roland said. "That bastard is likely to go after her if he thinks she can associate him with the missing weapons."

"So, what can we do?" Duff asked.

"I'm sorry, bud, but like I said, me and Spencer are out of here as soon as our orders come through."

"Does Spartan know you're leaving?"

"He will later today."

"What if he tries to stop your orders?"

"Won't happen. The colonel already talked with General Buckingham down at MACV. It's a done deal."

"Can I have one of those cigarettes?"

Roland pulled the pack from his pocket and tossed it to Duff.

"I've got to hang around awhile," Duff said.

Roland flipped open his lighter and lit the cigarette dangling from Duff's lips. "I thought you didn't smoke?"

"I'm fixin' to start," Duff said.

"You better tread softly and watch your back, little brother. Spartan is a twenty-four-carat nut-job, and he's got the backing of some big-shots at the OSA."

"What's the OSA?"

"Office of the Special Assistant. It's the name for the CIA station in Saigon."

Duff exhaled slowly, blowing the smoke across the room. "I'm running with the big dogs, aren't I?"

It was more of a statement than a question.

* * *

Call it a sense of duty or call it infatuation, but Duff wasn't about to let a sleaze-bag like Spartan hurt Lynn Dai. She was a woman as beautiful and complicated as this country she called her own. Problem was he'd stand a better chance fighting a mountain lion with a pocket knife than going up against Spartan and the company. It was late the next afternoon when he parked the jeep in the courtyard at the IOCC. They were having a pre-op meeting, one he was pretty sure wouldn't include Roland or Spencer.

Duff sat with his feet resting on the brake and clutch after turning off the ignition. The jeep's motor made quiet ticking sounds as it cooled, and he sat thinking. He had to have a plan. Waiting for Spartan to make the next move might be the answer, but he had to make sure Lynn Dai knew Spartan would likely come after her. At least that was what he had again threatened. She had to be warned.

When he stepped out of the jeep, the Vietnamese guard at the door recognized and saluted him. Duff wanted to explain to him that he was a grunt like him, but it was useless. He returned the salute. There were voices coming from the ops room in back, and as he walked down the hallway, they grew silent. Duff walked into the room.

Spartan sat with two uniformed Vietnamese Special Police officers and two PRU officers. He'd met the PRU officers previously, Captain Truc and his second in command, Lieutenant Tri. He also knew the Special Police commander, Colonel Tranh.

"Come on in, Coleridge," Spartan said. "Grab a beer and a chair. You know Colonel Tranh."

Several men held cans of 33. Duff wasn't much of a beer drinker, and if the Vietnamese Ba Moui Ba - Biere 33 was his only choice, he would pass. The only thing worse was Tiger beer. It tasted like formaldehyde.

Duff nodded to Tranh, then turned to Spartan. "Thanks, but I'll pass on the beer."

"This," Spartan said, motioning toward the other uniformed officer, "is one of his men, Captain Nguyen. His second in command, Major Loc, is on leave and won't be participating on this mission. Captain Truc and Lieutenant Tri here head the PRU company.

"So, I suppose you know your buddies Rocky and Speed are trying to bug-out on us?"

Duff nodded. "Yeah, Roland told me."

"Chickenshits can't stand a little heat, but I'm not letting them go. They'll be back by the end of the week. Meanwhile, for this next op it's going to be just me, you and Dibbs.

"Tomorrow we're going into a village about fourteen klicks southwest of here on the other side of the Song Yen River. About ten days ago a truckload of medical supplies going to a an RVN base disappeared, and the driver was assumed dead, but he turned up in this village. It's where he's originally from. He was seen there Friday. There's no doubt our boy is VC, and the Special Police think those medical supplies are being distributed to the enemy from that village. It's right at the base of the mountains with a good road all the way in.

"The people there are no doubt VC sympathizers. We're going in and bust them up. Colonel Tranh and the Special Police along with a detachment of RVN troops will cordon and search the village while we hook up with a platoon from the Regional Defense Force and pull some ambushes for anyone trying to sneak out the back way.

"There are several trails leading back into the hills from the village, and we're pretty sure there's tunnels coming out of the village near them. These are where we expect to catch the VC. Coleridge and I will set up with two squads on the most heavily used trail. Dibbs and the other squads will watch a secondary trail. The plan is to be in position at daylight. Out where we're going is a free fire zone. Anyone coming that way gets his shit blown away.

"We'll coordinate frequencies with the Special Police and the ARVN unit. There'll also be a couple of American Cobra gunships and a dust-off on call from the airbase if we need them.

"Questions?"

No one spoke.

"We'll assemble and move out of here at oh-three-hundred hours. Let's make certain we brief every man and tell them to put on their best game-faces. Contact is just about a hundred-percent certainty."

* * *

The convoy headed inland that morning, the dim lights of the military vehicles barely penetrating the mist. Up front were the ARVN vehicles, followed by those of the Special Police. Duff rode in the jeep with Spartan and Dibbs. The morning air was cool, and Dibbs dozed in back with his fatigue jacket pulled over his head. He was surrounded by a jumble of radios, rucksacks, and other gear.

"Once we get to our assembly area, we have some serious humping to do before daylight," Spartan said. His voice was tight with tension. "I'm putting you on point, but you've got to stay on your toes. This is Indian country, so pay attention and don't walk us into an ambush."

Duff cut his eyes over at him, wanting to ask if he got demoted if they walked into one. He decided against antagonizing the jerk further. Hopefully, this op would be another dud. He needed to get back and warn Lynn Dai of Spartan's threats.

After passing miles of rice paddies and an almost continuous chain of villages, the convoy arrived at an intersection where another road came in from the west. Here they stopped, and the engines went silent. The village was less than two klicks away. No one spoke above a whisper as ARVN soldiers, Special Police, and the PRU assembled and trotted away down the road to the west. The morning darkness quickly swallowed them. Duff had studied the map, storing it like a picture in his mind. He knew exactly how to reach the ambush point. He shouldered his gear and looked toward Spartan.

"Let's go," Spartan said.

Duff started up the road with Dibbs walking slack, followed by Spartan and twenty Regional Defense Force militiamen. He didn't care for working with the militiamen. Although most were loyal, there were some he didn't trust, and Roland said he'd been left hanging more than once when the shit hit the fan. He described their disappearance as a retrograde *di di mau* to parts unknown.

Duff raised his hand to stop the column. He had reached the first trail leading southward around the back of the village. He motioned for Spartan to come up.

"This is the wrong trail," Spartan whispered.

"It's the one we need to take," Duff said.

"Why?" Spartan hissed. "The one further up the road is a hell of a lot shorter and takes us right behind the village."

"That's right. It's a hell of a lot closer to the village, and it's likely to be booby trapped. It also takes us over that rise up there. If they have lookouts, that's probably where they'll be."

Spartan looked at Dibbs. Dibbs shrugged. "If I were you, I'd listen to the man. Sounds to me like he knows his shit."

Dibbs looked at Duff and smiled. The Vietnamese militia knelt in a curious cluster watching them. Spartan always depended on Roland and Spencer to guide him, something Duff had recognized all too quickly. Now that Spartan was trying to call his own shots, he was fucking up by the numbers. Duff didn't wait for his order, but turned and headed down the footpath. He heard the scuffing of boots and clop of sandals as the militiamen came down the embankment behind him.

The foot path skirted the rise, then led across a series of dikes between the rice paddies. After covering nearly a klick, Duff spotted his first marker silhouetted against the night sky, a pagoda. This was where Dibbs and half the RDF militiamen would set up the first ambush along a dike. This was where the footpath intersected with one coming from the village. Duff silently nodded at Dibbs, who quickly motioned for his group to spread out along the dike.

"Good luck," Duff whispered.

Several hundred meters to the west was the end of a ridge extending from the Nui Son Ga mountains. Duff crossed the last rice paddy and made his way up the ridge, crossing to the other side. He spotted his second marker, its mass rising from the palm trees below. It was an old Buddhist temple ruin. The main trail coming from the village crossed a palm flat behind the ruin and turned directly up the ridge. Duff spread his men in a tight line and found the Vietnamese interpreter.

"No one talks. All weapons on safe. I don't want any accidental shots. If someone shoots, we shoot them because we know they are warning the VC. You understand?"

The interpreter nodded.

"I'm going to set out two claymores down the ridge. If we pull the ambush, no one shoots until we blow the claymores. Is that clear?"

The interpreter nodded again.

"Say it back to me."

"Jesus, Coleridge, I think he got it," Spartan said.

Duff ignored him.

"Say it back to me."

"All weapon on safe. You shoot anyone who make accidental shot to warn VC. Do not shoot for ambush until claymore blow."

"Thanks. Now, go and keep them quiet."

"This isn't their first rodeo," Spartan said.

"They sounded like a herd of cattle walking in here this morning," Duff said. "They've been doing this a lot longer than you have."

Duff ignored him as he grabbed the cords and detonators for the claymores. Trailing the cords, he worked his way down the hill parallel to the trail, where he set the mines. Within minutes they were ready. He found Spartan hunkered down in the darkness and gave him the detonators. The ground mist below was thinning and overhead the stars were fading. Dawn was quickly approaching.

CHAPTER SIXTEEN

Heartbreak Ambush
April, 1967

The men lay still as stones in the grassy undergrowth as the misty light of dawn revealed the gray stone ruins of the temple far below. A heavy green moss grew on its lower portions while a labyrinth of vines snaked over its ancient walls. Only a portion of its red-tiled roof remained. A half-kilometer to the east the thatched roofs of the village jutted through the mist. The ARVN troops and Special Police were no doubt moving into position at that very moment, but the surrounding countryside was strangely quiet.

Beyond the village the horizon glowed with a thin streak of orange, the first hint of the coming sunrise. The dank odor of the rice paddies drifted up the ridge. Duff studied the palms and undergrowth with his binoculars. From the direction of the village came a faint shout. The soldiers were awakening the inhabitants. It was only a few moments before he spotted movement on the trail. A single man appeared about three hundred meters away, but he was standing, looking back toward the village.

Wearing black pajamas and a conical tan hat, the man had an AK-47 slung over his shoulder. More men appeared trotting up the trail toward him. First there were two, then three more. All wore the same black pajamas and tan conical hats, and all carried AK-47s, but they, too, stopped and looked back. A moment later more guerrillas appeared, a single-file line of at least eight more in the same garb coming up the trail, except these were unarmed. Instead they leaned forward as they struggled under the burden of enormous backpacks.

"Holy shit," Spartan whispered. "I hope we didn't bite off more than we can chew. How many are there?"

Duff glassed the column with his binoculars. "Fourteen, so far," he said, "but only six are carrying weapons."

The guerrillas quickly organized into a single-file column and hurried up the trail, straight toward the ambush.

"I'm guessing those are the stolen medical supplies they're packing," Spartan whispered.

"Get those clackers in your hands and remove the safeties," Duff said.

Spartan picked up the detonators for the claymores.

"When the point man reaches the claymores we'll pop the ambush," Duff said.

With the six carrying weapons in the lead, the guerrillas quickly closed the distance and started up the side of the ridge. From the corner of his eye Duff noticed Spartan's hands trembling.

"Steady," he said. "Not yet."

The point man was still thirty meters from the claymores. The sound of their sandals slapping the hard-packed clay on the trail was distinct.

"Waaaiitt," Duff muttered.

Fifteen meters. The sound of their labored breathing was distinct.

"Now!" Duff said.

The explosions of the claymores shattered the morning stillness as smoke, leaves, and debris filled the air. The first six guerrillas were shredded like rag dolls as the two claymores struck them with fourteen hundred ball-bearing-size steel pellets. Several more in the column were also struck and lay writhing in the trail as the Popular militia showered them with automatic weapons fire. Scattering in the palms below, others dropped their huge packs as they ran for their lives.

Spartan rose to a crouch as he sprayed the bodies below, but Duff noticed one guerrilla who had escaped, still running with the giant backpack up the trail near the temple ruins. Duff raised his rifle and centered the crosshairs on the pack. The target was just over three hundred meters out when he squeezed off the round. The guerrilla pitched forward and disappeared. It was suddenly quiet except for the faint moans of the wounded. The smoke, dust, and odor of burnt cordite drifted across the ridgetop.

"Let's clean up and look for intel," Spartan said.

"There may be more show up," Duff said. "You may want to swap magazines."

Spartan looked down at his weapon. The bolt was locked back, the magazine empty. "Uh, yeah, sure," he said, but he didn't make eye contact with Duff.

Duff shook his head. It had to be blind luck that this idiot had survived a previous tour. The RDF militia spread in a skirmish line and filtered through the trees as they made their way down the ridge. Spartan followed Duff down the trail to where the first bodies lay.

"We need to search them for papers," Spartan said.

"Have at it," Duff replied. "I'm going to ease on down the trail and see if we have any potential prisoners."

It was obvious Spartan wanted him to search the mutilated bodies, but Duff smiled as he walked away. He was feeling a little cantankerous this morning. Let super-spy search his own bodies. He eased down the trail to where the first of the pack bearers lay dead. This one had fallen backward and was lying with an arched back over the top of the pack. Duff pushed the conical hat back, and shoulder-length black hair spilled out on the ground.

She lay, arms spread with her eyes wide open, her back arched over the huge load she had been carrying. Her body was riddled with holes, and she was very dead. It caught him off guard, that this was a woman. He knew they were common amongst the VC, but this was the first time he'd actually seen one. War or no war, killing a woman seemed unnatural. He sucked down a deep breath. What was done was done. He eased further down the trail.

The next one had fallen under the backpack, face down in the hat. Blood pooled in the trail on either side of the body. The hair wasn't as long, but it was another woman. Duff felt a nausea rising from within. Surely they weren't all… He hurried to the next. This one had made it several meters off the trail before falling. Duff dropped to his knees and pulled the hat from her head. She couldn't have been more than fifteen years old.

A Ruff-Puff appeared beside him as Duff stood up. He glanced at the militiaman, and quickly turned away lest his eyes reveal the revulsion he held inside for what they had done. They were all nurses. Granted they were the enemy, but none had been carrying a weapon. He walked out to the trail but stopped and looked back. The Ruff-Puff had snatched the black pajama pants from the girl's body and unbuckled his belt. He was removing his pants.

"No!" Duff shouted.

He raised his rifle and pointed it at the militiaman. The Ruff-Puff glanced at the girl's body, then at his weapon lying on the ground beside her.

"Go ahead. Pick up your weapon and get the hell out of here."

The Ruff-Puff remained frozen staring back at him.

"Spartan," Duff shouted, still holding his rifle on the militiaman. "Send me that goddamned interpreter."

He looked further down the trail. Another Ruff-Puff straddled a body with his pants down. Duff raised his M-14 and sent a round within inches of the militiaman's head. The interpreter trotted up.

Duff wheeled around and grabbed the man's shirt. "You tell these sorry animals they *will* respect the dead, or I'll kill every last damned one of them. You fucking hear me?"

"Không cưỡng hiếp phụ nữ!" the interpreter shouted.

Duff turned and walked down the trail. His heart was a drum pounding in his ears. He passed the Ruff-Puff he'd fired the warning shot at. The militiaman held up his hands as if to surrender. The interpreter continued shouting at them. Down the trail, somewhere in the undergrowth Duff heard the whimpering moans of one of the wounded. He eased carefully in that direction. It was another young girl, one who had shed her pack. She was sitting in the grass. She had removed her shirt and held it wadded over a hole in her right breast.

Duff stared down at her. She seemed hardly able to breathe as she looked up at him with defiant eyes. Big and brown, her eyes reminded him of Lacey's. The bullet had passed through a lung, and frothy pink blood leaked from the corner of her mouth. Her lips were purple and her face already wore the gray mask of impending death. He knelt beside her. Setting his rifle aside, he gently pushed her backward and removed her hat.

"Lie down," he softly whispered. "You are dying."

Her eyes changed from defiance to a plea—but for what? She tried to speak, but managed only a weak murmur. The blood gurgled in her one remaining lung.

"What?" Duff said, pulling her closer. "Tell me what it is. What did you say? What can I do?"

More blood trickled from the corner of her mouth, and she grasped the waist of her pajamas with one hand, and looked at him with pleading eyes. He knew what it was. He heard someone behind him and turned. It was the interpreter. He turned back to the girl and looked into her eyes as he spoke.

"Tell her that her body will be respected in death."

The interpreter hesitated.

"Tell her, now!"

The interpreter said something Duff could not understand, except he saw it in the girl's eyes. She looked at him, and he at her, and he saw what words could never say as peace came to her. The light slowly faded from her eyes, until they no longer stared at anything.

Duff stood and turned, coming face to face with Spartan.

"Just what the fuck are you doing?" Spartan said. "The fucking interpreter said you threatened one of his men and shot at another one."

"These animals are trying to rape the bodies."

"Jesus Christ, Coleridge! Let them have their fun. They're just bodies. We need these boys. Hell, you might want to try a little gook pussy yourself before it gets cold."

Duff had seldom been given to a quick temper. Always able to think through things no matter the circumstances, he normally used his head, but his mind was no longer in charge. He shoved the butt of the M-14 at an upward angle toward Spartan's head. Despite being totally impulsive, Duff maintained enough control to take him with only a glancing blow. Spartan fell backward, sitting dazed in the trail. He shook his head and reached for his shoulder holster. Duff placed the tip of his rifle barrel on Spartan's nose.

"I will gladly go to Leavenworth, if that's what it takes. So, go ahead, skin that forty-five, you sonofabitch."

"You're totally out of control, asshole," Spartan said. "And Leavenworth will be a dream compared to what I'm going to do if you don't get that fucking gun out of my face."

He stood and dusted off his fatigues.

"Don't ever say something like that to me again," Duff said.

"You really don't have a clue what war is about, do you?" Spartan said.

Duff headed down the trail, but stopped and looked back.

"War is war, and we're going to kill a lot of people, but we don't have to lower ourselves to being animals. There has to be some level of decency."

"I have news for you, shithead. There is no decency in war. They show us no mercy, and we show them no mercy. We put fear in them. If we don't stop them here, we'll be fighting them in the Philippines next. Then what? Hawaii? Mexico? I'm going to do whatever it takes to stop these fuckers, and anyone who isn't one-hundred percent on my team is going to get the same medicine these bitches got."

Spartan's eyes narrowed as he fixed Duff with a hard stare.

"You understand what I'm saying, right?"

Duff looked off to the hills in the west. There were a few thousand North Vietnamese Army regulars out there who weren't on Spartan's team.

"Right?" Spartan said.

"I'll follow orders, but I'm not raping dead women, and I'm not going to let it happen on any operation I'm part of. It's as simple as that."

Duff turned and walked up the trail. He had screwed up royally, but he refused to remain silent in the presence of such depravity. He could never be a spy or even a lookout for Lynn Dai. He was a soldier, nothing more, and now, Spartan had his number. He should have listened to Roland and gotten the hell out while he could.

* * *

The sun had risen above the morning mist, sending a luminescent orange haze amongst the palms as Duff and the Ruff-Puffs searched for another body. They had accounted for all but one, the one Duff had shot while she ran back toward the village. Yes, the other seven had all been female, and he was certain this one, too, would be no different. He was heartsick, but he had a job to perform.

One of the things he'd learned back in the Overhill was how to mark the spot when he took a distant shot at a deer. The last guerrilla was thirty meters to the right of a lone tamarind tree growing amongst the palms. He circled, but there were no signs of a blood trail. She had angled out toward the old temple ruin. He silently eased through the palms, carefully searching the undergrowth.

Up ahead the stark gray mass of the ruins rose above the trees. He carefully parted a large frond with the barrel of his M-14. She was sitting with her back against a mossy stone wall. Her large pack lay beside her as she stared into the undergrowth. She had no idea she was spotted. Duff let the palm leaf settle back into place and circled to the right until he emerged beside the temple wall. With one eye, he looked around the corner. The woman still sat looking off in the other direction. He edged her way.

She turned as he stepped up beside her, his M-14 trained on her head. Her hands were both in plain sight, but if she had a grenade, she might be sitting on it. What better way to go than taking an American with you? Leastwise, that was what he would do. Duff motioned for her to stand. The woman slowly rolled to one side and reached for the stone wall behind her as she struggled to pull herself to her feet. She stood with her back to him, her hands against the wall, unmoving.

Duff lifted the bottom of her pajama blouse with the barrel of his M-14. Her back was bruised and bleeding from several small wounds. The 7.62mm round had apparently shattered on something in her back pack. Carefully, he patted her pajamas for weapons. He found a hemostat clamped to a small pouch of bandages and surgical supplies. Stepping back, he motioned for the woman to turn around, then for her to raise her blouse.

She grasped it with both hands, raising her shirt to neck level exposing her breasts. There was one jagged exit wound at the edge of her chest near her left armpit. Blood seeped from it down her side. Duff opened the pouch and gave the woman a bandage. She unwrapped it and pushed it in place. He heard something behind him. A moment later Spartan and the interpreter stepped out of the undergrowth.

Duff leaned his M-14 against the stone wall and motioned for the interpreter. "Tell her to lie down so I can bandage her wounds."

"Nằm xuống," he said.

"Cảnh sát đặc biệt sẽ tra tấn tôi. Tôi thà chết," she said.

"What did she say?"

"She say Special Police torture her. She rather die."

"No, they won't," Duff said.

"Don't make promises you can't keep," Spartan said. He was smiling.

"Why would they torture a nurse?"

"Look, you fool. This is *their* fucking war. We're just here to help out. Our job is to advise. These slope-headed fuckers have been fighting like this since before recorded history. If you want to make some moral cause out of this shit, go ahead, but you're going to do it somewhere besides my unit."

Spartan turned to the interpreter. "Tell your men to tie her up. We'll work our way back over to—"

A sudden crackle of small arms fire came from the direction of the other ambush team. The echoing *karoomphs* of impacting mortar rounds quickly followed. The handset on the radio scratched and broke squelch as Spartan pressed it to his ear.

"Go ahead," Spartan said. He listened for several seconds. "Roger."

He turned to Duff. "Your boy Dibbs is getting hit with machine gun and mortar fire from that high ground to the southeast. We need to head in toward the village and see if we can flank them."

"Call for the gunships," Duff said.

"Yeah," Spartan answered.

Kneeling, he pulled the radio from his back and changed frequencies. Dibbs was already in contact with the ops center, calling in the enemy's coordinates. ETA for the choppers was less than fifteen minutes.

* * *

By the time they reached the back of the village and turned east toward the high ground, the shooting had ceased. The gunships had arrived, and the attack ended as the VC scattered at the sound of the approaching choppers. Dibbs was unscathed, but he had lost one of his militiamen. Two others were wounded. Spartan and Dibbs walked together as they made their way back to the vehicles. Spartan, no doubt, was giving Dibbs his version of events back at the temple ruins.

Duff insisted they bandage the VC nurse's wounds, but the Special Police had her blindfolded and placed in the back of a jeep. Before they drove away, he did it himself, carefully tightening the gauze bandage around her chest. When he was done, he touched the back of her hand, then turned away.

"Tôi cảm ơn bạn," she said.

"She said she thanks you," someone said.

Duff turned. It was Colonel Tranh. Tranh nodded, as if he respected what he had done, but Duff wondered if he'd only strengthened her for coming torture.

"Will she be tortured?" he asked.

"No, she will not be," Tranh said.

And Duff looked into his eyes. He was telling the truth.

* * *

The ride back into Da Nang that afternoon was a quiet one, as Duff considered the things he had done. The VC were vicious bastards who had tortured and slain their own countrymen unmercifully, and they would do him the same way if he were captured. It wasn't right, but he would not lower himself to be like them, or worse, like Spartan.

The sun was hanging low over the Annamese Cordillera mountains as the convoy approached Da Nang late that afternoon, and Duff was feeling lost. Fighting Spartan and the Special Police was useless. It was an unwinnable battle, because he was unwilling to play by their rules. Worse, he'd given Spartan the power to rule him. Spartan could send him to prison for life if he chose. Duff could no longer hide it. He had to tell Lynn Dai that he couldn't help her. He had to leave—if it wasn't already too late.

CHAPTER SEVENTEEN

Charge of the Light Brigade
April, 1967

Sometime after midnight Duff fell into a fitful sleep. It had been less than twenty hours since the ambush at the temple ruins, but it wasn't the residual effects of adrenaline that kept him awake. It was the eyes he saw—the eyes of the young nurse draped backward over her pack, arms spread wide open, staring into the green palms overhead. It was the eyes of the young nurse who'd died in his arms beside the trail, young, defiant and yet, fearful. It was the eyes of the captured nurse, calm even in the face of possible torture and death. He dozed only to jerk awake, and again he heard the soft moans of the dying. And it occurred to him that he had seen but a glimmer of the determination the enemy possessed.

The night finally ended, and when the sun shone outside his window, Duff sat up, rubbing his eyes. He tried, but he couldn't get the VC nurses out of his mind. It was war. Their deaths were unavoidable. And though he was part of it, he'd done nothing wrong. His thoughts of the ambush were a cancer eating his soul. And there was the impending showdown with Spartan, who could use the Vietnamese interpreter as a witness at a court martial. But perhaps too many other things would come out at a military tribunal—things Spartan didn't want known.

There came a slight knock at the door. Having someone to talk with was better than being left alone with his thoughts. Duff got out of bed and opened the door. It was Dibbs.

"What's up?" Duff said.

"Why don't *you* tell me? What the hell happened yesterday?"

Duff sat back on the bunk.

"Hell, I don't know. I guess I lost it."

"Spartan said you freaked out because you guys shot a bunch of VC nurses."

"Yeah, I reckon so," Duff said. "What else did he tell you?"

"He said you might not be cut out for special ops."

"Maybe, he's right. Did he tell you I decked him, when he said I should join the Ruff-Puffs raping the dead bodies?"

"Oh shit, man. No, he left that little detail out. What happened? Did you stop them?"

"After firing a warning shot at one."

"That explains why he was so hot. He said you were too worried about shooting the wrong gooks, but he didn't say anything about that shit."

"I just couldn't stand by and let them rape the bodies."

Dibbs walked over and sat in a chair against the wall. "Yeah, I don't blame you. Most of the Ruff-Puffs are okay, but there's a couple who were in prison before they got put in the Regional Defense Forces, and they're about as sick as he is."

"That explains why they work so well together," Duff said.

"Better watch your ass, partner. The crazy fucker told me to keep an eye on you. If I were you, I'd do like Rocky and Speed, and put in a 1059, book out of here and don't look back."

Duff nodded. He certainly needed to do something, but what if he transferred and Lynn Dai was killed? That would be another nightmare he would have to live with. Dibbs left, and Duff showered and dressed. He had to find Lynn Dai.

* * *

When life was simpler, Duff was the big brother Brady and Lacey always came to with their problems. They looked up to him. He was their protector, the one with all the answers, but now he had his own problems, and there were no answers—no good ones. He had never faced someone so utterly amoral as Spartan.

Catching a ride into Da Nang City that morning, Duff made his way to Lynn Dai's apartment, but her car was gone. She was probably at the Embassy House, a place he hoped to avoid, but he was running out of options. He began walking.

Being seen at the Embassy House was sure to elicit more questions from Spartan, but what the hell, he was already up to his neck in a dark and dangerous swamp with no islands. It took less than thirty minutes to get there, and Duff flashed his ID card at the Nung sentries as he made his way inside.

Lynn Dai looked up as he walked into the Naval Claims office. Her face became an instant mixture of surprise and concern, and she stood up behind her desk.

"Your face—what is it, Duff?"

"We need to talk," he said.

She grabbed her umbrella and bag and followed him out the door. Within minutes they were parked near her apartment. Duff remained silent, and they didn't speak until safely inside. She dropped her bag and threw her arms around his neck, kissing him urgently, then again softly with passion. After a few moments she drew back.

"What is it, Duff? What has happened?"

"I blew it," he said. "I confronted Spartan."

"What happened?"

Duff told her about the ambush and the Vietcong nurses and the attempted rape of the bodies.

She touched his face.

"You are a good man, Duff. This is a terrible war, and we are amongst some terrible people, but you have done nothing wrong."

Duff fought back the emotions welling inside. "My mind tells me you're right, but I can't believe we killed seven women—nurses. I mean I know they were Vietcong, but…" He shook his head and looked away.

"I understand your feelings, but if you stop fighting now, you allow not only the enemy an uncontested victory, but those like Mr. Spartan as well."

He turned and looked back at Lynn Dai. "What makes you think I want to stop fighting?"

"Duff, your eyes betray you. They are beautiful eyes, but I knew the moment you walked into my office that something terrible had occurred. Even now I see that your spirit is nearly broken."

"They were all so young. One girl couldn't have been more than fifteen years old. I don't want to see that happen to you."

She took his hand. "Come."

Duff sat on Lynn Dai's bed. It was a large bed with an aged and tarnished brass frame. She slipped out of her shoes and dropped her dress to the floor. Duff admired her beautiful body as she removed her lace slip. All the energy and all the heartbreak suddenly drained from his body as if someone had opened a floodgate. Lynn Dai unbuttoned his shirt and pulled it over his head. His physical and emotional exhaustion was so complete that making love seemed impossible, and he wanted to stop her.

"Stand up," she said.

As he stood, she peeled down her bra straps and let it too fall to the floor. She then released his belt buckle.

"Sit back, now," she said.

He sat back on the bed, and she unlaced his boots, removing them, along with his socks, shorts, and trousers. When he was completely naked, she stood, removed her lace panties and straddled him, resting on his abdomen. She bent forward, and her breath was hot against his neck as she gently grasped and pushed him deep inside her body. Duff thought he had not a bit of feeling left in his heart, but something made him reach for her. She was his only hope for sanity, but she grasped his hand.

258 | RICK DESTEFANIS

"No," she said.

She sat upright, taking an involuntary breath as he sank deeper up into her.

"Lie still," she said, almost breathlessly. "Rest."

She bent forward again, caressing his ear with her lips and tongue as she slowly began raising and lowering her hips, drawing back to the very brink of losing him, before slowly and deliberately pushing downward, softly massaging his body with hers. If only for a while, he became lost in a dream-world, free from the previous day's nightmare.

* * *

Duff's eyes opened, and he realized that he had been sleeping for several hours. Lynn Dai lay beneath the sheet beside him, watching him with a sad smile on her face. He reached out and pulled her closer. As he turned up on his side, she lay back, and he pulled the sheet from her breasts. Her breasts were neither large nor small, but they were firm. With only the gentlest pressure he outlined her jutting nipples then drew a line softly down her abdomen along the slightest downy shadow of hair leading to her navel.

"Do you believe there may be a future for us together?" she asked.

Duff stopped, and their eyes met.

"There could be," he said, "but it would take some pretty big sacrifices on your part."

Her lips formed a tight circle. "Oh?"

"Well, yeah. First, you would have to come home with me to the United States to live, and second, you'd have to have lots of babies that are as beautiful as you are."

She smiled and pulled his head toward hers as their lips met once again. "I knew I was right about you," she said.

"How's that?"

Her eyes dropped, and she looked suddenly embarrassed. "My mother would often say I was too much of a romanticist like my father, and he would say I was too much the pragmatist like my mother. I think, perhaps, she was right. I am too much the romanticist. After the first moment when I spoke with you, something in my heart told me you were a man with whom I could spend my life."

"And you're a woman I can love," Duff said.

They held one another for a long while, but the world outside intruded on his thoughts, and Duff eventually sat up on the side of the bed. He reached to the floor for his underwear and socks. "We need to talk about this situation with Spartan," he said.

Lynn Dai threw the sheet back, swung her legs from the bed and stood beside him. She pulled his face into her breasts with one hand and gently pulled the socks and boxers from his grasp with the other.

"We will talk while we bathe," she said.

Duff smiled. "Sounds like your father was right as well."

"I am as much a part of my mother's culture as my father's, and I am here with you and we need to bathe, therefore I shall be the pragmatist for the moment. Join me in my bath. We will talk there."

Duff grinned as he stood and placed one arm behind his back and one across his abdomen, then bowed. "Certainly, Mademoiselle."

The tub was a large free-standing one of yellowed porcelain. Duff and Lynn Dai sat facing one another in a mass of soapy bubbles.

"Do you know if my brother saw me taking a bubble bath, I would never hear the end of it."

Lynn Dai tilted her head to one side. "Really? Why do you say that?"

"Most men where I come from don't take bubble baths. It's considered a girl thing. You know?"

She laughed. "You are saying then, that paratroopers are too much the man to take a bubble bath?"

"Exactly."

"That is probably why so many of you smell like water buffalo," she said.

Duff smiled, then sighed. His mind had wondered back to Spartan.

"You are still worried," Lynn Dai said.

"Yeah, I have to tell you something. Spartan made more threats against you. You may be in danger."

Lynn Dai nodded. "That doesn't surprise me, but it no longer worries me. The people for whom I work have said they will protect me."

"That guy is a total wacko," Duff said.

"A wacko?"

"Yeah, a nut job. I mean he's insane, crazy."

"Oh, yes, I agree, but you shouldn't worry about me. I am more concerned for you."

"Yeah, my teammates said I need to get the hell out of Dodge."

"Dodge?"

Duff smiled. "Sorry. They said I need to put in for a transfer to get away from him."

"Why would you *not* do that?"

"Because I said I would help you, and as long as I'm around I don't think that bastard will try to hurt you."

"No. You must not stay. If you feel you are in danger I want you to go. I will continue my investigation with whatever means I have available, but I do not want you hurt."

Lynn Dai braced her arms on either side of the tub and stood.

"I have someone from the Special Police who is aiding me. I believe he is to be trusted. He has given me several pieces of paper, telex messages and such as that. They have handwritten notes by Mr. Spartan on them. I am going to give these things to you for safekeeping."

"I wonder if we aren't both making The Charge of the Light Brigade." Duff said.

"You mean we are charging like the British Cavalry at Balaclava into too many cannons?"

"Yes," Duff said.

Lynn Dai looked down. "We must try."

After rinsing and toweling off, they dressed, and Lynn Dai drove Duff back to his quarters at the airbase. The sun was already low in the western sky when he kissed her good-bye and she drove away. The SOG team jeep was parked beside the building, but it was quiet as he walked inside. There was a note thumb-tacked to his door. He snatched it down and read:

Coleridge,

Come to the operations center ASAP.

Spartan

14:00 hours

He glanced around. The door to Roland's room was ajar. Stepping across the hall, he tapped on the door. There was no response. He pushed it open. The room was empty. All Roland's gear was gone. He glanced down the hall toward Spencer's room. The door there was open as well. He walked down and looked inside. It, too, was empty.

Dibbs's door was closed. After knocking there, Duff listened as there came a shuffling sound from inside. Dibbs opened the door. He glanced down at the note still in Duff's hand.

"I see you found it."

Duff nodded.

Dibbs slowly wagged his head. "Well, someone told the sonofabitch you were with the Bouchet girl this morning. He gave me ten kinds of hell, like it was my fault. Said if I saw you to tell you to get your ass out to the ops center ASAP."

"How do I apply for that transfer we talked about?" Duff asked.

"Smart move," Dibbs said. "Roland and Spencer sent a telex from the ops center to Colonel Adler. He reports directly to General Buckingham at MACV."

* * *

Duff drove the jeep to the IOCC, and went inside to find Spartan sitting at his desk. Expecting the usual bombastic fit, he was surprised when Spartan simply motioned him toward one of the chairs on the wall.

"Come in and sit down," he said.

There were two ladder-back chairs with woven straw seats and a plush but seedy-looking burgundy easy chair with high padded arms. Duff chose one of the ladder-backs.

"You talk with Dibbs?" Spartan asked.

"Yes."

"So, why did you go back to see the Bouchet girl after I ordered you not to?"

"I'm ready to transfer out," Duff said.

Spartan's facade showed instant signs of another melt-down as the veins on his temples grew larger.

"You'll transfer when I say you can. What kind of questions is that woman asking you?"

"She's not asking questions about anything except matters pertaining to her job—wrongful or accidental death claims by Vietnamese civilians. Problem is the villagers are telling her that a lot of their people are being killed by you—intentionally."

"Don't you have enough fucking sense to know that nosey bitch is probably VC? I'd have taken her out a long time ago if she wasn't protected by her friends."

Duff shook his head. "No. You're wrong. Her father was a professor from France, and her mother was from a wealthy Catholic family in Hue. She also had an uncle who was an officer with the French paratroops. He died at Dien Bien Phu. I guarantee you she's *not* VC."

"Okay, Mister know-it-all. I'm going to make this clear in no uncertain terms, so listen up. You are in way over your head. There is more to this than you will ever know. And I'm beginning to see a pattern here. Every time you get around women you lose your head. Yesterday, you stepped way out of line. Do you realize I have a witness who saw you assault me with your rifle and shoot at another man in our unit? You said you were willing to go to Leavenworth. Well, I can send you there for twenty years if I want. You hear me?"

Duff stood and stepped up to the desk, planting his hands palms down.

"Maybe we can get adjoining cells when they figure out you're running guns for profit on the black market."

Spartan blinked. "You don't know what the fuck you're talking about."

"Oh? I know weapons from that warehouse were sold to the VC. Why do you think Roland and Speed got the hell out of here?"

"You better be damn careful what you're saying, Coleridge, because you're in this, too, all the way up to your neck. Remember the money you took from me?"

Duff was ready. Reaching in his pocket, he pulled out the three one-hundred-dollar bills and let them flutter down onto the desk. "You can shove your money up your ass."

"Doesn't mean shit," Spartan said. "There were others who saw you there."

"Yeah, the Vietcong. I'm sure their testimony will go a long way."

"They weren't Vietcong. They were South Vietnamese businessmen."

"And who the hell do you think is *really* buying that stuff?" Duff asked.

"Idiot GIs like you, hunting for souvenirs, and province chiefs outfitting their Popular forces, that's who."

Duff shook his head. "I'm not the brightest person around, but even I'm not stupid enough to believe that bullshit."

"You're right. You aren't very bright, and you don't know shit about what's going on behind the scenes. Like I said, there's a lot more to this than you know or are allowed to know, but I'm going to give you a hint about who you're fucking with.

"Do you know what the National Security Act is?"

Duff didn't answer, but remained steadfastly poker-faced.

"That's what I thought," Spartan said. "The National Security Act overrides all civil and military legal procedures. It governs most of what I do. To put it in terms that even you can understand, I have the authority as judge, jury, and executioner in this 'ville. If you present a threat to the national security of the United States or The Republic of South Vietnam, I have the authority to take you out. Do you understand what I am saying?"

Duff didn't blink or change expressions. "So, why not keep it simple and let me transfer out?"

"I'll tell you what I'm going to do," Spartan said. "I'm going to put in a request for your transfer, but in the meantime, I want you to move your sorry ass over here to the IOCC where I can keep an eye on you. That Quonset hut across the courtyard is the Special Police barracks, and it has several empty rooms. Get your shit from the base and move out here tonight. From now on you don't come or go without checking with me. You understand?

"And you better think about what I said about the National Security Act, because until you're gone, you're going to pull ops and keep your mouth shut."

Duff turned and walked out. He'd made a mistake. His anger had gotten the best of him, and he had frightened the bogus bastard. He saw it in his eyes. What to do next, that was the question. He had to get help, but where?

Should he go to Crandall Reeves? He seemed like an intelligent man, and surely he wasn't as crazy as Spartan. But then, if Spartan was his executioner, Reeves might try to cover for him. He had to come up with some way of telling someone what was happening.

It was after nightfall when he got back to the base, but as he drove the jeep past the front of the building, he saw three men in camouflaged fatigues standing in the hallway near his room. Duff drove around the side of the barracks where he parked the jeep and ran down the opening between the buildings. Circling, he came up on the opposite side of the front door. Un-holstering his forty-five, he peeked around the front corner of the building. The men had apparently heard the jeep and opened the screened door to look outside. Duff drew back and thumbed the safety off on his forty-five. There came the sound of footsteps. He cocked the hammer.

CHAPTER EIGHTEEN

The Help of A Friend
April, 1967

D uff peeked around the corner of the building as one of the men came outside. The man, an American, walked to the opposite corner of the building, peering at the parked jeep. His tiger-striped fatigues had no insignia. He was either a LRRP, SOG or one of Spartan's spook buddies. Duff held the forty-five at the ready as he remained concealed.

"I told you so. It's a jeep. It's parked right back there, but there's no one around."

Another soldier stepped out of the door behind the first. Both men stood with their backs to Duff. The second soldier looked at his partner standing at the corner of the building and shrugged. "I reckon it wasn't him."

268 | RICK DESTEFANIS

Duff lowered the forty-five. The voice was eerily familiar. "Jimmy?" he said.

The man turned his way.

"Duff! What the hell, dude?"

It was Jimmy Nobles. Duff slid the forty-five back into the holster and walked around the building. Wrapping his arms around Jimmy's shoulders, he slapped his back.

"Damn it, man, it's good to see you," Duff said.

They clutched one another for several seconds.

"Okay, fellas, I'm startin' to worry about you two," one of the men said.

Jimmy turned, looking over his shoulder at the soldier standing behind him.

"You'd hug him, too, if he'd saved your ass. Matter of fact, this fucker saved our whole team on an op in the Song Con River Valley."

Duff extended his hand to Jimmy's buddy. "Duff Coleridge," he said.

"Banks, Ernie Banks. Nobles has told me about you. It's an honor."

"I think the legend is somewhat embellished," Duff said.

"Don't listen to that shit," Nobles replied. "He got a Silver Star for it."

"Yeah, whatever," Duff said. "Me and you gotta talk."

"About what?" Jimmy said.

"I've gotten myself into some shit, and I need your help."

Their eyes met. Nobles cocked his head back and studied Duff's face.

"Is there an EM or NCO club around this place?" Nobles asked.

* * *

Duff sat with Jimmy and the other two lurps at a table in a dark corner of the NCO club. An oasis of air-conditioning, the club provided relief from the humid coastal air outside. The odor of cigarettes and stale beer provided an ambiance appreciated only by men who spent their days inhaling jet-A and diesel fumes. Patsy Cline was singing *Sweet Dreams* from a juke box glowing on the back wall. Other than the music and muted conversations of men sitting at the bar, the club was quiet.

"So, how long are you guys going to be around?" Duff asked.

"Not sure," Jimmy said. "We're supporting some ops over in the A Shau Valley. Two, maybe three weeks at least, if we're lucky."

"If you're lucky?" Duff said. "I've heard some bad shit about the A Shau."

"Yeah, but it'll be worth it if we can get over to China Beach and check it out."

"Oh, yeah, I hear it's nice."

"You mean you haven't been to China Beach yet?" Jimmy said.

"I've been too busy. Besides, like I said earlier, I've gotten myself into some serious shit."

Duff began explaining the situation to Jimmy and his friends. When he was done, they sat in silence. Jimmy flipped the cap on his Zippo and scratched a flame. He stared steadily at Duff while lighting the cigarette. His face glowed orange and his eyes were sharp and piercing. He said nothing as he dropped the lighter back into his pocket and exhaled a cloud of smoke.

Duff shrugged. "So, do you guys want to make any suggestions?"

"If I were you," Jimmy said. "I'd start by getting a pen and some paper. I'd write down every last bit of that shit. Then I'd send it to someone I could trust for safekeeping. Then I'd tell that sonofabitch what I did. It might be life insurance for you and your girl."

"Haven't thought of that," Duff said. "But I'm not sure who I can trust around here."

"That brother of yours you talked about, mail it to him. Tell him to hang on to it, and if something happens to you, take it to a newspaper or maybe a senator. Somebody who won't cover it up."

"He'd be the one I trust most, but I can't send it to him. All my outgoing mail is being read by these people. If I don't write something that says we're all drinking bubble-up soda and eating rainbow pie, they get their panties in a wad."

"You write the letter and get it to me. My DEROS is a couple weeks away. I'll get it to him."

Duff shook his head. "Don't you understand that these bastards are dangerous? You don't want them to find out you're involved."

"Just write the damned letter," Jimmy said. "I'll watch my back."

* * *

Spartan sat in his office at the IOCC staring up at the ceiling fan above his desk. His head was spinning like the fan, and the cinder-block walls were becoming a claustrophobic trap. Coleridge was out of control. He couldn't be managed. If he ran his mouth it might cost him everything he'd worked for. The stupid fucker didn't realize he had the world by the tail. All he had to do was name his price, but he had some screwed-up idea that he could change the world into Disneyland. Dumbass probably still believed in Santa Claus, too.

Coleridge had some pompous idea that he was smarter than the men running this war, he was an idiot. Spartan was out of options. He had no choice but to silence him, if not through intimidation, then by whatever means necessary. He was determined to leave this war financially set for life, and if possible, with a top-notch analyst's job, and no dumbass hillbilly was going to take it from him. Besides, it was in the national interest to see that the new ICEX program was protected. If a fool like Coleridge spilled his guts, the program could be compromised before it was rolled out.

He also needed to silence the Bouchet bitch, but that simply required putting a little fear in her. After all, she was just a woman, and a young one at that. Scare the shit out of her, and she'd probably hightail it to another neighborhood where she could cause someone else trouble. He had to be careful, though. She was a GVN employee working for Naval Claims. He bent across the desk and scribbled a note to send his boss at the OSA in Saigon.

Suspected infiltration of operations group by enemy agent requires interrogation of local GVN employee Lynn Dai Bouchet, possibly other suspected enemy collaborators. Request permission to proceed.
Spartan

His hope was to get the "go-ahead" so he could put the alligator clips on her tits and shock some sense into her. If nothing else, getting her name on a list of suspected VC collaborators would make her back off. The big problem was how to handle Coleridge. He was going to be a harder nut to crack. Getting the Special Police involved by twisting their arms a little was his first thought, but he quickly dismissed that idea. Major Loc and his cohorts didn't mind making a little money on the black market, but he was pretty sure they wouldn't participate in any plan to off an American.

Loc was a hardcore sonofabitch, but he wasn't stupid. He knew there was more money to be made selling weapons, but he wouldn't risk direct involvement with an American supposedly killed by friendly fire. There was only one other who might be willing. It was the former VC guerrilla in the PRU unit—the Chieu Hoi. He was the one who was most likely the spy, still switch-hitting and tipping off his buddies about all the Special Police operations. If he took the offer and followed through there would be no doubt. The Special Police could nail his ass.

Spartan tossed his pen on the desk and sat back. Recruiting the VC spy to kill Coleridge was a stroke of genius, and it would also bring the spy out into the open. Sometimes he was surprised at how the details fell into place with a little analytical thinking. The company needed more men like him.

* * *

It had been two days since Duff had moved into the Quonset hut at the IOCC, and he hadn't heard a word from anyone. He looked out through the screened door at the dusty courtyard and tried to think through his situation, but his mind was clouded with exhaustion. Every time he dozed he saw those eyes. He was at the temple ruins with the young VC nurse dying in his arms. Her eyes were locked with his, unable to forgive him for what he had done, but thankful for what he promised. And the nightmare ended the same way every time, with the light of life fading from her eyes as they became cold and still, staring without focus. It had gotten so he fought to stay awake to avoid the nightmares, but the sleep deprivation left him unable to think.

He had written the letter that Jimmy suggested, and included with it the Telex messages containing Spartan's handwritten comments including one that appeared to be a hit-list of South Vietnamese citizens. Probably the most damning piece of evidence, the list had several of the names already marked through. Duff put it in the envelope with the letter and other documents. Now, he had to find a way to deliver it to Jimmy.

Folding the large envelope, Duff pushed it into the cargo pocket of his fatigue pants and walked across the courtyard to the ops center. He looked first into the darkened ops room, then Spartan's office. All was quiet. With no one around, this was his opportunity to sneak away, but he had to move quickly. Walking back outside, he crossed the courtyard toward the jeep.

Duff glanced over his shoulder. If he could get outside the IOCC compound, he'd take the letter to Jimmy on the base, but he froze mid-stride. The guards at the front gate had suddenly stood upright. There came the sound of a vehicle approaching from outside the wall. He waited, and a moment later Spartan drove through the main gate. The letter wouldn't be delivered this morning. Spartan stepped from his jeep, motioning for Duff to follow him inside to his office.

"Come on in and sit down," Spartan said.

He studied Duff's face. "You look like shit. You been getting any sleep?"

"I keep thinking about those VC nurses we killed, and the way I freaked out."

Duff pulled a cigarette from his shirt pocket and lit it.

"Look, Coleridge, all that's water under the bridge. I'm letting bygones be bygones till you leave. We've got to look ahead because whether we like it or not, this war isn't waiting for us to settle our differences, and until your transfer orders come through, I need your help around here."

He cut his eyes off to one side then looked up at Duff with the wide-eyed innocence of one overcompensating for a lie. The bullshit alarms were clanging in Duff's head.

"Think you can help?"

"What do you need?" Duff asked.

"The Special Police are trying to nail a gook they think is high-level VC cadre. They have some pretty reliable intel. My bosses want it handled on a local level. We're the guinea pigs for a new program they're trying to come up with called ICEX."

"ICEX?"

"Yeah. It hasn't been approved or implemented yet, and it's still probably a month or two out, but it stands for Intelligence Coordination and Exploitation. The idea is that we work together with the military, my people and the gooks, to gather evidence on these scumbags. Hell, we're using computers now. Every gook is going to have his own punch card that we'll update as we get more intel. You know?

"The key is all the combined intel is pushed down to us on the local level and we decide when and how to go after the suspects. We take the intelligence they give us, pull our own surveillance, gather more information, and when one of these guys shows himself, we nail his ass. Can you can do your part?"

"Where is this surveillance supposed to take place?"

"Our boy has been recruiting in some villages southeast of here, down toward Hoi an. He's pretty well connected, and the special police think if we arrest him, he'll probably just Chieu Hoi, hit the revolving door and be back at it again tomorrow. And it's not going to be simply reconnaissance. That's where you come in."

"Oh? What's the plan?"

"You, the Special Police, and the PRU detachment are going to stake out those villages for the next few days, to see if you can spot this guy or any other suspicious activity. It's going to be pretty simple. We've got cooperation from the locals, so you'll set up in an abandoned hooch after dark to pull reconnaissance. If you spot activity, we'll have the PRU and a larger Special Police field force detachment on standby to move in, but if you spot this particular guy you need to be ready to take him out."

"What if he's not armed?"

Spartan reached into the desk drawer and retrieved several eight-by-ten black and white photos. He pushed them across the desk toward Duff. There were close-ups of mutilated corpses in a ditch along with a close-up of a Vietnamese man brandishing an M-16.

"This is our boy when he was in a PRU outfit south of here, and these are his handiwork after he joined the VC. If you don't want to see more of this kind of shit, you take him out, armed or not."

Duff nodded, but he wasn't about to shoot an unarmed man.

"Other than the VC recruiting in these villages, there hasn't been any enemy activity, so you won't need security. You'll ride with Colonel Tranh and Major Loc to the ops area, and they'll assign you to your specific recon location. Colonel Tranh and the Special Police will question the locals during the day, then give the impression they are leaving the area, but they will be doing the same thing you're doing. We think our boy will show after he thinks they are gone. Questions?"

"Where will you be?"

"I'm staying here. We're not looking for enemy contact, mostly just surveillance. I'll be in the ops room monitoring the mission."

The alarm bells continued ringing in Duff's head. Spartan seldom stayed behind. He was too much of a glory-hog.

"I take it you trust the Special Police to do this without you?"

"Shit, Coleridge, this is their fucking country. I can only advise them, but I'm not going to babysit them. Besides, you'll be my eyes and ears if anything goes sideways."

"And you think you can trust *me*?"

"What the fuck is that supposed to mean?"

Duff shook his head. "I think you need to go along. I'm exhausted. Besides, do you really think Colonel Tranh is going to do what I suggest?"

Whatever this mission was about, the central objective wasn't arresting this VC recruiter, and Spartan was too intent on staying in Da Nang.

"Look, maybe you've had a rough time lately, but I need you on this mission. I've got a lot of work to do back here. Tranh and his people know their shit, and they'll kick ass. Just go with me on this one. Your transfer orders will probably be here when you get back.

"We'll have a pre-op meeting at 0800 in the morning and you leave after that. Plan on three days in the field right now. If you end up staying longer, we'll resupply you with rations. Any more questions?"

Even the tone of Spartan's voice betrayed him. He was planning something, but what? Spartan continued staring across the desk with that same bogus look of wide-eyed innocence.

Duff was stymied. He was certain Spartan wanted to kill Lynn Dai, and what better time than while he was away on a mission? Yet there was something more. What if Spartan was setting him up to kill an innocent civilian? What proof was there that he was following orders if Spartan wasn't there? Whatever was happening, he needed to get the letter to Jimmy Nobles and warn Lynn Dai. It might be his only alibi, and as Jimmy said, it was a way to blackmail Spartan.

"Do you mind if I take the jeep over to the base PX? I need to pick up some extra snacks and cigarettes."

Spartan's face turned to stone, but just as quickly it morphed into another bogus smile. "I was going over there myself. Why don't you just ride with me?"

Duff realized he was no better at lying than Spartan. "Sure," he said. "That'll work fine. Maybe we can talk a little more about the mission."

Every move had become a chess match with Spartan, one where he controlled the board. For the moment, Duff was at a loss. If only he could talk with Lynn Dai, she might be able to help. She saw so much of what he missed, detecting the underlying currents and the purposes of men, the hidden nuance of intentions that often escaped him. It was something Lacey called female intuition, and he needed some now.

It was funny how Lynn Dai was able to read devious minds, especially since she was so blatantly honest herself. Despite her intuitive nature and ability to recognize evil intent, her honesty left her with an innocent vulnerability. Lacey was like that. Both women thought with their hearts, trusting in some hidden power to protect them from the evil of the world. Duff prayed that the power Lynn Dai so trusted would continue protecting her while he was away.

* * *

The pre-op briefing revealed nothing new, and Duff found himself examining the plan, not for its weaknesses against the enemy, but for its threat from within. Was he being set up to do a snuff and face a subsequent frame-up for an illegal assassination? He'd even considered that Spartan might enlist someone in his group to take him out, but that was too extreme, even for a nut-case like Spartan. Duff was certain his paranoia resulted from lack of sleep, a psychotic reaction to his nightmares. Spartan's bluster about the National Security Act was meant to scare him, and apparently it was working.

The convoy pulled out of the IOCC compound at 0900 under a cloudy sky. It promised to be a hot and muggy afternoon. Duff sat in the back of the jeep behind Colonel Tranh and Major Loc. He carefully examined his equipment—the PRC-25radio with an extra battery and long-distance antennae, a couple extra frags and several extra magazines of ammo for the M-14. Whatever happened, he intended to be prepared.

The wind and noise from the jeep prevented much conversation as they drove down Highway One, and despite his bleary-eyed fatigue, Duff once again tried to think through his situation. There were no answers. He couldn't bail and leave Lynn Dai alone, and he couldn't go to the military police without proof. He was unable to get the letter to Jimmy; it remained in his pocket. Spartan had check-mated his every move.

Duff was in over his head. He simply wasn't smart enough to play this cat and mouse game with so many lives at stake. What mattered most were the effects his actions might have on others. What if he *was* sent to Leavenworth, or perhaps killed? He thought of his mother, and how she would suffer if he didn't come home. He thought of Lacey, his beautiful, sweet little sister. It would break her heart. And there was Brady, his loyal foster brother, a fiercely faithful friend and companion. They all deserved better. Most of all, he worried about Lynn Dai. What if he caused her death?

The problem was he couldn't figure where the danger was hidden. Obviously, Spartan was the man behind the curtain, but despite all his bluster, he was a paper tiger, a dangerous one in many ways, but his behavior on the last mission had revealed his true character. He was a coward who depended on others to do his dirty work, as much as Crandall Reeves depended on him to do his. Spartan was a dumbass who failed to see that he was simply another pawn, another layer of insulation for those above him.

The convoy passed hamlets and villages one after another until Duff lost count, and he'd nearly dozed off when they came to a sudden stop. Up ahead a plume of black smoke rose above a roadside village. Several choppers circled above, and along the highway ARVN infantrymen stood tired and listless, their weapons at the ready. They waited with hollow stares of exhaustion, the same exhaustion that gripped him.

"What's going on?" Duff asked.

The traffic on the radio was all in Vietnamese. Major Loc didn't turn his head as he spoke. "The National Liberation Front has taken control of the highway," he said.

His response sounded strange, almost disconnected. Duff had little direct interaction with the Special Police, but there was something in Loc's words and his tone of voice—something that didn't quite ring true to the cause, almost as if he were proud of the NLF. Whatever it was, Duff's instincts suddenly led him to the raw and edgy realization that the men with whom he was riding might want him silenced as much as Spartan did. After all, it was one or both of them that had helped Spartan with the arms theft from the warehouse in Da Nang. There was also the mysterious Special Police captain, Nguyen, who never seemed to be around.

Artillery impacting on the highway up ahead shook the ground, and when the barrage stopped, the choppers dove in firing salvos of rockets and shredding the village with Vulcan machine guns. Eventually, the convoy again lurched forward as it headed down the highway into a haze of smoke and dust. Several Sky Raiders streaked overhead, following the highway southward as the battle seemed to recede.

"Looks like The National Liberation Front got their asses kicked," Duff said.

It was not something he blurted without thinking. Rather, it was calculated, but neither Colonel Tranh nor Major Loc responded. Duff waited. A nod from either of them would be sufficient, anything that indicated a positive response. After several seconds Major Loc turned his head slightly, only to quickly face ahead again. Tranh and Loc were both ones to watch.

* * *

The convoy entered the village, where the dust and smoke from the artillery barrage still hung in the air. There were no Americans there, only South Vietnamese soldiers and a rag-tag string of refugees fleeing northward. The bodies of several ARVN soldiers lay in the ditch beside the road, while the wounded were clustered in the grass nearby. A single Vietnamese medic worked feverishly, first on one, then another. The convoy ground to a halt once again as the chatter of automatic weapons came from beyond the village. Realizing the medic was overwhelmed, Duff leapt from the back of the jeep and trotted to him.

The medic raised his eyes revealing his desperation. He was holding a pressure bandage against a soldier's chest.

"Bạn có phải là một bác sĩ?"

"I can't understand you," Duff said.

The medic motioned with his chin. A few feet away sat another soldier, his left hand gone. The jagged ends of bones protruded from the stub of his lower arm, and despite the grip he held on it with his right hand the blood spurted through his fingers. Duff nodded and grabbed a rubber tourniquet from the medic's satchel. Wrapping it above the man's elbow, he knotted and cinched it tight.

"Cảm ơn bạn," the soldier said in a shaky voice.

Recognizing the soldier was weak from his loss of blood, he helped him lie back. Duff again went to the medic's satchel and grabbed a bag of plasma and some tape. He found a vein, and inserted the IV needle into the soldier's good arm. After pressing a strip of tape over the needle, he looked around for something to support the bag. He spotted an entrenching tool nearby. Grabbing it, he opened it, drove it into the ground and taped the bag to the handle.

There came a shout from Major Loc. The convoy was beginning to move. Duff scrambled toward the jeep, but a sudden thought occurred to him. Glancing about, he found another entrenching tool in a pile of abandoned gear. Neither Tranh nor Loc seemed to notice as he carried it with him back to the jeep, but for Duff the little shovel was just another bit of insurance in case he needed cover.

* * *

The sun had dropped into the treetops when they reached a series of small hamlets surrounding a larger village west of the highway. The plan was to send patrols through the village to act as diversions while Duff and the others took up positions in the abandoned hooches at nightfall. While he waited, Duff checked his gear, and it was dusk when Tranh and Loc led him to an empty hooch. Other than a small contingent of PRU on the trail near the hamlet, they were alone. Duff slipped inside, and the others disappeared into the twilight shadows.

Peering out through one of several holes in the walls, he studied his surroundings in the fading light. From his vantage point he had a clear view of two rice paddies and the trail running atop a dike leading from the highway into the hamlet. The terrain behind him was overgrown scrub and palms, ideal cover for someone wanting to sneak up on the hooch. Lost in a flood of paranoia, Duff was determined to follow his instincts.

If he were attacked, the straw walls of the hooch would provide little protection. Opening the entrenching tool, he began digging through the dirt floor inside the hooch. The ground was sandy and made for easy digging. Within thirty minutes he had a waist-deep hole dug in one corner. He mounded the loose dirt around the rim for added protection. When he was done, he looked at it. It was a stupid idea. The hole might offer some momentary cover, but it might also end up as his grave.

The night, hot and still, was without the hint of a breeze. The sing-song voices of the people in the village eventually faded into silence. Easing to the door of the hooch, he looked out into the night. A sliver of a crescent moon hung overhead, but it did little more than add texture to the shadows. It was simply too dark to see much of anything. He listened. The cricking of tree frogs and the drone of insects filled the night air. He had already begun second-guessing himself. Was he prepared for what might come? Or perhaps nothing would come.

Duff paced silently making the rounds, peering first through the holes in the walls, then from the door of the hooch. As the moon traveled up into the night sky, it occurred to him that he was no better than a chicken tethered to a string, waiting for a predator to pounce from the darkness. Why sit and wait? Why give them the advantage? Turning, he grabbed the radio and other gear and returned to the door. Gazing into the darkness, he heard nothing, he saw nothing.

Stepping outside the door, Duff ducked as he ran across the trail. Silently pushing his way through the chest-high grass, he found a spot twenty meters from the hooch. There, he turned and looked back. The hooch was outlined against the night sky, and though he could see little else, he was close enough to hear anyone approaching on the trail. He knelt and waited. This was better than being holed-up like a rat, and he was out in the open with at least a fighting chance against any would-be attackers. He again felt like the hunter rather than the hunted.

Holding his watch to catch the light of the moon, he studied it until he made out the time. It was after midnight. If someone was going to do something, they were in no hurry. After a few minutes he noticed something. It was subtle, but there had been a change in the night sounds. The insects and frogs up the trail to the north had suddenly become silent. Duff strained as he listened. So far there was only the permanent ringing in his ears, the result of one too many exploding mortar and rocket rounds, but there was a definite shift in the sounds of the night.

After a while he heard a very subtle but gradually increasing sound. It didn't come from the trail. He listened and finally recognized there was an engine idling out on the highway east of the hamlet. There were no lights, but it sounded like a jeep, and it was moving very slowly. It came to a stop, and the engine went silent. Whether the threat came from the highway or from the trail, Duff was certain of one thing. He was about to have company.

CHAPTER NINETEEN

A Hidden Danger
May, 1967

D uff was certain he had heard a jeep, and it was likely one of the Special Police vehicles or perhaps even Spartan. His mind raced as a faint shuffling came from the trail near the hooch. Rising to his feet, he peered over the top of the grass. Shadows shifted and moved before his eyes—people. The distinct pop and hiss of a grenade fuse made him flinch, but he was frozen in place. Perhaps it was the overwhelming realization that it wasn't simply paranoia. This was really happening. Someone on the trail had thrown a grenade into the hooch where they thought he was hiding, someone who knew he was there. And only with the help of the Special Police or the PRU could they have known.

The grenade blast lit the night, and the sting of shrapnel grazed Duff's cheek. A moment later from mere feet away the automatic weapons of the ones responsible opened fire on the hooch. Their muzzle flashes silhouetted the men, three of them. Duff raised his M-14 and began firing as he walked up out of the grass, straight toward them. He dropped all three in seconds and was standing on the trail as the ping of the last piece of spent brass quickly faded into silence.

The instantaneous return of the night-time silence was as jarring at the sudden attack. He stood on the trail in front of the hooch doorway. One of the wounded attackers exhaled a last gurgling breath. The adrenaline coursed through Duff's veins as he dropped the empty magazine from his M-14 and jammed another into place. A baby began crying in the hamlet, and there came the subdued voices of terrified villagers cowering in their hooches. They, no doubt, wondered if their home would be next.

The ringing in his ears grew louder, and Duff for the first time felt an abysmal fear. He had been a blind idiot. Despite his every instinct telling him otherwise, he had been in denial that this could really happen. He thought there were lines no one would cross, especially another American, but he was now witness to the naïveté of his thinking. Someone wanted him dead, and everything pointed to Spartan, but he wasn't here.

Duff examined the bodies in the darkness. They appeared to be VC. Someone had told them he would be in the hooch, but who? A small white card lay on the ground beside one of the bodies. He picked it up and put it in his pocket. As the adrenaline subsided, he felt something warm and wet running down his neck. At first it felt like sweat, but it didn't stop as it trickled onto his shoulder.

Duff touched his jaw. He'd been hit by shrapnel from the grenade blast. Pulling the green bandanna from around his neck, he pressed it against his face. There came another tightness, not quite a sting, but a definite discomfort as he felt more dampness. It was on the upper right side of his chest near his armpit. The discomfort grew into pain.

Unsure how bad he was hit, Duff began walking toward the highway. After circling the hooch, he was about to start across the dike between the rice paddies when he spotted two figures coming from the opposite direction. He squatted in the shadows beside the trail, watching and waiting as two men came across the dike from the highway. They were apparently coming from the jeep he had heard earlier. One carried an M-16, the other a .45. Both wore the black berets and the camouflaged fatigues of the Special Police, but they were unrecognizable in the darkness. Passing within a few meters, the two men silently made their way toward the hooch where he had been hidden.

When they disappeared in the shadows, Duff bent low and trotted across the dike to the highway. The jeep was parked on the shoulder of the road with no one guarding it. Jumping into the driver's seat, he cranked the engine and jammed it into gear. Making a rapid U-turn, he headed back to Da Nang. With the accelerator mashed to the floor, he drove through sleepy villages, across bridges, past grazing water buffalo, bouncing, swerving, desperate to escape. But to where? It would be blind luck if he didn't hit a mine or drive into a VC ambush, and he had no idea exactly where he was going or who he hoped to find. He only wanted to reach the safety of the base.

* * *

By the time Duff reached the Naval Hospital at China Beach, dawn was near. His fatigue shirt and bandanna were soaked with blood. Dizzy and disoriented, he stumbled up a sandy wooden walkway and made his way inside, where a nurse spotted him. She shouted for help and ran to him as an orderly came running up a hallway. Another nurse appeared from a nearby room. After hours in the darkened countryside, he squinted his eyes in the bright lights of the hospital.

"Where are you wounded?" the nurse asked.

Duff pulled the soggy bandanna from his face to show her the wound. "I'm hit here, too." He pointed to his right shoulder. His jungle fatigues were soaked crimson.

An orderly rolled a gurney beside him, and they helped him lie back as they began removing his clothes.

"Who are you? Where did this happen? How did you get here? What caused these wounds?"

The questions came rapid-fire as they pushed him to a triage area.

"I work for a special operations group in Da Nang, and I was on a mission in a village southeast of here. Shrapnel from a grenade."

They scissored away the remainder of his clothes and removed his boots. A few moments later a doctor appeared, and the nurse prepared a syringe of morphine, but Duff stopped her. "No. Wait. There's a brown envelope in the cargo pocket of my fatigue pants. It has to stay with me. There's also a small card in my shirt pocket. I need that too."

She picked up the fatigues from the floor and ran her hand in the pockets. After putting the card in the envelope, she placed it on the gurney beside him. Several harried minutes passed while they probed and examined his wounds. The nurse checked his blood pressure, and after getting X-rays Duff lay quietly, but he continued to refuse sedation. Instead he asked for a pen and paper.

He could barely focus his eyes as he wrote a note to Lynn Dai. When it was complete he explained to the nurse that it had to be delivered to her personally at the Naval Claims office. Despite his near delirium, Duff opened the envelope and examined the card he had picked up at the ambush site. Only then in the light of the room did he realize that it wasn't white. It was yellow. It was also stained with blood—his—but the emblem and words remained plainly visible. A green, blue, and yellow bird with the Vietnamese words "Phung Hoang" were printed on the card.

He dropped it back inside the envelope. It was a kill card. Roland had told him about them. They were used to intimidate the enemy, but this one was meant for him. He had to get it and the rest of the evidence to Lynn Dai. The sound of footsteps came from the hallway, and Duff shoved the other items back into the envelope with the card.

"Mostly good news," the doctor said. "There's no major trauma from your wounds. It'll take a couple sutures to close that cut on your cheek, and there's a very small piece of shrapnel just below your right shoulder. We'll leave it for the time being, but we're putting you on an IV for the day to replenish your fluids and give you an anti-biotic. You'll need to stay with us for a day or two."

* * *

Duff held the dying nurse in his arms, a girl really, a teenager, but she was Vietcong. Her eyes locked with his, and he saw the pride and defiance even in the face of impending death as her breast rose and sank less with each breath. The dying moans of her comrades drifted through the palms and undergrowth, all women, all non-combatants, all slain.

Duff found himself caressing the girl's hair, and gently massaging her cheek. "No, no, you can't close your eyes. Please. I didn't know."

Logic said things like this happen in a war, but logic couldn't repair his heart. He was immersed in the reality of an unending nightmare, and her eyes refused to release him. They refused to forgive him. He wanted to look heavenward and shout "Why? Why, God, did you let me do this?"

He opened his eyes, and she was there, standing over him, tears in her eyes, but it wasn't the young VC nurse. It was Lynn Dai. He had fallen asleep, and the disorientation was unsettling as he shook his head to clear away the fog and confusion. He looked around the room. There were other soldiers in beds, and orderlies and nurses working on the ward. An odd mix of body odor, iodine, and alcohol permeated the air.

"It is okay," Lynn Dai said. "We are alone, at least for the moment. What happened?"

She softly touched a bandage on his cheek where the stitches were apparently already in place. He took her hand.

"They tried to get me," he said.

"Who?" she said. "Who did this?"

"I know what my instincts tell me, but I'm not absolutely certain."

"Spartan?" she said.

"My gut tells me he's involved, but I could be wrong. It could be that spy you've been trying to find."

"Why do you say this?"

"Because it was VC that tried to ambush me, but someone in our group had to tell them I was there. A spy or maybe someone working for Spartan, I don't know, but the only ones around when I slipped into the hooch were the Special Police and some PRU. It was too dark for anyone else to see me."

Another tear trickled from her eye. "I spoke with my people in Saigon and asked for their help."

Duff nodded, but Lynn Dai lowered her eyes as if she were ashamed.

"They refuse to interfere with what they say is an American problem, that is your conflict with Mr. Spartan. I do not know what to do, or to whom I can turn."

Duff found the envelope still lying beside him on the bed.

"I need to finish this letter. I want you to take it to a friend of mine. His name is Jimmy Nobles. He's with a LRRP Unit from the Hundred and First Airborne. They're temporarily quartered at the airbase. He'll know what to do with it, but you've got to warn him to watch his back."

"But what will you do? Where will you go?"

Duff held her hand.

"I've got to go back," he said. "I know Spartan has a real name, and I have to know for certain if he's involved."

"You mustn't. He may kill you. You should go to your military police. They can protect you."

"That's probably the smart thing, but that bastard will wriggle out of this if his bosses cover for him. Then what? You may be next."

"Duff, you are taking too great a risk."

"So are you," Duff said, "and I'm not leaving you here alone to fight this battle."

"But I have the protection of my countrymen. You have no one's protection."

Duff held up the envelope. "Put this in your bag. Don't let anyone see you with it."

Lynn Dai shoved it into her purse.

"See if you can round up some clothes," Duff said. "I need to get out of here."

* * *

Despite Lynn Dai's objections, Duff was determined to expose Spartan and the An Ninh agent in their midst. Driving the jeep, he returned to the IOCC the following morning at first light. It was quiet, and he saluted the Nung guards as he drove through the gate. He parked in front of the ops building, and as the dust settled, it grew quiet again. Other than the guards, there was no one around. He went inside, directly to Spartan's office and sat behind the desk.

Propping his feet, he pulled his forty-five and laid it across his lap. Then he waited.

It was only a few minutes before he heard the sound of another jeep arriving out in the courtyard. Duff released the safety on his forty-five. A moment later Spartan came through the office door. He froze mid-stride. His lips parted with the involuntary response of a man seeing a ghost. Duff smiled. His hand rested on the forty-five in his lap.

"Hey boss, what's happening?"

"What the fuck?" Spartan said. "Where have you been?"

Spartan's eyes darted around the room.

"I've been over at the naval hospital getting patched up. Got a few holes in me, but I'm not dead."

Duff dropped his feet from the desk and stood as he slipped the forty-five back into the holster.

"What were you going to do with that?" Spartan asked, nodding at the forty-five.

"We still have that spy in our midst, and I'm not taking any chances."

"What the hell happened down there?"

Despite looking like a startled deer, Spartan tried to affect the appearance of genuine curiosity. Duff saw it in his eyes. The bastard knew exactly what had happened, but he played along, hoping he would somehow tip his hand.

"Somebody in the unit set us up again. The enemy knew right where I was hiding, and if I hadn't gone outside in the middle of the night, they'd have ambushed me right there. Instead, I hosed them down, got three of them, but I caught a little shrapnel in the process."

Spartan shook his head with a grim look of concern. "Goddammit, Coleridge, you are one lucky sonofabitch. You know that?"

Duff wanted to laugh at the bogus bastard, but resisted. "Yeah, reckon I am, but we need to catch this guy before he gets one of us. He sure seems to know a lot about our business."

Spartan nodded. "Uh, yeah, right."

Walking over to the wall, Duff looked up at a photo hanging in a cheap frame. It was a black and white of Spartan shaking hands with President Johnson, and it was signed, "To Max, A hell of a Warrior, Lyndon B. Johnson."

"So 'Spartan' is obviously not your real name?"

Spartan looked around. "Uh, yeah. Some of my friends call me Max."

Duff walked over to another wall where several more photos hung. There was another black and white of Spartan standing in a group with Crandall Reeves, a province chief, Colonel Tranh, and some Vietnamese civilians he didn't recognize.

"Can I call you Max?"

Spartan stood fidgeting with papers on his desk. He seemed momentarily rattled. "Let's stick with Spartan for now."

"Not a problem," Duff said.

He turned from the wall.

"So how are we gonna nail this spy?"

Spartan shrugged. "Hell, I don't know. Let me think on it. This shit is crazy."

Duff's facade seemed to be working. Spartan was rowing with one oar in the water, unsure of himself, but he seemed to be regaining control of his wits as he sat in his chair.

Another of the photographs showed Spartan shaking hands with a man wearing a white shirt and tie. It was inscribed, "To 'Spartan' from Blowtorch. Ha! Go get 'em."

"Who's Blowtorch?"

"What's with this sudden interest in the chain of command?"

"Seems natural to me," Duff said. "You always want to know the people you're working for. I mean, I do. Don't you?"

"Well, I suppose, but in this business, sometimes the less you know the better off you are."

Duff nodded. If nothing else, the sonofabitch's jargon was predictable.

"Okay, I'm going to get some sleep and try to heal some. Let me know if you come up with any ideas. By the way, have you heard anything on my transfer orders?"

Duff already knew the answer.

"Uh, no, I haven't. I'll check on them first thing and let you know something later. Is that okay?"

"Sure," Duff said. "And there's something else I want to say."

Spartan raised his eyebrows.

"Look, I really freaked out that day when we killed all those nurses. I just want to tell you how sorry I am. It's just that raping dead bodies sounded so, I don't know, bad…"

Spartan pressed his lips together, raised his chin and nodded with a look of smug satisfaction. "You'll learn. You stay over here long enough with these animals, and nothing will surprise you."

Spartan winked as he reached into the drawer and tossed two envelopes out onto the desk. They had been cut open. "There's a couple letters that came for you the other day. We've already checked them out. Sounds like a little brother-sister love affair is cranking up back home in the hills."

Spartan smiled and winked. Duff dead-panned him as he held his anger in check.

"Brady is a foster brother. He came to live with us when his mama and daddy died. Him and Lacey aren't blood kin."

"Just checking," Spartan said. "You know what they say about you hillbillies."

Duff stood and picked up the letters from the desk. "No, I don't know what they say. Why don't you fucking tell me."

Spartan drew back. "I was just kidding, Coleridge. Get control, and calm your ass down."

Duff smiled. "Oh, I'm in control, but if you're going to stick your nose in my mail, don't talk about my family."

Spartan sat tight-lipped, and Duff wanted to drag him across the desk and stomp his ass, but he would let him slide for now. Sooner or later, Spartan's time would come.

* * *

Spartan wasn't sure why, but as soon as Coleridge left his office that morning, he pulled the forty-five from his shoulder holster and laid it on the desk. He'd been caught totally off guard by Coleridge being in his office. It had rattled the shit out of him, but he was feeling better now that he was gone. And he wasn't buying all of Coleridge's bullshit, but he *did* seem to be coming around. Perhaps the little ambush helped him see the light.

Coleridge was right about one thing—the spy. Spartan rubbed his chin as he thought about it. Prior to the mission he mentioned to Loc that Coleridge had become a problem with the arms deal. Loc expressed his concern, but the conversation pretty much ended there as he seemed unwilling to discuss the next step. That's why Spartan had gone to the Chieu Hoi in the PRU and asked about a possible favor for cash.

Problem was when he mentioned killing Coleridge the PRU soldier balked. He probably smelled a set-up. That had to be the answer. The Chieu Hoi was the An Ninh agent, but he didn't want to tip his hand by taking the cash. He had to be the spy, because he'd gone ahead with the ambush. He saw an opportunity and went for it on his own. Problem was Coleridge had the luck of a cur escaping the pound.

Spartan looked around his office at the photos with LBJ, McNamara and the others. He had built too much to let some shithead like Coleridge take it all away. He had to go back to the Special Police and tell them to watch the PRU soldier, because he was a suspected An Ninh Agent. If it worked, one of them would kill him after he nailed Coleridge.

That was it. Colonel Tranh and Captain Nguyen would gladly go after a VC spy, and Loc would help if for no other reason than to hide his involvement with the weapons deal. He was unwilling to go after Coleridge himself, but he would sure as hell kill a VC spy, especially one who had just murdered a SOG member. Spartan nodded and smiled. Sometimes he surprised even himself with the cleverness of his plans.

* * *

Duff returned to his room at the back of the Quonset hut. Lying back on his cot, he opened the letters from home. He read Lacey's first.

May, 1967

Dear Duff,

I miss you a lot, and I wish you would write home more. We haven't gotten a letter in weeks. I know you don't like me worrying, but I can't help it. You are my only big brother, so be careful over there. Brady and I had a really great senior year, but it wasn't the same without you here. Graduation day is only a few weeks off, and I met with Hugh Langston the other day. Don't worry. I'm not dumb. He's getting me that job in Nashville, and letting me sing in his club on the weekends. It's a big chance for me to do something really good with my life. I know you aren't happy about it, and neither is Brady, but y'all worry too much. Anyway, I guess you know by now Brady and I are closer than ever, and I really love him, but he's just like you, stubborn as an old mule. He doesn't want me to go to Nashville, but he won't go with me either. I'm still trying to convince him, but I hope you can come home soon and talk some sense into that boy. Maybe, he'll listen. Until then, please take care of yourself, and write home more. We don't hear from you enough. I say a prayer for you every night.

Love you,
Lacey
PS I bought a really cool car with the money you gave me. Can't wait for you to see it.

Duff set her letter aside. At one time he would have said his little sister was a worrywart. He opened Brady's letter next.

May, 1967

Dear Duff,
Well, graduation day is in a couple weeks, and I can't hardly wait. I'm not sure what I'm going to do, but Lacey is still planning on moving to Nashville. That jerk Hugh Langston offered her the job singing in his club there. I still don't know if I should sign up for the National Guard or try college, but I sure as heck don't want her to go to Nashville. I wish you were here to referee. You already know how much I love her. She also bought a Chevy Malibu, SS, 396 cubic inch V8 with a Holley 4-barrel on it. They used it as a pace car up at Bristol last year, and it's the fastest thing anywhere around Polk County. I tried to talk her out of it, and she almost wrecked it the first time she drove it, but she drives like a pro now.

Mama Emma is doing good, but she's just like Lacey, always worrying about you. I suppose I do too. I know you're having a hell of an experience, and you're going to have some stories to tell when you get home, but be careful. I reckon that's all for now. Please write me when you get a chance.

Your Brother,
Brady

Duff lay back and closed his eyes. If only he could talk with them one more time, the things he would tell them, but the one he worried most about was his mother. If something happened to him, she wouldn't do well at all. His only hope was that his motivations were the right ones, because he was gambling with a lot more lives than his own.

He glanced at his watch. It was too early yet, but later after Spartan was gone, he planned to sneak out. If he could get past the guards at the gate without being challenged, he was going to see Lynn Dai and make sure she delivered his letter to Jimmy Nobles. With spies everywhere, Spartan was certain to know he had left the IOCC, and there would be another confrontation, but it would be too late by then. The letter would be delivered. Only then would he go to the military police and ask for protection.

CHAPTER TWENTY

The Letter
May, 1967

I t was late in the day when Duff stretched and walked outside
into the IOCC courtyard. Spartan's jeep was gone, and the
only people around were the guards at the ops center building
and the main gate. He fired up his Zippo, cupped his hands and lit
a cigarette. Smoking had become one of the little stress relievers
he allowed himself. Exhaling into the stagnant air, he looked about.
The late afternoon sun reflected an amber glow from the guard
tower and along the top of the buildings. Inside the courtyard the
shadows stretched long across the empty lot and up the sides of the
buildings.

He needed to get out of here, and try to find Lynn Dai, but taking
a jeep would make his absence obvious. He decided to walk, maybe

hitch a ride to her apartment, but as he started across the courtyard there came a scream, a gut-wrenching scream that made the back of his neck tingle. Duff froze in his tracks. It was like none he'd ever heard, the scream of a man in so much pain he was without hope.

It had come from beyond the main building. Out back there was another Quonset hut that served as the PRU barracks, some storage sheds and a building with holding cells. He'd only seen them from a distance. Another less audible but extended moan broke the afternoon silence. It was that of a broken man, resigned to the inevitability of suffering until death. It turned his stomach, and Duff instinctively ran his hand over the holster that held his forty-five. This person needed help, but the reality was he could do nothing. He could do nothing, because he instinctively knew what was happening.

Walking around the side of the ops center, Duff stared at a small cinder-block building near the rear wall of the courtyard. It was enveloped in the late afternoon shadows, but a dim light shone through two small windows on either side of a heavy metal door. This was where Spartan had said the holding cells were located. Someone was being tortured there, and Duff felt his arms hanging like lead. What could he do?

Without warning the metal door thudded and swung open as Colonel Tranh charged stiff-legged across the yard toward the ops center. Spotting Duff, he stopped. They stood staring at one another for several seconds. Tranh was sweating, and his eyes were narrowed and jittery. He had the pained look of a man who'd seen something he abhorred. After a moment, he broke eye contact and walked into the back door of the ops center.

Duff walked to where the metal door stood open. A dim bulb burned inside, and a man sat strapped in a chair. He was totally naked, his chin on his chest and his mop of black hair singed and hanging. Perhaps a young man before he'd been brought here and strapped in the chair, he now looked very old. He'd been beaten until he was drained and devoid of all but the barest signs of life. Duff stared, both sickened and angered.

A young Vietnamese policeman in a black T-shirt and camouflaged fatigue pants stood beside the chair, staring at Duff with the stone-hard eyes of a man without a soul. He was one of the Special Police cadre, not an officer, but one of their many young enforcers. On a table in front of him were a hammer, pliers and an array of alligator clips and electrical cables.

With firmly clenched jaws and cold dead eyes, the young soldier slowly broke into a smile. Duff felt something deep inside break—perhaps his last hope for sanity. Without breaking eye contact, he spat on the floor. And after a moment, he walked over to the man in the chair, took him by his chin and carefully raised his head. It was dead weight. The man's eyeballs were gorged with blood, his face a purple pulp, his jaws and teeth broken and sagging. He was all but dead. He slowly let the man's head down again, and turned to the young Special Policeman. A nauseating bile rose in Duff's throat, and he drew his forty-five, shoving it against the policeman's nose.

The man's glower of intimidation shattered into a wild-eyed look of fear and uncertainty. This policeman was just another little person who had found the reckless pleasure of power amongst the insanities of war. He had inflicted unspeakable torture on another human being, seemingly with satisfaction. And the look of frustration on Tranh's face when he came out the door moments before told the rest of the story. They'd been unable to break the man in the chair, or worse, the man had never possessed the information they sought. He was innocent.

Duff released the safety on the pistol and held it steady as he stared hard at the Vietnamese policeman. His finger caressed the trigger. He would make an example of this ruthless bastard, but he wanted to make him suffer first. He dropped the pistol and shoved it into the man's crotch. He would blow this little bastard's balls off and let him die a slow death. That's what he deserved, but the policeman's eyes began showing an element of humanity as they filled with tears. Duff hesitated. He would be no different from any of these filthy bastards if he pulled the trigger.

"Someday," Duff said, "you will end up like this man."

With that he turned and walked out the door. Crossing the courtyard, he holstered his forty-five and quickly made his way toward the gate. His mind was a roiling cauldron of anger and confusion. How could he ever go home and live a normal life after this? He had stared into the depths of hell and realized there would never again be anything "normal."

* * *

The Nung guard at the gate glanced about as Duff approached, then stepped forward and handed him a folded piece of paper. Duff quickly pushed it into his pocket, nodded, and continued walking. When he was a safe distance from prying eyes he unfolded the paper.

Duff

Meet me in the garden at the Blue Dahlia. If I am not there,
wait. I will come.

Lynn Dai

But when he arrived she was there, and they embraced as he
buried his face in her hair. Inhaling deeply, he smelled her scent, one
he had grown to love. It was one of life, one of hope.

"Can we go to your apartment?"

She smiled and pressed her head against his chest. "Yes, of course."

She motioned toward her car parked down at the end of the
street near the market, and they began walking.

"I want to make sure you get the letter to Jimmy, but first I want
to rewrite it," Duff said. "Do you still have it?"

"Yes, I have it. Has something else happened?"

"The Special Police had a prisoner at the IOCC this afternoon.
They were torturing him. I'm pretty sure he'll die. From what I
saw, it looks like something they do a lot."

Lynn Dai stared straight ahead. With dusk fading into nightfall,
she switched on the car's headlights as they drove back to the
apartment.

"The Special Police are fools. We can never win the people's
hearts if we do the same as the Communists. I have been told that
this was happening, but you are the first person with whom I have
spoken who actually witnessed it. You must get away from there,
Duff."

"I will as soon as I'm sure Jimmy is gone with the letter. Do you
carry a weapon, a pistol or something?" he asked.

Lynn Dai took her eyes off the road, turning toward him. "When I find that I must carry a weapon, I will no longer remain in this country."

They parked near the apartment, walked across the small courtyard and went inside. After Lynn Dai gave him the envelope, a pen, and several sheets of paper, Duff sat on the couch and began writing. It took nearly a half-hour, and when he finished he signed the letter and put it in the envelope. On the envelope he wrote Brady's name, the telephone number at his mother's house, and 'Melody Hill, Tennessee.'

"Please try to get this to Jimmy as soon as you can," he said. "He's supposed to be leaving soon, and I don't want to miss my chance."

"I spoke with a contact two days ago," Lynn Dai said. "He told me Jimmy Nobles was on a mission, but he was supposed to return yesterday to the base. I will deliver it to him this evening."

Duff pulled the Hog's Tooth necklace over his head. "I want you to give this to him as well. Tell him I said to wear it. It will protect him."

Lynn Dai held the necklace and studied it with furrowed brows.

"It's a tradition with snipers," Duff said. "It's a bullet taken from an enemy weapon, and it protects the sniper."

She slowly nodded, and curled the tarnished brass bullet and leather necklace into the palm of her hand.

Duff stood. "I suppose I'd better get back to the IOCC before Spartan comes looking for me."

Lynn Dai grasped his hands and pulled him down on the couch beside her. "I will drive you there later," she said. "Right now, I need you."

Their lips met, and they embraced, but after a few moments Duff pushed her back.

"I don't want to hurt your feelings, but I have a question."

She looked up at him, already breathless with anticipation.

"Are you certain you will go home to America with me, I mean, as my wife?"

Her eyes glistened with a sudden moisture. "Are you asking me to marry you?"

Duff had already begun unbuttoning her blouse, but he stopped. It had caught him off guard, this simple statement of what he had assumed all along. Lynn Dai was his. He saw it in her eyes every time they were together, but he had never put his commitment into words. It was something he meant to say, but never had, and it came from his deepest emotions. He had asked her to spend her life with him; it was what he wanted. Her eyes met his, and he paused on the last button of her blouse.

"Yes," he said.

She looked up at him, her huge brown eyes shining in the dim light. "Before now, I was willing to fight alone for the country my mother and father hoped to make of Vietnam, but I will follow you, Duff. I will go wherever you go, because I know we can do more together than either of us can do alone."

Duff pushed his hand gently between her legs, and with the gentlest care pulled his fingers upward into her body. She breathed a soft groan, and their lips met again.

He had never felt so drawn to a woman, and telling anyone how he felt never came easy, but Lynn Dai was not just anyone.

"And I will always love you," he said.

* * *

When Spartan got the call from the Special Police that evening, he realized that Bouchet and Coleridge were up to something more than their usual love-nesting, because she had dropped him outside the IOCC at an early hour. He decided to get out and see if he could find her.

Driving into the city, he searched out an alley on the main drag near her apartment and backed the jeep into the shadows. He'd been there only a few minutes when a car's headlights appeared, slowly weaving through the clot of scooters and rickshaws. It was Bouchet, and after she passed, he pulled out. Trailing a block or two behind, he followed her to the gate at Da Nang Airbase. Stopping well back, he watched. He had never known she had access to the base, but the guards at the gate didn't hesitate as they checked her identification and motioned her through. It was as if they knew her.

He continued, and after passing through the gate, followed her as she drove down a back street paralleling the runways. She stopped outside of an enlisted men's barracks. Spartan pulled his jeep to the side of the road nearly a block away and watched as she got out of the car. Bouchet paused to look around before walking to the door. She was up to something, but what? Someone came to the barracks door.

The meeting lasted no more than a minute, before she quickly returned to the car and left again. He could not make out the other person in the dim light, nor whether anything changed hands. After Bouchet's taillights disappeared, Spartan pulled down to the barracks and walked to the door. Letting himself inside, he walked into an open bay area where several soldiers were lying around on bunks.

"Who just met with the woman at the door?" he asked.

The men shrugged, but one slowly came to his feet. "That would be me," the man said.

Spartan cast a quick glance back at the door, before looking at the man. "What did she want with you?"

"She said a friend of mine sent me something he wanted me to have. Who the hell are you?"

Spartan hesitated. The soldier standing in front of him had the hardened eyes of one who had seen a lot of combat.

"Here's my ID," Spartan said.

The soldier studied the card. "CIA, huh?"

Spartan looked around at the other soldiers lounging about. "Are all of you in the same outfit?"

"This is a transit barracks," the soldier said.

Spartan sized him up. The soldier didn't look smart enough to bullshit him. "So what did she give you?"

"Just this," the soldier said. He pulled a bullet hanging on a leather lanyard from inside his shirt.

"That's it?"

"It has a lot of sentimental value. We both started out together in the same lurp platoon."

"She didn't give you anything else?"

"No."

Spartan stared hard at the soldier. This fucker wasn't much help, but he didn't seem to be lying either. He turned and walked out.

Bouchet was no doubt up to something with Coleridge, but what? He had to find out, but she had become a tougher nut to crack than he first realized. With the "hands-off" message from the big boys in Saigon, she was off limits, but there had to be a way to get to her without anyone knowing he was involved. He had to think this one through before going to Reeves.

* * *

When the man left the barracks, Jimmy Nobles breathed a sigh of relief. Pulling the envelope from beneath the pillow, he pushed it down inside his duffle bag. Duff had gotten it to him just in time. He was heading down to Phan Rang in the morning for out-processing, then boarding the freedom bird. He was going home, back to the world and glad of it, but there was this last favor he had promised Duff. He intended on keeping it.

"Who was that asshole?" another lurp asked.

Ernie, his closest buddy since Duff had left the unit, dropped the Playboy he was reading on his chest and peered at Nobles.

"Let me put it this way," Jimmy said. "It'll be better for your health if you don't know."

Jimmy continued packing his duffle bag.

"Was that one of the people your buddy Duff said was were after him?"

Jimmy didn't look over at Ernie, but glanced at the door instead. It was still closed. Duff's paranoia was becoming contagious.

"Yeah, I reckon so, but I'm telling you, if you don't want to get involved, don't say anything. Just act stupid if he comes around again. The way Duff talked, those people are a bunch of crazies who don't mind killing anyone on either side."

"Pulls any shit with me, and I'll smoke his ass," Ernie said.

Jimmy slowly shook his head in resignation. "I have no doubt you would, Ernie, but it might land your ass in Leavenworth. Just act like you never saw or heard any of this. I really didn't mean to get you guys involved."

"Long as you get safely on that freedom bird in the morning and get the hell out of here, I'm good," Ernie said.

Jimmy smiled. "Read your damned Playboy, Ernie. I got this. In a couple days, I'll be back in the world. And in a few weeks, I'll be out of this man's army and on my way home to Georgia."

Jimmy hoped he was convincing, because his confidence was shaken. Startled when the scar-faced bastard barged into the barracks, he barely had time to slide the envelope beneath the pillow. And now that he'd turned in his weapons, he *really* felt naked.

* * *

Spartan was determined to act before it was too late. He was heading into Da Nang City to have a talk with Crandall Reeves, but that wasn't all he intended to do. Having let matters get out of control, he had no choice but to act quickly. He had to do something that would turn the tide in his favor. He had to silence Coleridge. If he could do that, Bouchet would probably see the writing on the wall. She'd probably turn tail and run, or at least she'd shut her mouth and stop fucking with his business.

He stopped by the Embassy House to inform Reeves of the incident between Coleridge's lurp buddy and Bouchet. Reeves said he would follow up personally and instructed him to keep an eye on Bouchet and Coleridge. Spartan already had plans.

Return to Melody Hill
May, 1967

A sun-splintered bank of morning clouds hung in the eastern sky as Duff stretched and yawned with exhaustion. Spartan had sent a message saying they were having another pre-op meeting that morning, but he had yet to arrive. Duff stood in the IOCC courtyard smoking a cigarette and wondering if he would ever again sleep without seeing the young Vietcong nurse there dying in his arms. It had been another restless night of drinking and trying to sleep, but mostly staring into her eyes. The bourbon brought relief, but it was fool's gold. He had to leave it alone. He had to protect Lynn Dai and face the unresolved business with Spartan.

Sooner or later a reckoning would come, and someone would answer for the things that had been done. Duff's fear was that he had become as much a part of the corruption as Spartan. He feared he had already crossed the line into a dark place from which there was no return. It wasn't intentional, but that didn't matter. He had allowed himself to be drawn into the killing. Someday he would have to face his actions, but his only hope now was to save Lynn Dai, bring her home to Tennessee, and never again return to this godforsaken place.

Putting it all together, that was the problem. There was no doubt that Spartan intended to kill Lynn Dai, but that wasn't going to happen. Whatever it took, Duff would find a way to stop him, but his mind struggled in a vortex of confusion. The youthful assumptions of immortality that were once his no longer remained. He remembered that day in the Dak Akoi Valley when his buddies were killed by the booby trap, and the sudden realization that came to him as he pushed their bloody corpses aboard the chopper. His eighteen years seemed suddenly very old, and he had forever become a part of this nightmare that was Vietnam.

Since that day he had become a person who shot female nurses and stood by as innocent civilians were slaughtered. He had witnessed unarmed men arbitrarily shot, and he took orders from the ones who did these things. Even so, there was this last opportunity for some small degree of redemption, a chance to stop Spartan, to protect Lynn Dai, and to salvage something from his tour of duty—if only he could think clearly enough to come up with a plan.

Duff ground his cigarette into the gravel and looked around the IOCC courtyard. The Nung guards stood watch in the tower and at the front gate. A young ARVN soldier stood with his M-16 at the door to the ops center. It felt almost as if he were being held prisoner, but he had to wait until Jimmy had plenty of time to deliver the letter. After that, he would confront Spartan and demand an immediate transfer.

The morning breeze filtered through the trees along the courtyard walls, causing the leaves to flutter and sparkle in the morning sunlight. Still refreshing at this early hour, it was destined to become a hot wind later in the day. Of this Duff was certain.

* * *

Jimmy Nobles had noticed some strange characters around Da Nang for the few weeks he had been here, but as he checked in for his flight that morning there were some that made the hair rise on his neck. There was the grim-faced Vietnamese man wearing dark gold-rimmed Ray-Bans and a side arm. He stood at a nearby window the entire time, smoking a cigarette and staring out at the runways. A couple hundred yards down the tarmac a jeep was parked beside a hangar. Inside, a man with binoculars sat watching the line of men boarding the C-130. Jimmy was fairly certain they were spooks, and they were watching him.

Apparently they still suspected he had the documents, but when the C-130 lifted off the runway later that morning, he exhaled. Hopefully that was the end of it, but he refused to lower his guard. He hadn't gotten through his tour of duty by being stupid. Glancing up and down the aircraft cabin, he studied the other men lounging on the red nylon-webbed benches. Most were

GIs wearing fatigues with unit patches. None of them appeared particularly suspicious.

After the aircraft landed, Jimmy held back, letting the others deplane. The crew was still in the cockpit as he looked around and slid his hand inside the duffle bag. Retrieving the envelope, he quickly shoved it down inside the back of his trousers, then stood and tossed the bag over his shoulder. He caught up to the last man crossing the tarmac.

As he walked into the building someone called his name. "Sergeant Nobles."

A man holding a briefcase stood with two Army MPs. He was wearing a pressed poplin shirt, civilian khakis, and round wire-rimmed spectacles. His appearance was that of a physician, or perhaps a college professor, things Jimmy was pretty sure he wasn't.

"That would be me," Jimmy said.

It was just as he thought. They were still following him.

"Step over here in this room, please, where we can talk in private."

The man motioned toward a small side room, and Jimmy nodded. The MPs followed, and the man who was carrying the briefcase closed the door. The room was hot and claustrophobic.

"Sergeant, I must talk with you about a very important matter involving national security. I believe you met with a friend of yours in Da Nang named Duff Coleridge?"

"That's right," Jimmy said.

"Did Specialist Coleridge, or anyone he may have been associated with, give you any documents, photos, or other information?"

"The only thing Duff told me was that he was having a rough time with some advisor he worked for. Said the guy was a real asshole, but when I ask him more about it, he said he couldn't talk."

The man cut his eyes to Jimmy's duffle bag. "So, you would have no problem if these men went through your bag, right?"

"What for?"

"To make certain there have been no documents placed there, perhaps without your knowledge."

Jimmy dropped the bag at his feet. "Have at it."

One of the MPs picked up the duffle bag, opened it and dumped the contents on a table. After a minute or two, the man in the civilian clothes directed the contents be returned to the bag. He turned to Jimmy. The man nonchalantly looked him up and down.

"I need for you to empty your pockets."

Nobles pulled his wallet, a girlfriend's letter and a green bandanna from his pockets. He tossed them on the table. The man took the girlfriend's letter from its pink envelope, glanced at it and tossed it back on the table.

"So, is Duff in some kind of trouble?" Jimmy asked.

"I'm not sure, but anyone holding any documents, classified information or—"

"All right, look," Jimmy said. "I already went through this with some wild-eyed-looking fucker who came around last night. The only thing I got from Duff was this."

Jimmy pulled the bullet hanging around his neck from inside his shirt and showed it to the man. "We were on the same lurp team, and he gave it to me as a memento."

"When did he give it to you?"

"His girlfriend came by and gave it to me yesterday evening. She said he was restricted to quarters, but wanted to make sure I got it before leaving."

After a long moment, the man nodded. "I apologize, sergeant. We appreciate your cooperation. We're done here."

With that the man walked out of the room. One of the MPs looked at Jimmy and shrugged, then followed the others out the door.

* * *

Duff felt himself slipping into a near psychotic state. Despite his love for Lynn Dai and the comfort she brought him, the specter of the young VC nurse's face returned every night. He saw the bodies of the old people floating amongst the shattered remnants of their boats down the Song Thu Bon River. He saw the village chief's grandsons lying in the dust, slaughtered by Spartan before his very eyes. What he no longer saw was the possibility of life as it once was. He owed too much to too many. But those who ran the war controlled him, and he had let it happen.

The meeting that morning was typical of what Spartan passed off as pre-op planning—short, vague, and pretty much void of detail or contingency plans. Duff and Dibbs were assigned with different groups of PRU soldiers to watch trails outside of a village while Spartan and the Special Police interrogated the inhabitants. The village, west of Da Nang, was a known hotbed of enemy activity and one of the last populated areas before the hills gave way to the highlands. Beyond were miles of mountainous jungle.

In a convoy moving west on Highway 1 to Provincial Highway 545, Duff and Dibbs rode with Spartan in his jeep. They arrived in the operations area sometime around midmorning. Duff tried to make sense of the situation. With Dibbs along, it didn't make sense that Spartan would try anything, but there was no guarantee. He had to stay alert.

Overhead was a rare clear blue sky, and the normally oppressive heat of the day was still held at bay by a cool breeze drifting from the high mountains beyond the village. Duff and Dibbs stood near the main road with a contingent of PRU, while Spartan and Tranh made individual assignments.

"Dibbs," Spartan said, "You take these men and head up northwest of the village and watch the trail going around that ridge. Coleridge, you take these two and head across that dike and up that trail into the high ground southwest of the village. Captain Truc and the rest of the PRU will pull security for Colonel Tranh, Major Loc, and the Special Police inside the village. We'll all meet back here at 1100 hours."

Duff sized up the situation. On the ridge behind the village was a solid wall of trees and undergrowth. A well-worn trail crossed a small dike, then led up into the lush undergrowth of palms. It was prime terrain for an enemy ambush, but nowhere in Nam ever seemed without threat, and this place was no different. He had a job to do. Duff motioned for the two PRU soldiers to follow.

Taking point, he led them across the dike toward the ridge. They followed several meters behind as he moved carefully, studying the ground, searching for trip wires, loose dirt, or other indications of a booby trap. When he reached the base of the ridge where the jungle began, Duff paused and searched the undergrowth. It was soundless. Not even a bird chirped. The wind was quartering, and he inhaled deeply attempting to catch the telltale odor of humans. Nothing. After a few moments, he began moving slowly up the trail.

Call it a premonition that comes from a sixth sense, or simply a bad feeling, but something wasn't right. Duff felt an increasing tension as he took each step up the trail. He glanced back at the two PRU soldiers. Their eyes were like those of antelopes on the African savanna, wide and nervous. Duff pushed the selector switch on his M-14 to fire. He was twenty meters up the trail, hoping to find a place for his security watch, but the jungle pressed in from all sides. The entire setup was bad.

There came a rustling sound from behind, and he glanced over his shoulder. The two PRU soldiers were running wildly back down the trail toward the village. His body went cold. Duff dove into a shallow depression beside the trail as a sudden explosion of gunfire shattered the silence. Showers of green tracers sent the leaves fluttering down like confetti. He'd allowed his physical and mental exhaustion to walk him into a trap. Duff lay on his back holding his M-14 above his head as he sprayed the hillside above with random shots, but the enemy fire intensified.

The two PRU soldiers were nearly halfway across the rice paddy dike when he saw first one then the other stumble and fall. On the far side of the paddy, standing beside a hooch in the village, was one of the National Police officers with an M-16 firing at the two PRU soldiers. At first it seemed a friendly fire incident, but Duff quickly realized the man who shot them knew who they were.

A grenade thumped onto the trail beside him. Duff picked it up and tossed it away. He buried his head under his arm as the explosion ripped through the trees above. He was in a hornet's nest, but didn't know which way to turn. Although confused, he was certain that running back toward the village wasn't an option. He quickly loaded a fresh magazine into the M-14.

Grabbing two frags, he pulled the pins and flung first one then the other up the hillside into the undergrowth. As soon as they exploded he came to his feet and sprinted up the trail, firing his M-14 as he tried to escape the ambush. He ran, but the guerrillas pursued him, crashing through the undergrowth on the ridge above. There were a dozen or more, their voices coming from everywhere at once, and they were close.

Duff crouched as he ran, but he felt bullets cracking close, clipping the undergrowth. The skin on one arm burned as a round passed through his shirt sleeve, but he didn't look back. He had to reach the crest of the hill. It was his only hope, but a sledge-hammer force slammed him to the ground. He was face-down in the trail, the world spinning upside down and out of control around him.

The impact of the bullet had knocked the breath from his lungs, and he saw stars as he struggled to regain control. His legs responded, and he staggered to his feet. Dazed and still unable to draw a breath, he continued up the trail. Over the next hill was home. Over the hill, not too far, was Melody Hill. He thought he could see the mist rising from Reliance Gorge and the titanium white steeple of the church rising through the treetops. In the distance was the Cherokee Ridge where the mountain laurel grew so thick it was parted only by streams of clear waters spilling over the rocks. More bullets tore his fatigues, and he turned and sprayed his attackers with the last rounds from his M-14, but the guerrillas kept coming, leaping over their fallen comrades.

Duff dropped his rifle and continued up the trail. He could see Melody Hill clearly now. Reliance Gorge thundered in the distance, its cool mist rising above the trees and disappearing into a crystalline blue sky. Another Tennessee morning awaited him. And he could see his mother and Lacey and Brady, and now, even his daddy. He walked to the top of the rise, but he was tired. He heard the chimes coming from the church. They were playing his favorite hymn, Amazing Grace, and it seemed almost as if they were calling him.

His shredded fatigues were soaked with blood, and all he wanted to do was to lie down and go to sleep, but there came to him at that moment something he had heard Brady say long ago. "Never give up." With his last fragmentation grenade in hand, Duff dropped to his knees and pulled the pin. Behind him he heard the clip-clop of sandals on the beaten trail.

The enemy soldiers chattered excitedly as they ran toward him, but he didn't throw the grenade, and they didn't see it. Dropping his arm to his side, he let the spoon flip away into the undergrowth, and looked up as several Vietcong guerrillas gathered around panting and smiling. Talking excitedly, they held their weapons on him, unaware the grenade was there, until he held it up, smiled, and dropped it at their feet.

* * *

Captain Truc had watched from the edge of the village as his two men came running across the dike. They were fleeing the ambush. He thought they would reach safety, but there came a sudden burst of gunfire from within the village. His men tumbled and fell, and he began running along the backside of the village in their direction, but he stopped as a figure appeared, walking from the village toward the bodies. It was one of the Special Police officers, one he knew well.

Truc hid and watched as the Special Policeman approached the bodies, nudged them both with his M-16, then looked across the paddy in the direction of the ambush. There had come one last grenade blast, then silence. A single figure limped to the edge of the jungle and raised his AK-47 above his head. The Special Policeman glanced over his shoulder at the village, then raised his M-16 in salute to the guerrilla standing on the trail. This was insanity. This Special Police officer was an enemy agent. There was no other explanation.

Truc brought his rifle to his shoulder, and was about to fire when the officer turned back toward the village and nodded. There was yet another, someone else inside the village that Truc couldn't see. He stood frozen with fear. How many were there? Who had the Special Policeman signaled? Was it another Special Policeman, or perhaps one of his own men? There was a sudden void in the pit of his stomach as he realized there was no hope. For all he had done to fight the enemies of his country, they had infiltrated his organization to its very core.

* * *

Spartan returned to the road near his jeep and waited. The radio crackled as Dibbs called in that he was moving toward Coleridge's position. A few minutes later someone ran from the village and reported that two PRU soldiers had been shot dead. Spartan already knew this. The VC spy had been eliminated. Now, he waited and hoped to hear from Dibbs that the other problem was resolved as well.

A few minutes later Dibbs called in asking Spartan to send more men. It seems there were bodies stacked in the trail and along the ridge, sixteen in all. Spartan sent no one. Instead, he waited, and the minutes crept by. It was something he had to do. He had to protect the national security. He had no choice, but the waiting was unbearable. What if Coleridge was only wounded? Spartan grabbed the handset and called for Dibbs over the radio, but there was no answer. Colonel Tranh and Major Loc returned to the road outside the village, but Captain Truc was nowhere to be seen.

"What the fuck is happening? What's taking Dibbs so long?" Spartan shouted to no one in particular.

It had been nearly thirty minutes, and Spartan again grabbed the handset on the radio, but he spotted Dibbs coming through the village. Flanked by Captain Truc and several of the PRU, Dibbs had Coleridge draped across his shoulders. Both were drenched with blood.

"Do I need to call for a dust-off?" Spartan shouted.

Dibbs didn't answer as he walked out to the jeep. With the help of Captain Truc and his men, Dibbs put Coleridge in the back seat of the jeep. Coleridge's eyes were open. Spartan's lungs were cold lumps of stone. He couldn't breathe.

"Is he still alive?"

Dibbs looked at Coleridge, but he said nothing. Spartan felt his heart pounding in his ears as Coleridge fixed him with a cold stare. His brown eyes seemed to bore through him. They were the same eyes he had seen that day at the temple ruins when Coleridge held his rifle against his nose—honest eyes, locked on him.

"Why are you staring at me that way?"

"Calm down," Dibbs said. "He's not staring at you. He's dead."

Dibbs gently used his fingers to close Coleridge's eyes.

"Jesus Christ! I thought—it looked… hell, I thought he was.…"

Dibbs unrolled a poncho and draped it over the body, carefully tucking the edges underneath.

Spartan realized he had nearly lost it, and looked away. After a few moments he turned back to Dibbs. "Was he alive when you found him?"

"No," Dibbs said, "but he made those bastards pay before he went. Looks like he was wounded and surrounded, and he took out six of them and himself with a grenade. There's six more stacked up on the trail and three or four on the ridge above it. We found at least three more blood trails, too."

"What about Truc's two men who were with him? They were shot out on the dike. Did you confirm them KIA?"

Spartan realized as soon as he said it that there was no way he should have known Truc's men had been shot on the dike.

"Uh, I mean, Tranh and Loc said there were two PRUs shot on the dike."

Although his eyes were bloodshot and moist, Dibbs got a quizzical look on his face, almost as if he suspected something. "They're dead, except Truc is saying someone shot them from inside the village."

Spartan looked around. Truc had come out of the village and was down the road near the other vehicles, surrounded by several of his men. "Did he say who shot them?"

"Apparently he didn't see who it was. He saw his men running back toward the village on the dike and someone shot them."

"He's probably confused," Spartan said. He glanced around at the two Special Police officers, Tranh and Loc. Both spoke fluent English, but neither reacted. "He doesn't know what he's talking about. They were probably shot by someone in the ambush."

Dibbs eyed him, furrowing his brow. Spartan looked away.

As the convoy headed back to the IOCC that afternoon, Spartan realized that his plan had come together with lethal perfection. The special police had taken out the Chieu Hoi, who no doubt was the An Ninh Agent who had been compromising his every operation, but not before he had eliminated Coleridge. Despite Dibbs's look of doubt, it had all worked out, and he had no direct involvement. He glanced over his shoulder. Dibbs sat in the back of the Jeep, hollow-eyed and cradling the poncho-wrapped body of Coleridge.

The only problem remaining was Bouchet. With her boyfriend dead, perhaps she would see the light and disappear from his life. Black ops was a nasty business, but there was no place in it for people with weak minds, people who couldn't keep their mouths shut, people like Bouchet and Coleridge. Before long, it would again be business as usual in the district, and he could go back to killing gooks and making money.

CHAPTER TWENTY-TWO

The Face of Evil
May, 1967

A fter her mother and father were slain by the Viet Minh, Lynn Dai thought she could never again weep so hard, but for two days she wept uncontrollably. The old mansion outside Da Nang City, her childhood home, had become her refuge, and she slept beneath the canopy of mosquito netting above her bed. When she wasn't sleeping, she stood on the balcony outside her room, staring into the jungle, but the tears still came in torrents. She wished she were dead.

Besides her father, Duff was the only man she had ever truly loved, a brave and loyal man, a man who refused to leave a dangerous situation all because of his love for her. Now, she considered leaving Vietnam and going to France to live with her father's people, but she couldn't. She had to stay. She would stay for him. She would stay and face the dangers just as Duff had, and she would bring to justice the savages that murdered him. An impossible hope, perhaps, but it was one she would not surrender.

As she pulled the brush through her hair that morning, Lynn Dai gazed into the mirror at her swollen and bloodshot eyes. She was determined to overcome her grief. She had no choice. To delay meant those responsible would have more time to hide the evidence and influence possible witnesses. She had to question the PRU soldiers that were in the village when Duff and their two comrades were slain. Her investigation meant going back to the very ones responsible, because it was Spartan who arranged such meetings when they were approved.

* * *

As Lynn Dai expected, the first response to her meeting request was refusal. Only after her superiors in Saigon contacted the OSA did she receive cooperation. Her first request was for nine PRU soldiers to be brought to the Embassy House for questioning. She wasn't surprised when that took several days, but she hadn't planned for Spartan's and Captain Truc's presence in the room. Her frustration was giving way to hopelessness.

The paranoia was palpable as the soldiers' eyes darted about like trapped cats. That they cowered in silence was not surprising. After all, two of their own had just been slain, and it was evident they knew it was no simple act of war. Spartan sat glowering, with his boots propped on the table, manicuring his fingernails with a bayonet. The futility of the exercise did not escape her, but Lynn Dai refused to give up. She locked eyes with Spartan, and after several seconds she slowly turned away.

Lynn Dai asked if anyone had seen how the two soldiers were slain or if anyone had heard talk about it, then studied the PRU soldiers' reactions. Several exchanged furtive glances, but none made eye contact with her. It was evident they knew something. They cast glances toward their leader, Captain Truc, as if they expected he would speak for them. Truc's conduct was most telling. He simply stared down at the table.

Lynn Dai again looked toward Spartan. His patronizing smile might have added to her frustration, but she had prepared herself for the caged silence she now faced. She maintained total composure. This would take time, but she was prepared to wait. As it was with the people of her mother's country, she was prepared to be patient, to bend with the force and to return when the position of strength was hers. For now, she would allow Spartan his arrogant satisfaction.

"You seem happy, Mr. Spartan, no?" Lynn Dai said.

"No, Ms. Bouchet. I'm amused."

"At what, the deaths of the two men I am investigating, at their families who are now without fathers and husbands, or perhaps you are amused at the death of your own man, Duff Coleridge?"

Spartan's grin morphed to a tooth-grinding grimace. He dropped his feet from the table. For the first time, Captain Truc looked up.

"I'm amused at your ignorance. I'm amused at your constant questions about our business, a business you'd avoid if you were smart. This is a special operations group, and we operate under oaths of secrecy."

With that he brought the bayonet down point-first with his fist, jamming it forcefully into the table. Every man at the table stared wide-eyed as Spartan slowly removed his hand, leaving the bayonet standing. He casually turned to face Lynn Dai. His scarred face was hard as stone.

"Like these men, you too might be better off if you understood how things work around here."

Lynn Dai was unshaken. Fear and intimidation were the tools of those who were frightened by something much larger than themselves. She'd lost her parents. She'd lost Duff. The only thing left to lose was her life, and that no longer seemed like such a terrible consequence. With forced but well-controlled nonchalance she gazed at Spartan.

"How things work, as you say, has become very clear to me, Mr. Spartan, but perhaps that advice would benefit you as well."

Spartan stood, grasped the bayonet and wrenched it from the table.

"Okay, that's enough bullshit for one day. If you're done with your questions, we have work to do."

Lynn Dai nodded. "I am done with my questions for today, Mr. Spartan, but my investigation will be complete only when the truth is eventually discovered, and you can be assured that if not tomorrow, it will be revealed, some day."

Spartan had begun walking toward the door, but he stopped and looked over his shoulder.

"The *truth* is that war is a bitch and people die, lady. Truc, get your men loaded, and let's get them back to the IOCC."

Lynn Dai walked down the hallway to her office and closed the door. Although emotionally exhausted from the meeting, she felt her grief again rising from within, but she fought it back. When she was alone at her apartment or at her home outside Da Nang she could afford the luxury of tears, but not here. Here she would not let them see her grief. Here she would let them see only steadfast determination.

There came a knock at her door.

"Yes?" she said.

The door opened. Captain Truc was there. After glancing back down the hallway, he quickly stepped inside.

"Forgive my cowardice, but I felt I could not speak freely in our meeting."

Lynn Dai stood. Truc's face wore a sheen of perspiration, and it was lined with the fine creases of inner tension. His eyes, at once fearful and defiant, were those of a glaring bull awaiting the *estacada*, that moment when the matador thrusts the sword into its neck. She was elated with this opportunity, yet sickened by the fear she saw in this man's eyes.

"What is it?" Lynn Dai asked. "What do you know?"

"I am afraid my time has come, because I have witnessed too much. I can no longer remain silent. The questions you were asking tell me you are not merely a liaison for the Americans, but perhaps in the service of our government. You are seeking the An Ninh agent in our midst, and I may be able to help you. My men were slain by the Special Police, but I also believe it was with the knowledge of Mr. Spartan."

Lynn Dai grabbed her notepad from the desk. "Tell me what you saw."

"I believe Mr. Spartan knew in advance what would happen because he came a few days ago to one of my men asking if he knew of someone who would kill an American in return for money. My soldier came to me afterward and told me about this. It was Spartan who sent him and another of my men with Specialist Coleridge across the rice paddy into the ambush, but they escaped.

"I saw them running back to the village, but one of the Special Police officers raised his rifle and killed them both. I believe this officer may have been indirectly responsible for the killing of Specialist Coleridge as well, because after he killed my men, he raised his rifle as if to salute one of those who ambushed the American. It was an NLF guerilla."

"You saw the NLF there?"

"Yes, there was one whom I saw standing on the hill beyond the rice paddy, and he signaled the Special Police officer."

"Who was the Special Police officer that you saw?" Lynn Dai asked.

"It was—"

Captain Truc looked back at the door. There came the sound of footsteps in the hallway. Someone pushed the door open. Standing there was Spartan.

"Captain Truc, your men are out there roasting in the hot sun. We have a mission in the morning, and you need to get back to the operations center. Report to Colonel Tranh for the mission briefing."

"I need a few more minutes with the Captain," Lynn Dai said.

"Sorry, lady, but it won't be today. He has orders. You can meet with him later."

Spartan pushed the door open wider. "Let's go, captain, *now*."

"You are only an advisor, not this man's commander," Lynn Dai said.

Truc glanced at her. His eyes were wide with fear. He slowly turned and walked out the door. Spartan watched as the PRU captain walked down the hallway and out the door. Lynn Dai's heart pounded with frustration. She had been so close, but she had failed to get the name she needed. Spartan stepped inside and closed the door. Her frustration turned to fear. His face boiled with hatred as he walked toward her and shoved his finger in her face.

"I'm going to make this clear to you one last time. If I hear you asking my men any more questions about our operations, I am going to turn your ass over to the Special Police, and let them ask *you* questions. They have some very unique interrogation methods, and you don't want to experience them. Now, do I make myself clear?"

Lynn Dai picked up the phone on her desk, but the line was dead. Setting it carefully back into the receiver, she took a deep breath and exhaled.

"That's right," Spartan said. "You may have some big-shot friends in Saigon, but they can't protect you here. Figure it out, but do it real quick before you end up like..." Spartan seemed to catch himself, "...the rest of the gooks around here."

Lynn Dai had felt a similar hatred when the NLF killed her parents, and she now fought to maintain her composure. "These people you call 'gooks' are my countrymen, Mr. Spartan. They deserve better than your version of arbitrary justice."

Spartan slammed his fist down on her desk, upsetting the telephone and scattering papers. "They deserve what they fucking get, bitch, and if you don't keep your fucking mouth shut, someone's going to mistake you for a VC."

With that he turned and walked out. Lynn Dai felt the hot tears in her eyes, but they were no longer tears of grief. These were tears spawned by rage. When he was gone, she walked down to the communications room. It was as she thought. The door there was locked.

Lynn Dai raised her head and stared down the hallway at the window where sunbeams filtered through the dust. Her father, the romantic French intellectual, always seemed puzzled with her mother's Asian stoicism, but it was this trait that served Lynn Dai all too well in times of crisis. She took another deep breath to quell her emotions. Her mother's example would guide her. Her mother's life, as Duff's, would live through her.

These setbacks would only serve to increase her determination. It could take weeks, possibly months, perhaps even years, but she would never give up. She would see that those responsible for Duff's death received the justice they deserved. His love for her would not be in vain, and his memory would be honored.

* * *

It was late afternoon when Lynn Dai finally contacted her superiors in Saigon. After explaining that she was close to identifying the An Ninh agent and needed only to speak with Captain Truc, they assured her of their support. She further explained the imminent threat to

Truc's life, but when she told them that the American advisor might be involved and that she was certain he was responsible for his own countryman's death, they balked with disbelief. It suddenly became a very delicate matter, one that perhaps would take some time to resolve, they said. They promised to contact her with instructions as soon as possible.

CHAPTER TWENTY-THREE

The Awakening of Xảo Quyệt Hồ
May, 1967

S pring in the Tennessee Overhill had always been a time of optimism and rebirth, but Duff was gone, and Brady was lost in a world without meaning. Spinning in confusion, he was lost in a downward spiral toward oblivion. His psyche was that of a barely conscious prizefighter crashing to the canvas. Life was suddenly a huge shadow, a darkened abyss, and he had no compass, no Duff to show him the way. The tears had already come and gone several times.

Brady had come home one afternoon to find Mama Emma on the living room floor, and he instantly knew the reason. Helping her to the couch, he took the telegram from her hand and read that Duff had been killed in action in the Republic of Vietnam. Brady held his foster mother in his arms that afternoon until Lacey came home. He was so young when his father was killed and later when his mother died, he never quite understood the depth of those losses until now.

That Duff would not come home was something Brady never truly believed, something he had never truly considered. The futility of trying to comfort Mama Emma and Lacey at the funeral was like none he'd ever experienced. Life was suddenly pointless. He and Lacey had become isolated in their grief, and they had hardly spoken for days. Now, there was this letter. It was in the envelope on the seat of the truck beside him, yet unread.

The soldier at the bus stop told him that Duff might not have died the way the army said, and despite his chest full of ribbons and paratrooper jump wings, the soldier was undoubtedly afraid. What was it that was so ominous that it frightened even a man who had survived a war? The soldier had warned him, but of what, of whom? The letter lying on the seat beside him held the answers.

Crossing down 411, Brady headed back up into the hills. He drove in a daze with tear-blurred eyes, searching for a place to pull over. An over-look appeared on the road ahead. Slowing, he pulled the pickup off the road and parked against a low stone wall. The river valley spread below him, miles of wilderness broken only by an occasional homestead or small farm. He sat with the truck windows open as the gentle spring breeze carried the scent of the pines and spring flowers up the mountainside.

Far across the valley on a distant mountain that he knew well, the steeple of the Melody Hill church rose through the trees. On the rise behind the church was Duff's grave. It was so new, the only markers were a mound of red dirt and a few rock shards. A hawk rode the afternoon thermals across the valley, while Brady opened his pocket knife and slit the top of the envelope. He removed the largest piece of paper and unfolded it. It was the letter.

* * *

Brady had sat in his truck the entire afternoon staring out at the valley below. The distant church spire had turned from white to amber as the evening sun set in the west. He picked up the letter again, and he wasn't sure how many times he had read it that afternoon, but he read it again.

May, 1967

Dear Brady,

Do not let Mama or Lacey read this letter, and don't write back about it, because all my mail is being read. A friend of mine from my old LRRP unit is going to deliver it to you when he gets back home from Nam. I don't want to violate my oath of secrecy, but I know I can trust you with this information. I think I am in trouble. A couple months ago I was recruited to a special operations group by a man named Spartan. He is an American civilian advisor for a Vietnamese Special Police detachment near Da Nang. He also has charge of a Provincial Reconnaissance Unit. That's a bunch of local Vietnamese militia guys working under him.

The reason I'm sending you this information is because if I don't come home, I think these people will cover up what really happens. If that happens I want you to send copies of this letter and everything in the envelope to the Army and maybe a newspaper or anyone else who can help find out why. Just do it anonymously because the people I am working for are very dangerous.

I'm afraid I've gotten in over my head here in Vietnam. Someone tried to ambush me the other night, and I'm not sure if it was the people I'm working for or a spy. It's crazy over here. I thought I came to fight the communists, but there are so many different groups I don't know who to trust any more. This guy Spartan is a total psychopath who seems to hate everybody. He knows that I know he stole some American weapons from a warehouse near here and sold them on the black market. He tried to bribe me, and when I refused, he said I was as much a part of it as he was. I've done some terrible things, but I didn't do anything I knew wasn't right. I also saw him kill innocent Vietnamese civilians two different times, and today I witnessed the Vietnamese Special Police he advises torture a prisoner to death. It was a bad thing to see. The Americans here are involved with the killings and torture, but claim they are only advisors, and if word gets out, they might just cover everything up.

This whole situation is bad. Lynn Dai says there is a Vietcong spy working under Spartan, and he has been compromising all our missions. Two of our SOG team have already quit. They transferred out, and I'm trying to do the same thing, but I think Spartan is blocking it because he's afraid I'll go to the authorities on him.

I haven't told anyone here in Nam because I'm afraid they'll try to protect him, and just cover up the whole mess, or try to say I did these things on my own. There are several Telex messages with his handwriting on them inside the envelope. One of the Telex messages is a hit-list of local civilians with Spartan's handwriting on it. Several of the people on the list have already been killed. I have met a beautiful French and Vietnamese woman named Lynn Dai Bouchet. I love her, and she is going to come home with me. She works for the South Vietnamese government as an investigator and liaison to the Naval Claims office at the Embassy House in Da Nang. She also knows a lot about what is happening, and she is trying to help me, but Spartan has threatened her and ordered me to stay away from her. When you get this letter keep it in a safe place, and make some copies. Hopefully, you won't need them. I love you, little brother, and I will be home to see you soon. Until then, take care of Mama and Lacey.

Your brother,
Duff

It was as the soldier at the bus stop had said, Duff might not have been killed the way the army said. And the letter was proof that someone was already trying to cover up the facts. They said Duff had been killed in action, but it wasn't so. Someone, probably the one named Spartan, had murdered him, but the letter provided no proof, and it wouldn't prevent a cover-up, unless there were more names to put with it.

Brady sat that afternoon thinking about the situation. If he gave the letter to the military, a newspaper, or anyone else, could they find the truth? These were powerful people Duff had faced. They would do anything to avoid being caught. It had taken most of the afternoon to think it through, but Brady knew now what had to be done. Duff stood up for what was right, and they killed him. Someone had to go and find these people, find them and put names with faces. It was up to him.

Brady slammed his fist against the dashboard. His knuckles bled, but there was no pain. There was no pain because he no longer had feelings. If vengeance was God's, then he was God's messenger. He was determined. He would go to the Army recruiter and find out what it would take for him to go to Vietnam. He would go there, and he would find these people. He would find them and look them in the eye, and if his government didn't back him, he'd meet them on his terms. They would face a damnation the likes of which no one could ever imagine.

CHAPTER TWENTY-FOUR

The Art of War
May 1967

T he call Lynn Dai expected from her superiors about Captain Truc did not come that day. Nor had it come the next
morning. Lynn Dai knelt before the crucifix in her apartment, before the fading photos of her mother and father, and she
prayed. The news she expected had come, but it was not until two
days later. Captain Truc was reported killed in action while on the
mission. It had happened as she had feared. Truc, too, was murdered.

Truc was dead, but her determination to find the identity of
Duff's killers would not die with him. And there was still an An Nihn
agent amongst them. She would continue quietly and unobtrusively

with her investigation. She would not give up. She would continue until justice was served or they murdered her, too.

* * *

As long as she had the trust and support of her superiors in Saigon, Lynn Dai was determined to continue her fight, but hers was not a position of strength. Her enemies were formidable. She thought of her studies at the university when she read of the ancient Chinese military general, strategist and tactician, Sun-Tzu. They said his tactics and strategies were studied even today by modern armies, and though dutiful in her studies, she never imagined she might someday utilize those teachings.

Spartan and his band of misguided rogues now owned without challenge their share of the province around Da Nang, and if she was to continue her fight, she had no choice but to assume the mantle of weakness. Confronting them directly was out of the question if she hoped to ever bring these killers into the open. She had no choice but to continue her normal activities and present the illusion of humility and surrender.

Standing before the mirror Lynn Dai smoothed her black dress and adjusted the straps on her shoulders. It was one of her nicer dresses, not formal but suitable for mourning, and equally for an evening at the Embassy House. She would allow Spartan to believe he had won, but she would not hide from him. She had to be there when he made that fatal mistake. Only then could she stop him once and for all. In the interim, her only hope was that her presence might at least give him pause before he committed more acts of violence. She had been unable to save Duff, but she hoped to save others and bear for him the fruit of his endeavors.

After applying her makeup, she slipped on her heels and grabbed a handbag. It was time for the ritual they called 'Friday Night Depressurization' at the Embassy House. Everyone would be there, the province chiefs, the Special Police officers, embassy staff, Marines, Army, the hospital nurses, and a mob of people who rushed to this oasis of alcohol and music nearly every weekend.

Going there was the last thing she wanted to do, but to catch a jackal, one had to go into the jungle. She had to walk amongst the vultures, scavengers, and predators to show them she wouldn't be intimidated. She parked her car and walked down a narrow lane past several houses. When she arrived, the guard there opened the door for her, but she froze. From inside came the music of The Platters, *Smoke Gets in Your Eyes*. The silhouettes of the people clinging to one another became visible in the dim light. It struck her that she could no longer dance with Duff. Her first impulse was to turn around, to run back to the safety and serenity of her apartment where her tears would go unnoticed. But that was a coward's way out.

She had to be brave like Duff. Taking a deep breath, she steeled herself and walked through the door. Eyes around the room locked on her. Lynn Dai quickly made her way to a cluster of chairs and a couch in an alcove, where she found several of the nurses from the hospital at China Beach.

The nurses stopped talking and looked up at her, seemingly stunned. One of them stood. They had heard about Duff and began offering their condolences while one of their group hurried to the bar. She returned a few moments later with a glass of liquor. Lynn

Dai had made up her mind not to drink, but she quickly took a gulp from the glass. Presenting some semblance of normalcy was all she hoped to accomplish, something that would be noted by the power brokers across the room.

"How could you come here tonight?" one of the nurses asked.

It was Katherine, the girl closest to her age.

"I had no choice," Lynn Dai said. "I had to."

Katherine nodded. "Yes. I understand. I suppose it is better this way."

Lynn Dai smiled. Katherine was trying to be kind, but she had no idea of the motivations that drove her, nor did she understand the anguish she faced by disguising her feelings. Certain that she had found with Duff the relationship she most sought in life, Lynn Dai now struggled with the reality of having lost him. The Skyliners began singing *Since I Don't Have You*, and she wondered if it was some form of punishment from God. *"I don't have anything, since I don't have you."* She took another gulp from the glass. The liquor softened her pain, but it wasn't part of the plan. She could ill afford a drunken display of grief.

At the center of the room, Crandall Reeves was dancing, and he looked in her direction, then looked again. He had seen her. That was enough. As long as they knew she wouldn't be intimidated, that she wasn't going to run and hide, then her mission was accomplished. It would worry them, and perhaps make them reluctant to murder more innocent people. She finished the drink and stood. She had to go before she broke into tears in front of them all.

"Please forgive me," she said to the nurses. "Perhaps you were right. It will be better if I return another time."

Katherine stood with her.

"You poor thing. Let me walk you to your car," she said.

"I truly appreciate your offer," Lynn Dai said, "but that will not be necessary."

She started across the room, but one of the Vietnamese waiters stopped her before she reached the door. He nodded respectfully and motioned toward a table across the room. Crandall Reeves was there, and he held up his glass and smiled as he motioned her over. There with him were Spartan and Colonel Greer, along with several staffers and nurses.

"Mister Reeves said he is honored you to come sit at table with his friends," the waiter said.

Her first impulse was to say no. Walking in the jungle with jackals was one thing, but to sit at the table with them was reprehensible. She'd rather dine with pigs.

Lynn Dai smiled at the waiter and thanked him. To refuse this invitation would counter the impression she wished to leave. She turned and walked toward the table. Reeves stood as she approached.

"Please, come join us," he said.

"I am honored, Mr. Reeves, but I have no choice but to decline. I am meeting friends for a late dinner."

"Oh, how unfortunate," he said. "Perhaps another time, but before you leave us I want to express my condolences. I understand you had a special friendship with Specialist Coleridge."

Lynn Dai forced the lump in her throat back down into her chest. "That is true."

"Here," Reeves said. He grabbed a glass and poured a shot of Scotch.

Handing her the glass, he said, "I would like to propose a toast to a brave soldier who gave his life in the service of his country and yours."

The others at the table stood and held their glasses high.

"Here's to the memory of Specialist Coleridge," Reeves said.

Lynn Dai would gladly have thrown the whiskey into his face, but her duties with the Military Security Service prevented it. Another song began playing, and her love for music turned to profound regret as she realized how close to her heart it had become. Gerry and The Pacemakers had begun singing *Don't Let the Sun Catch You Cryin'*. She forced herself not to hear the lyrics.

She had to be strong. She would be strong for Duff. She would wait and watch. She would watch them, and sooner or later her opportunity would come. The new Phung Hoang program that Reeves was about to implement with the Special Police was named after the mythical Vietnamese bird of a thousand eyes. It saw all, but what Reeves didn't realize, nor Spartan, was that the Phung Hoang was already watching *them*. She drank the Scotch, and set the glass on the table.

As she nodded and turned to leave, the music stopped, and Lynn Dai heard Spartan's voice. "Didn't take her long to get over him, did it?"

She stopped. After a momentary pause to gather her emotions, Lynn Dai slowly turned back toward the table. She would not blink, nor would she react with anger. She did not smile, nor did she frown, but she stepped closer and looked down at him with clear-eyed honesty.

"A man who gloats in victory loses. This may escape you for the moment, but I truly believe you will face the consequences of your deeds. I have seen with clarity that you will someday be called to a reckoning by one with such determination that it will escape even the depravity of your small mind until it is too late. He will come, and you will once again look into the eyes of the one you have slain, but it is the one with the eyes of a tiger who will deliver you to hell."

* * *

Spartan felt his face flush with heat, and his temples suddenly pounded. The bitch was threatening him, but given the presence of his boss and the others, he couldn't react. He attempted a nonchalant smirk, but his facial muscles were frozen—unresponsive. Perhaps it was this sudden incapacitation that enabled him a brief moment of clarity, one in which he experienced something unlike anything he'd ever experienced before. It came as a vision, something rushing from out of the jungle toward him, an apocalyptic figure in the form of an angry tiger. It bore down on him with a fury, its huge claws splayed, its fangs bared. Then it was gone as quickly as it came. Only then did he realize Lynn Dai had turned and walked away.

"Are you still with us? Hello."

After a few moments Spartan realized it was his boss's voice he was hearing.

"You look as if you've seen a ghost. Are you all right?"

Spartan turned to face Reeves, but he could not make his mouth form words. The vision was too real.

"Surely, you didn't let that woman spook you? Here, let me freshen your glass."

Spartan grabbed the newly refilled glass and downed the contents. Taking the bottle from his boss, he filled the glass again.

* * *

Before she closed her eyes that night, Lynn Dai once again thought of Duff and that first night when they danced together to that old Chad and Jeremy song:

They say that all good things must end some day
Autumn leaves must fall
But don't you know that it hurts me so
To say goodbye to you
Wish you didn't have to go

She said a prayer, not one of revenge, but that God's will be served, and that Duff's spirit live on within her. She prayed that she be given the strength to endure the long struggle ahead. And she asked God only that Duff's letter fall into capable hands.

When her prayer was done, Lynn Dai closed her eyes, and a peace settled over her and comforted her heart. She felt it with certainty. Someday her prayer *would* be answered. Her efforts would not have been in vain. She saw it as clearly as she saw the sunrise in the east. Someday someone would come again to challenge those who had taken Duff from her.

The End

A Final Note to The Reader

If you enjoyed this story, your written review of Melody Hill will be greatly appreciated. By posting your comments on such venues as Amazon.com and Goodreads.com you can tell others what you liked about this book. It is the single best way for spreading the word to other readers. Regardless, I deeply appreciate your having read this novel.

About The Author

Writer, photographer, and avid outdoorsman Rick DeStefanis lives in northern Mississippi with his wife of forty years, Janet. While his nonfiction writing, such as *The Philosophy of Big Buck Hunting*, focuses on his outdoor excursions, it is his military expertise that informs his novels. His latest work, *Melody Hill*, the prequel to his award-winning novel *The Gomorrah Principle*, draws from his experiences as a paratrooper and infantry light weapons specialist serving from 1970 to 1972 with the 82nd Airborne Division. Learn more about DeStefanis and his books at http:// www.rickdestefanis.com/.

Glossary

105 & 155mm	Standard US military Howitzer artillery rounds
3X–9X	A zoom lens rifle scope adjustable from three- to nine-power magnification
30.06	"Thirty aught six," original high-powered rifle caliber used by US military during first and second world wars
.45	Refers to the 1911 Forty-five caliber semi-automatic pistol (standard military-issue side arm during the Vietnam conflict)
A-Team	Army Special Forces team with specific infiltration skills and specialized training
Airborne	The United States Army's designation for its paratroops
An Ninh	Vietcong counterintelligence and propaganda group
AK-47	Russian-made assault rifle, the standard weapon used by the North Vietnamese
AO	Area of operation
ARVN	Army of the Republic of Vietnam (the South Vietnamese Army)
Booby traps	Improvised explosive devices, usually hidden, meant to cause injury or death
C-130	US military four-engine turboprop cargo and troop transport aircraft

C-119	Flying Box Car, 1950s era transport aircraft
Cherry	Derogatory term for new replacements
Chieu Hoi	Amnesty program set up for VC defectors
Chopper	American military slang for helicopter
CIA	Central Intelligence Agency
CID	Criminal Investigation Department (US Army)
CO	Commanding Officer
Cobra Gunship	A fast and lethal attack helicopter first utilized in the Vietnam War
CP	Command post (usually for field operations)
C- rations	Combat field rations for individual use (US military)
E-6	A staff sergeant, usually the NCO in charge of a platoon
FNG	F---ing New Guy, Derogatory term for new replacements
ICEX	Intelligence coordination and exploitations: original name for the Phoenix Program
IOCC	Intelligence Operations Coordination Center
DEROS	Date of Estimated Return from Overseas Service
Deuce and a Half	
	Slang for an American military two-and-a-half-ton truck
Di du mau	Vietnamese for "move quickly" (literally, "travel quickly")
Dừng Lại	Vietnamese for "halt"
GVN	Government of Vietnam

HQ	Headquarters
I Corps	"Eye" Corps, the northernmost operations sector during the Vietnam War
Ka-Bar	Combat knife first adopted by the United States Marine Corps
KIA	Killed In Action
Klick	Military slang for a kilometer, or one thousand meters
Lại đây	Vietnamese for "Come here"
LOCH	Light observation helicopter
LP	Listening Post, a forward post beyond friendly lines to detect enemy activity
LRRP or Lurp	Long-range reconnaissance patrol
LT	Jargon reference for a Lieutenant
LZ	Landing zone
MACV	Military Assistance Command, Vietnam
MIA	Missing In Action
MOS	Military Occupational Specialty (B112P is an airborne infantryman)
MP	Military Police
MSS	Military Security Service, counterintelligence group for the Vietnamese armed forces
M-14	US military assault rifle (308/7.62 mm caliber), predecessor to the M-16
NCO	Noncommissioned officer (the sergeants)
NDP	Night Defensive Position
NLF	National Liberation Front (the Vietcong)
NPFF	National Police Field Force (South Vietnamese)

Nùng	Ethnic Chinese the CIA utilized to guard its facilities
NVA	North Vietnamese Army
OD	Olive Drab Green, standard U.S. Army color
OP	Observation Post
op	(lower case) abbreviation for "operation"
OSA	Office of the Special Assistant (CIA headquarters, Republic of Vietnam)
Phung Hoang	Vietnamese mythological bird of love, name given to the Vietnamese version of the Phoenix Program
PRC-25	The standard US military portable field radio carried by ground troops in Vietnam
PRU	Provincial Reconnaissance Unit, local mercenary forces controlled by the CIA
PX	Post exchange, military department store
RDF	Regional Defense Forces, Vietnamese mercenary forces controlled by the CIA
REMF	Rear-echelon motherf——r (term used by combat troops to describe their noncombat counterparts)
RPG	Rocket propelled grenade
R&R	Leave granted for rest and recuperation
RTO	Radio telephone operator (the man who carried the radio)
S2	Military designation for an intelligence unit
SEAL	U.S. Navy's special operations Sea, Air, Land Teams

Section 8   A military provision for discharge for reasons of mental instability

SKS   Chinese assault rifle

SOG   Strategic Operations Group (covert military units)

Sky Raider   A propeller driven attack aircraft used mostly by the South Vietnamese Airforce

Special Forces   US Army green berets

Special Police   CIA advised and funded branch of the South Vietnamese National Police

SWAG   Acronym for Scientific Wild Ass Guess, tongue in cheek term used by snipers for making estimates.

TAC   Tactical Air Cover, often referred to by ground troops as "TAC air."

TDY   Temporary duty

TOC   Tactical Operations Center, also referred to as C&C: Command and Control.

VC   Vietcong, Civilian Communist insurgents in South Vietnam

Xảo Quyệt Hổ   Vietnamese term "The Cunning Tiger"

XO   Executive officer (second-in-command)